Witch[illegible] The Hardest Pill To Swallow

Published by Implode Publishing Ltd

Chapter 1

"You have to let it go, Jill," Jack said, not for the first time this morning. "You have to let the police do their job."

"Oh yeah. Because they did such a brilliant job of protecting her."

Goldie Barr, one of our neighbours, had been found murdered in her house. Prior to that, there had been a number of weird, if trivial, incidents at her property: milk bottles mysteriously being taken into her house, bowls being taken from the cupboard and placed onto the kitchen table, and beds apparently having been slept in. Understandably, she had become increasingly upset by these weird goings on, and she'd shared her concerns with me. I had encouraged her to contact the police, which she'd done, but according to Goldie, they had shown very little interest. She'd told me that they didn't seem to take her seriously and there had been some suggestion that it was all in her mind. Was I really supposed to trust the same people, who had dismissed her earlier appeal for help, to solve her murder?

I think you already know the answer to that.

"They couldn't have foreseen what would happen," Jack said.

"Why are you defending them?"

"I'm not. I'm just saying that I can understand why they didn't do more about the earlier incidents."

"Because they wrote Goldie off as a silly, paranoid woman?"

"That's not what I said."

"It's what you meant, though."

"I'm not arguing with you, Jill. It's pointless, anyway because you'll do what you want. You always do. I'm going to the store." He started for the door.

"Don't I get a kiss?"

"Sorry." He gave me a quick peck on the lips. "I'll see you tonight."

It had been like that every day since Detective Archie McDonald, AKA Big Mac, had informed us about Goldie's murder. That was a week ago now and there had been precious little news about their investigation since then. I knew Jack was becoming increasingly frustrated by what he saw as my obsession with Goldie's murder, but that was because I felt like I could have done more when she came to me originally.

I was still lost in my thoughts when I got a call from Pearl.

"We've done it, Jill," she screeched.

"You have to come and see," Amber shouted from somewhere in the background.

"Done what? See what?"

"Cuppy C is now Cuppy C again. Come and see the new sign."

"How did you manage to get a new sign up so quickly?"

Memories, bad ones, came flooding back of my ordeal when I'd tried to get a new sign installed at my old office building. What a nightmare that had turned out to be. There were many pros and cons about my new office, but one of the biggest pros was that none of the businesses were allowed to install signs on the exterior of the building.

"We decided to revert to the original name a few weeks ago," Amber said. "But we didn't want to tell anyone until the new sign was ready. Come and see it."

Any other time, I might have blown them off. After all, just how excited was I meant to be about a sign? But at that particular moment, it sounded like the ideal way to take my mind off Goldie.

"I'm on my way."

Moments later, I was standing outside Cuppy C.

"Well, what do you think of the new sign?" asked Amber, who along with her sister had been waiting for me outside the door.

"It's big."

"Isn't it brilliant?" Pearl said.

"It's *very* big."

"Don't keep saying that." Amber sighed. "Tell us what you think of the new design."

"It's very different to the original sign, isn't it? Much bigger for a start."

"Cooler, though?"

"What made you decide to incorporate those butterflies into the design?"

"Those aren't butterflies!" Pearl snapped. "They're winged cupcakes."

"Oh, right, yeah. Of course."

"You don't like it, do you?" Amber pouted.

"Of course I do."

"Honestly?"

"Yeah, it's just not what I was expecting. I thought it would be similar to the old one."

"We designed this one ourselves," Pearl said.

Why wasn't I surprised by that?

"We spent ages coming up with the flying cupcakes idea," Amber said. "The sign maker said he thought it was a touch of genius."

"He did? I mean, yeah, I bet he did. It is. I'll guarantee no one else will have thought of it."

"That's what we said." Pearl puffed out her chest with pride. "So, you do really like it? Honestly?"

"I love it," I lied. "The old one didn't used to have any lights, did it?"

"We didn't need them because Cuppy C wasn't open in the evenings back then. Since we extended the shop, we're open until late, so we figured that we needed an illuminated sign. It's a pity it isn't dark, so you could see it in its full glory. It's pretty spectacular."

"I bet."

"Saturday is going to be amazeballs," Amber said.

Amazeballs?

"Why? What's happening on Saturday?"

"It's the official relaunch party for Cuppy C."

"But you never actually closed."

"We're relaunching the *name,* silly. You have to come. It's going to be epic."

Epic?

"What's with the *amazeballs* and *epic*?"

"That must be the kids." Amber smiled. "Lily is always saying stuff like that."

"L too," Pearl said.

"L?"

"Oh yeah, I didn't tell you, did I? Lil now insists on being called L."

"Right. How are those two doing at their new school?"

"*Amazeballs,* apparently," Pearl said. "L has made loads

of new friends."

"Lily loves it too." Amber nodded.

"That's good. I know you were both worried about how they'd make the transition to senior school. Do they get a lot of homework?"

"Yeah, and it's really hard." Pearl sighed. "L keeps asking me to help her, but I haven't got a clue how to do any of the maths stuff."

"Same here," Amber said. "I tell Lily to ask her dad."

Although I was proud of Florence for being accepted into CASS, a part of me envied the twins for having their daughters still living with them.

"So?" Pearl said. "Are you going to come to the relaunch party?"

"I—err—"

"There'll be lots of free cake."

"I'll be there."

"What about Florence? Will she be able to come?"

"I doubt it. She doesn't get to come home many weekends, but I'll mention it to her on Friday when I take my weekly lesson at CASS."

"Tell her it's going to be *amazeballs*." Amber grinned.

***

"Good morning, Jules."

"Morning," she whispered in reply. "Your sister is in your office. I tried to get her to wait out here, but she said you wouldn't mind her going through."

"Okay."

"Shall I make you both a drink?"

"No, I don't want to encourage her to stay any longer

than necessary."

Kathy, who was seated on the sofa, was totally oblivious to the fact that Winky, my ghost cat, was sitting by her side.

"You really have to do something about this sofa, Jill," Kathy said.

"What's wrong with it? It's really comfortable."

She stood up and then sat down again, causing the sofa to make the unfortunate sound it made every time someone sat on it.

"It's embarrassing, Jill. What must your clients think when they sit on it?"

"They rarely do. Winky's the only one—" I stopped as soon as I realised what I was about to say.

"Winky? Wasn't that that flea-bitten old cat of yours? He died, didn't he?"

"Yeah, I meant *Vinky*."

"Who's *Vinky*?"

"He's a friend of Mrs V's."

"What kind of name is *Vinky*?"

"That's not actually his name. It's just what Mrs V calls him."

While I was spouting all this rubbish, Winky was rolling around on the sofa in hysterics.

"I came to give you this." Kathy handed me an envelope that looked like some kind of wedding invitation. It had Jack's and my name, written in beautiful calligraphy, on the front.

"What's this?"

"Open it."

The envelope looked so expensive that I felt as though I should be using a solid gold letter-opener, but in the absence of such an instrument, I resorted to tearing it open. It was an invitation to the grand opening of Gallery K.

"A week on Saturday? I didn't realise it was opening so soon."

"I did tell you. It's going to be the social event of the year."

"Right. Who's Gregor Leggor?"

"Please tell me you're joking." She rolled her eyes.

"No. Who is he?"

"Only one of this generation's most talented abstract artists. I'm incredibly lucky to have landed him for my first exhibition. And guess what."

I shrugged.

"He's agreed to attend in person during the opening weekend. I'm so excited I could burst."

"Sounds great, but I'm not sure we'll be able to make it. What with my workload and the store."

"You have to come, Jill. Both of you. This is really important to me."

"Will there be cake?"

"No, there *won't* be cake. We can't have sticky fingers touching the exhibits. There'll be a cheese platter and bubbly."

"Okay, we'll do our best."

"Promise?"

"I promise."

"Amazing."

"Don't you mean *amazeballs*?"

"Sorry?"

"It doesn't matter."

"I have to go. I have lots more invitations to deliver."

"I can't believe your sister has landed Gregor Leggor," Winky said, after Kathy had left.

"You've heard of him?"

"Of course I haven't. If he was any good, do you really think he'd have agreed to exhibit in your sister's gallery?"

"I've never really understood abstract art."

"It's pretty simple. Just throw a load of paint at a blank canvas, and then try to get some poor sucker to pay you a fortune for it."

"At least there'll be free bubbly."

"Your sister is right about one thing, though."

"What's that?"

"This sofa. Every time someone sits on it, it sounds like—"

"I know, but I don't see what I can do about it. I've tried changing the cushions around, but it doesn't make any difference."

"Have you tried oiling it?"

"Oiling it? I don't—oh, very funny."

Just then, Jules popped her head around the door.

"Jill, I have a Mr Beasley out here. He doesn't have an appointment, but he wondered if you could spare him a few minutes?"

Other than the Goldie Barr case, which strictly speaking wasn't an official case anyway, I had no work on at the moment, so I asked her to show him through.

"Bring him straight over to my desk, would you? Not to the sofa."

"Will do."

Mr Beasley was probably in his late thirties, but he walked like an old man. His unkempt hair and stubble added to the homeless chic look he seemed to be shooting for.

"Thanks for seeing me, Mrs Maxwell," he said. "Would you mind awfully if I sat on your sofa? I have a bad back and I find it very difficult to sit on firm chairs."

"Err, sure. Do you need a hand?"

"No, I'm fine." He hobbled over to the sofa and then very gingerly lowered himself down onto the seat.

I had my fingers crossed that, by sitting down so slowly, he would avoid the—

Nope. There it went.

My eyes met his but neither of us commented on the unfortunate sound. Instead, we carried on as if nothing had happened. Winky, meanwhile, was once again in hysterics.

There was no way I was going to risk further embarrassment by joining Mr Beasley on the sofa, so instead, I wheeled my chair across the room to be closer to him.

"Are you comfortable on there?" I asked.

"As comfortable as I can be under the circumstances."

"Would you care for a drink?"

"An iced caramel macchiato would go down a treat."

I almost asked him if he'd mistaken my office for Starbucks, but I was desperately short of paying work, so I didn't want to alienate him without at least knowing why he was here.

"Sure." I picked up the phone and buzzed Jules. "Jules, would you get Mr Beasley an iced caramel macchiato, please? Yes, I realise that. Try the one across the road. I'll have one too. Thanks."

"Please call me Bobby," he said.

"Okay, and I'm Jill. What is it I can do for you today?"

"I'm being blackmailed."

"By who? And what are they blackmailing you about?"

"It's rather delicate."

"Even so. If I'm going to help, I'll need to know the details."

"Do you promise not to share what I tell you with anyone else?"

"Of course. Anything you tell me is strictly confidential and will not go beyond these four walls."

"This isn't easy for me."

"Take your time. There's no rush."

"Okay." He took a deep breath. "My mother died recently."

"I'm sorry to hear that."

"Thank you. She was eighty-two."

"Right."

"She fell down the steps to the basement in the house we shared. The house where I still live."

"That's terrible."

"It was. I was just starting to get over it when this happened."

"The blackmail?"

"That's right."

We were interrupted by Jules, who had managed to get the two drinks in double-quick time.

"This is just what I needed." Beasley took a long drink. "Thank you."

"You were about to tell me who was blackmailing you and why."

"As I mentioned, my mother died in tragic circumstances just over a month ago, and now someone is blackmailing me."

This was like pulling teeth.

"About?"

"If I don't pay them, they say they'll go to the police, to tell them I killed her."

"Hold on. Can we back up a little? You said your mother died after she fell down the steps to the basement."

"That's right."

"And it was an accident?"

"Correct."

"Then I don't understand how someone can claim that you killed her."

"They have a recording of me saying that I wished she was dead."

"A recording? Is it real?"

"I—err—"

"I need you to be completely honest with me, Bobby."

"Yes, it's real, but I didn't mean it. We all say things we don't mean, don't we?"

"Sure. Who is blackmailing you?"

"I have no idea."

"You must know who made the recording."

"I don't."

"But you must at least know where you were when the recording was made."

"I have a good idea. It was in my local pub on my birthday. I'd had a few too many drinks that night."

"But you're sure it was you on the recording?"

"Positive."

"Who were you with that night?"

"No one. I was sitting by myself."

"On your birthday?"

"I'm a very private person. I prefer my own company."

"Who did you make the comment about your mother to?"

"No one. I was just talking to myself."

"Out loud?"

"Yes. As I've already said: I'd had a few drinks."

"Right. Here's the thing that I don't understand. If you didn't kill your mother, why are you worried about this? If someone was to pass the recording to the police, you could simply tell them what you've just told me: that it was just talk."

"It's not that simple."

"Why not?"

"Because I'm the sole beneficiary of my mother's estate. I get her house and her money, which is a not inconsiderable amount."

"That's not unusual in these circumstances."

"I know, but she also took out a life insurance policy a few years before she died. I had no idea she'd done it, but you have to admit it looks suspicious."

"I still think that if you have nothing to hide, you should go to the police and tell them about the blackmail."

"I can't take that risk. I really need you to find out who's behind this and to stop them."

"Okay, but I'm still not convinced this is your best course of action." I went to my desk and took out one of my standard contracts. "Read this, and if you're happy with the terms, sign it. I'll also need you to pay a retainer."

Ten minutes later, he'd signed the paperwork and made the initial payment.

"What happens now?" he asked.

"I'd like to start by paying a visit to your house, to see where your mother died."

"Why do you need to do that? I told you it was an accident."

"And I believe you, but I'd still like to see the steps down to the basement."

"Okay, but I'll be out all day tomorrow, so can we make it Wednesday?"

"Sure. What time?"

"Ten o'clock?"

"Okay, I'll see you then."

No sooner had he hobbled out of the office than Winky jumped onto my desk. "He definitely did it."

"What are you talking about?"

"The Weasley guy. He obviously pushed his old mum down the basement steps to get his hands on her money."

"His name is *Beasley*. And why would you say that?"

"You only have to look at him. He has murderer written all over his face."

Chapter 2

I caught a whiff of fish, and I was just about to accuse Winky of opening one of his cans of salmon (it wouldn't have been the first time) when Jules came through to my office, closing the door behind her.

"Mr Petty is out there." She pulled a face. "Why does he always smell of fish?"

"I've no idea. Maybe it's his aftershave. What does he want?"

"I did ask him, but he wouldn't tell me. I told him that you were extremely busy, but he insists it's urgent."

"It always is with him. Send him through, but if he's still here in ten minutes, come through and remind me of my urgent meeting across town."

"Will do."

Peter Petty marched into my office, wafting eau de mackerel as he did.

"Jill, there is a matter of some delicacy that I need to discuss with you."

"What's that, Peter?"

"Two-ply."

"Sorry?"

"You must have noticed."

"I'm sorry, Peter, but I have no idea what you're talking about."

"The management charges in this building are quite steep, I'm sure you'd agree."

"That's true."

"For that kind of money, the very least we should expect is three-ply."

Only then, did the penny drop. Although, given the

image it conjured up, I truly wished it hadn't.

"Are you talking about toilet rolls, Peter?"

"Indeed I am. Until recently, all the bathrooms were stocked with three-ply, but I noticed yesterday that the new stock are all two-ply. Now, I don't know about you, Jill, but I find the two-ply to be wholly inadequate for my needs. I'm forced to—"

"Stop there. I get the picture. Maybe, it's just a temporary measure. Perhaps they couldn't get hold of any three-ply."

Why was I even having this conversation?

"It's a slippery slope if you ask me. If we allow them to get away with this, then who knows what they'll do next." He opened his briefcase and took out a clipboard. "I've started a petition, which I intend to pass on to the management company, to get them to reinstate the three-ply." He pushed the petition across my desk.

I figured the quickest way to get him out of my office was to sign his stupid petition, so I scribbled my name and handed back the clipboard.

"Thanks, Jill. It's up to people like you and me to ensure standards around here don't fall. Did I tell you about the plants in reception?"

Fortunately, right on cue, Jules came through the door.

"Jill, you asked me to remind you about your urgent meeting on the other side of town."

"Oh yes. Thanks, Jules. Perhaps you could show Mr Petty out."

"What about the plants, Jill?" he said.

"I'm afraid that will have to wait for another day."

Somewhat reluctantly, he and his petition took their leave.

"I don't know why you put up with that idiot," Winky said.

"He's harmless enough."

"Toilet rolls, though? You should have told him that you didn't give a cr—"

"That's enough from you, thanks very much."

Suddenly, Winky shot across the room and dived under the sofa. That could mean only one thing. And, sure enough, moments later, Grandma appeared in front of my desk.

"Have you ever considered taking the lift like everyone else?" I sighed. "Or making an appointment?"

"I don't need an appointment to see my granddaughter, and that lift makes me dizzy. It travels much too fast."

"If this is a social call, I—"

"It isn't. A friend of mine needs your help."

"I'm too busy."

"You don't even know what she wants yet."

"Why don't *you* help her if she's a friend of yours?"

"Normally, I would, but I'm busy finalising the details on my patent application."

"*Patent application*? This is the first I've heard about that. What's it for?"

"I can't tell you."

"Why not?"

"Because you might rip off my idea."

"It's nice to know you have such trust in me. Anyway, like I said, I'm too busy to—"

"She's willing to pay for your services. I told her there was no need, but she insists."

"Who is it?" I asked.

"Her name is Joy Hoy."

"That's not really her name, is it?"

"It is, but only since she married Andy Hoy."

"Right."

"Before that, she was Joy Joy."

"You're making this up."

"I promise. You can ask her yourself."

"I assume Joy is a witch?"

"She is, but she doesn't practice much magic these days. She's too busy running her business."

"What kind of business does she have?"

"It's in the name: Joy's Toys. She runs it with her two boys."

"Joy's Toys is run by Joy and her two boys?"

"That's what I just said, isn't it? Roy and Troy."

"Roy and Troy are Joy's boys?"

"That's right, but they're not really boys anymore. They both have children of their own."

"What is it that Joy needs my help with?"

"It'll be easier for her to explain it herself. I told her that you'd pop over and see her this afternoon."

"Today?"

"It's not like you're doing anything else, is it? Apart from the pressing matter of the toilet rolls, that is."

"Okay, I'll go and talk to Joy. How can I find her?"

"This is her business card." She turned around and looked under the sofa. "I thought that mangy cat of yours had died."

"He did. Winky is a ghost now."

"You should ship him off to GT."

"I like having him around. He's got two eyes again now."

"Big whoop. By the way, did you hear my old hotel is

hosting its first convention this weekend?"

"No, I didn't. What is it? Do you know?"

"No idea. I have zero interest in what that bunch of saddos do." And with that, she disappeared.

When Winky came out from under the sofa, he had a stupid grin on his face. "You told your grandmother that you liked having me around."

"I just said that to annoy her. I didn't really mean it."

"Liar. You really *looooove* me." And with that he jumped straight at me, leaving me no option but to catch him in my arms.

"What do you think you're doing?"

"Give me a cuddle."

"Get lost." I dropped him onto the sofa, which made the obligatory rude noise. "That proves you're overweight."

"Rubbish. I'm a lean, mean loving machine."

"Talking of which, where is Daisy? I haven't seen her for a day or two."

"That's over."

"But I thought she was the one?"

"So did I, but those angels are more trouble than they're worth. I'm young, free and single again."

"Shouldn't that be dead, free and single?"

"Whatever. Let's just say every single lady cat in GT is hoping I'll come a calling."

"I see breaking up with Daisy hasn't dented your confidence."

"Why would it? I'm quite the catch."

"If you say so."

I magicked myself to the address on the business card that Grandma had left with me.

The multi-coloured building was so bright I could have done with a pair of sunglasses. The sign above the door read: **JOY'S TOYS.**

The display of toys in the window was nothing short of spectacular. There were no high-tech toys to be seen. Instead, it was full of amazing wooden toys. A chime announced my arrival as I stepped into the shop.

"Welcome to Joy's Toys."

The squeaky little voice came from over the other side of the shop, but I couldn't see anyone.

"Hello?"

"I'm over here. Behind the hill of cuddlies."

Smack bang in the centre of the shop was the biggest pile of cuddly toys I'd ever seen. In addition to all the usual favourites were some strange additions, including cuddly vampire bats and cuddly wood nymphs. I made my way around the hill, where I found a tiny pixie who was using a handheld device to add price stickers to the cuddly spiders she was placing on the hill.

"Hi, there." She smiled.

"Hi. The toys in here are amazing."

"Every one of them is handmade."

"Amazeballs, but do people really buy cuddly *spiders*?"

"They're one of our most popular lines. We've been waiting for this new batch to arrive. Is there anything in particular you're looking for today?"

"Actually, I'm not here to buy a toy. I'm here to see Joy. I believe she's expecting me."

"I see. What's your name, please?"

"Jill Maxwell."

"*The* Jill Maxwell?"

"I guess so."

"Wow. This is such an honour. My grandma thinks you're the bees' knees."

"That's—"

"My granddad doesn't like you, though. He said you can't ride a broom for toffee. I'm Leaf, by the way."

"*Leaf?*"

"Unusual, eh?" She smiled. "Still, I reckon I got the best end of the deal. My younger sister is called Twig. I'll go and tell Joy you're here."

"Thanks."

Moments later, Leaf reappeared, accompanied by a woman, who looked to be a similar age to Aunt Lucy. She was dressed from head to toe in pink, including pink jewellery and makeup. It was quite a look.

"Jill." She shook my hand. "It's good of you to come over so quickly. I only spoke to Mirabel this morning."

"No problem. I hope I can help."

"I was just about to have some iced tea," she said once we were in her office. "Would you care for some?"

"Thanks, that would be nice."

Using the intercom on her desk, she asked Leaf to bring iced tea and biscuits for both of us.

Biscuits. I liked the sound of that. I liked it even more when Leaf brought through a tin full of custard creams.

"Mirabel told me you were partial to these," Joy said. "So, I had someone nip over to the human world to buy them."

"You shouldn't have gone to all that trouble." I grabbed three of them. "Thanks."

"Did Mirabel tell you why I needed your help?"

"No, she said it would be better to hear it from you."

"In that case, I'd better start by telling you a little about

Joy's Toys."

"Okay."

"It all started out of my frustration at not being able to find quality toys for my own two boys."

"Roy and Troy?"

"That's right. When they were young, I spent ages visiting shop after shop, trying to find simple, but well-made toys. There weren't any. Everything was so cheap and tacky. I was convinced that I couldn't be the only parent in Candlefield who wanted something better for their children."

"Judging by how long you've been in business, I'd say you were proven right."

"Thankfully, yes, because I ploughed all our savings into the venture."

"The toys out there are fabulous."

"Thanks. Everything is handmade in our own factory. That way we can ensure it's of the highest quality. You have a daughter, don't you, Jill?"

"I do, but Florence is a little old for toys now, unfortunately."

"Your grandmother told me she's attending CASS."

"That's right. We're very proud of her."

"And rightly so. My boys were never very academic, which is why they both ended up working with me."

"Do they help you run this shop?"

"Good heavens, no." She laughed. "Roy and Troy have many good qualities, but working in a customer-facing role isn't one of them. Roy is in charge of manufacturing and Troy runs the warehouse."

"You have a warehouse too?"

"Yes. I should have said that we also supply most of the

toy shops here in the sup world."

"What about the human world?"

"No. I've considered it many times, but I always come to the same conclusion: it's best for us to stay focussed on the sup world."

"What prompted you to ask my grandmother to contact me?"

"As I mentioned before, we manufacture all the toys we sell. Until recently, that philosophy has paid dividends because the number of returns was practically zero."

"You said: *until recently*. What's changed?"

"Over the last couple of months, the number of faulty toys returned has increased ten-fold."

"Has something changed in your manufacturing process?"

"No. All the toys are made by highly trained operatives, and they go through a rigorous quality control check before being despatched to the warehouse."

"So the problem is at the warehouse?"

"I don't think so. I believe someone is sabotaging our toys."

"Would you care to elaborate?"

"I wish I could. I've racked my brain to try and figure out what's happening, but I'm none the wiser. When the toys leave the shop from which they're purchased, they're perfectly fine, but then within days, they develop faults."

"What kind of faults?"

"It varies. It might be easier for you to see for yourself. I've kept all the returns at the warehouse. If you agree to take the case, I'll arrange for Troy to show you."

"Do your sons know that you've contacted me?"

"Yes, and I'm afraid they weren't very happy when I

told them. They insist that they can sort out the problem themselves, but as I pointed out, this has been going on for far too long already. The conversation became a little heated, but I left them in no doubt that if you take the case, I will expect them to give you their full cooperation. So, what do you say, Jill? Can you help me?"

"I'm sure I can."

"Excellent. How do we proceed from here?"

I took a standard contract out of my bag and handed it to her. "Read this and if you're happy to proceed, sign it and let me have it back."

"I don't need to read it. Your reputation is good enough for me." She took out a pen, signed the contract and handed it back to me. "What now?"

"Can you arrange for me to visit the warehouse to see the toys that have been returned?"

"I'll get Troy to give you a call in the next day or two."

"Excellent."

Chapter 3

"Do you mind?" Jack said when I snatched his morning newspaper.

"I'm just checking if there's anything about Goldie."

"There isn't or I would have told you." He grabbed it back from me. "I want to check the bowling results."

"You shouldn't be reading at the table. Don't you know it's rude?"

"But you were—never mind." He folded the newspaper and placed it on the chair next to him. "Do you think I should buy a new suit?"

"Why on earth do you need a new suit?"

"For the gallery opening."

"Don't be ridiculous. It's only Kathy's shindig."

"It's in the creative quarter. It's likely to be a well posh affair."

"*Well posh*? When did you stop speaking English?"

"You know what I mean."

"I do, but I reckon it'll just be cheap plonk and a few cocktail sausages on sticks."

"I think I'll get my suit dry-cleaned, just in case."

"Please yourself. We'll probably be the only ones there."

We were interrupted by a loud knock at the door. Before either of us had the chance to react, there was an even louder pounding.

"Go and answer it, then," I said.

"You're the nearest."

"It might be a mad axeman."

"Fine." Jack huffed. "But if I get sliced up, it'll be your fault."

"Just don't get blood on the carpet."

I wasn't kidding. That new carpet had cost us an arm and a leg. And some idiot (me) had chosen light grey, which showed every mark.

In the absence of any blood curdling screams, I concluded that whoever was at the door wasn't wielding an axe. I could hear Jack talking to someone, but I couldn't hear what was being said. Probably some door-to-door salesman, in which case I should have answered the door because, soft-touch that he was, Jack would no doubt sign us up to buy a set of encyclopaedias.

As it turned out, it was much worse than that.

Jack walked back into the kitchen, followed by my nemesis, Mr Flatley, AKA Flat Head.

"Mr Flatley is here, Jill. He wondered if he might have a word with us."

"Good morning, Mrs Maxwell."

Flat Head had a smile that was much scarier than any vampire I'd ever encountered.

"Good morning, Mr Flatley."

"Is that toast I smell?" He sniffed the air. "My toaster broke yesterday."

Before I could suggest he go out and buy another one, Jack had jumped in. "Would you care for a slice, Mr Flatley?"

I shot Jack a look, but he ignored me.

"A couple of slices would go down a treat," Mr Flatley said. "Do you happen to have any marmalade?"

"Absolutely," Jack said. "Grab a seat while I make your toast."

Before I could stop him, Flat Head took the seat next to mine.

"Not too well done, please. I do hate burnt toast, don't

you?"

Not as much as I hated having a creepy little man invading my kitchen.

"No problem," Jack said.

"I hope you have butter. I don't hold with that spread nonsense."

"Butter it is."

Jack buttered the toast and handed the plate and marmalade to Flat Head who spent the longest moment examining it closely. If he so much as murmured one word of complaint, I would turn him into a cockroach, and gleefully crush him underfoot.

"Thank you, Mr Maxwell. That's just the way I like it." He began to spread the marmalade on the toast.

Just when I thought things couldn't get any worse, he began to chew the toast with his mouth wide open. I averted my gaze, but I couldn't escape the truly awful noise. Jack must have sensed that I was about to explode because he took the seat on the other side of me and put his hand on mine.

After what seemed like an age, Flat Head finished the last piece of toast.

"I don't suppose I could get a cup of tea to wash it down with, could I?"

"Sure." Jack jumped to his feet.

Needless to say, Flat Head's disgusting table manners were not confined to eating, so I was forced to listen to him slurping the tea.

"That was very kind of you both," Flat Head said. "Which makes what I have to say even more difficult." He hesitated. "You don't happen to have any toothpicks, do you?"

"No!" I snapped.

"Sorry, no," Jack said.

"Not to worry. I'll floss when I get home."

"You said you had something difficult to tell us," I prompted him.

"Oh yes. You'll both no doubt be aware of the rules regarding planning permission for fences, as they appertain to household dwellings."

"In English?"

Jack shot me a look, but I ignored him. This guy was pushing me to my limits.

"The maximum height allowed for a fence is two metres. Above that, and planning permission is required."

"That's all very interesting, Mr Flatley." I sighed. "But what does it have to do with anything?"

"I've always prided myself in my ability to judge heights, and so when I had occasion to walk past your fence the other day, it occurred to me that it seemed to be more than two metres high."

"That fence has been there for years. It was here when we bought this place. If it was too high, someone would have noticed at the time it was erected. You must be mistaken."

"I'm afraid not."

"How can you be so sure?" I was rapidly losing patience with the arrogant know-it-all.

"I'm sure because I took the liberty of measuring it."

"You did what?"

"Obviously, I wanted to be sure of my ground before I approached you."

"You must have measured it incorrectly."

"I'm afraid not. It's actually two metres and two

centimetres high."

"Even if you're right, and I'm not conceding that you are, we're only talking about a measly two centimetres." I used my thumb and forefinger to illustrate the point. "Who's to know?"

"That's what I wanted to tell you. I felt it was my civic duty to make the local authority aware of this breach of their regulations. I believe you'll be hearing from them shortly."

"You snitched on us?"

"I would hardly describe it as *snitching*, Jill. As I said, I felt honour bound to make the authorities aware. It's nothing personal." He stood up. "Now, I must get back. It's my day to water the tomato plants."

"I'll show you out." Jack jumped up and saw him to the door.

I was too stunned to move, so I was still in my seat when Jack returned.

"Can you believe the nerve of that man?" I exploded.

"Don't let him get you worked up."

"*Worked up*? I'm way beyond being *worked up*. I'm at Defcon One. He sits there, eating our toast and drinking our tea, and then he has the brass neck to tell us that he's grassed us up to the local authority."

"I doubt anything will come of it. Like you said, the fence has been there for years."

"Flat Head better hope nothing comes of it because if it does, he'll regret it."

***

"What's up with you?" Winky said.

"One of my neighbours is driving me insane. I hate him with a vengeance."

"What has he done?"

"Reported us to the local authority because our fence is two centimetres higher than is allowed without planning permission."

"Tut tut."

"It's not our doing. The fence was there when we bought the house."

"What are you going to do about it?"

"I'm debating whether to turn him into a cockroach or a rat."

"I meant about the fence?"

"Nothing. Jack reckons the local authority won't do anything about it after all this time."

"Hmm."

"What does that mean?"

"Never underestimate the pettiness of local bureaucrats. They get off on this kind of stuff."

It was as though Winky's mention of the word pettiness had somehow summoned him because, moments later, Jules popped her head through the door, to tell me Peter Petty wanted a quick word with me.

"He reckons it's very important."

Before I had the chance to say she should tell him to sling his hook, Petty appeared next to Jules in the doorway.

"Only me, Jill. I won't keep you a minute."

"Okay, but it will have to be very quick because I have an urgent appointment in five minutes, don't I, Jules?"

"Err, yeah, that's right. With Mr err—Sofadesk."

Jules had many strengths, but coming up with fake

names at the drop of a hat wasn't one of them.

Petty strolled across the room and took a seat.

"What's this about, Peter?"

"I thought you'd appreciate an update on the two-ply issue."

"We only spoke about it yesterday."

"Yes, but twenty-four hours is a long time to have to put up with inferior toilet tissue, don't you agree?"

"I can think of bigger problems."

"Guess how many signatures I have procured on my petition."

"I've no idea."

"Guess."

"Two million."

"Thirty-six."

Petty was clearly proud of the number of signatures he'd managed to get but given that I knew there were almost one thousand people working in Washbridge Central Point, I was less impressed.

"That's great, but I—"

"And that's only the first step."

"It is?"

"In the event that the management company sees fit to disregard the petition, as I suspect they might, then we will have no option but to take this story to the media. That's where you come in."

"Sorry?"

"I have many strengths, Jill, but dealing with the media isn't one of them. You would be perfect, though."

"Hang on. Even if the media were interested in a story about toilet rolls, which by the way they most certainly wouldn't be, there's no way I'm going to talk to them."

"Why not? You're not unattractive. You're articulate. And you have a certain presence. You'd be perfect as our spokesman."

Not unattractive? Something told me that wasn't quite the same as being attractive.

"I'm sorry, Peter, but you'll have to find someone else to do it, or better still, do it yourself."

"But you—"

"Sorry, that's my final word on the subject. We'll have to wind this up now because Mr Desksofa will be here any moment.

"Sofadesk."

"Sorry?"

"Jules said your appointment was with a Mr Sofadesk."

"That's what I meant." I stood up, walked over to the door, and held it open for him.

Why did I attract such obnoxious men? It was bad enough that I had Flat Head giving me grief about my fence, without having to listen to Petty's pettiness.

"I'm surprised you turned him down," Winky said.

"Of course I turned him down. I'm not going to go on TV, just to make a fool of myself over a few toilet rolls."

"I seem to remember you did just that a few years ago." He laughed.

He was referring to the awful TV advertisements I'd had the misfortune to take part in several years earlier. I still had nightmares about those giant toilet rolls.

Talking to Peter Petty had given me a headache, but I knew what would cure it, so I magicked myself over to Aunt Lucy's. I found her in the garden, weeding the borders. When she saw me, she got slowly to her feet, with a pained expression on her face.

"Are you okay, Aunt Lucy?"

"I'm fine. It's just my old knees. They tend to seize up when I've been on them for any length of time. To what do I owe this unexpected pleasure?"

"I've had a horrible morning, so I thought I'd pop over and see you. I hope you don't mind."

"Of course not. Shall we go inside and have a cup of tea?"

"That would be lovely."

"And a cupcake?"

"Even better. Where are the boys?"

"Old Mr Keentoe from next door but one has taken them to the park. He's all by himself since his wife ran away with the bread man, and he appreciates any excuse to get out of the house."

We took our drinks through to the lounge, and Aunt Lucy brought through a plate full of amazing looking cupcakes.

"I should warn you that these are experimental," she said.

"Sorry?"

"I was fed up of making the same old flavours all the time, so I went to the library and found this." She reached down the side of the chair and produced a book titled Extreme Cupcakes.

"What flavour is the blue one?" I asked.

"Sizzle berry."

"Never heard of it."

"Neither had I, but that's true for most of the ingredients in the book. I had to pay a visit to Grannie Harriet's to find them."

"Who's she?"

"It's a small shop, just around from the post office in the marketplace. Grannie Harriet herself is long gone, but the shop is still going from strength to strength. They sell all manner of exotic fruits and berries. You should check it out sometime."

"I'll do that." I hesitated. "Are you sure it's safe to eat sizzle berries?"

"Yes." She smiled. "All the recipes in the book are guaranteed to be free from any nasty side-effects."

"Okay." I was still a little nervous because I'd fallen foul of eating rare berries before. In the end, I threw caution to the wind and took a bite. "That's amazing. I've never tasted anything like it."

And to prove the point, I finished it off in double quick time.

"Would you like another one?"

"I shouldn't but go on then. What's the red one?"

"I forget. Let me just check." She flicked through the book. "Oh yes. How could I forget? That's Lunana."

"What's Lunana?"

"I asked the wonderful young man at Grannie Harriet's the same thing. Apparently, it's a fruit similar in shape to a banana but it's red and it tastes nothing like one. I ate one just before I started the gardening, and it was delicious."

Reassured, I took a bite.

"That's amazing." I managed to say through a mouthful of cake.

"You can take a couple home with you if you like."

"Thanks, I will, but not for me. I'll take them for Jack."

"Okay." She grinned, well aware that Jack wouldn't get

within a hundred yards of them. "It's always lovely to see you, Jill, but did you pop over for anything in particular?"

"Not really. I was just having a bad morning, and I figured this would cheer me up. And I was right." I took a slurp of tea to wash down the last of the cupcake.

"Are you as excited about Ringabell as I am? I can't believe it's almost fifty years since the last one, can you?"

"Sorry, Aunt Lucy, but I have no idea what you're talking about."

"Oh yes, I sometimes forget that you weren't around for the last one. It's one of the biggest celebrations in the sup calendar. Unlike most of the others, Ringabell is open to all sups."

"What happens, exactly?"

"Where do I begin? There's something for everyone. A funfair, music concerts, sports, amazing food, and of course, the centrepiece is the parade. Lester isn't one for carnivals, so he's agreed to stay home and watch the dogs while I watch the parade."

"What about the twins? Will they be taking part?"

"I wouldn't think so. The town will be heaving with people, and Cuppy C is likely to be busy all day. Do you think you'll be able to make it?"

"I hope so."

Chapter 4

I'd hoped I might hear from Joy's son, Troy, to arrange my visit to the warehouse to see the defective toys, but, so far, I had heard nothing from him. Joy had mentioned that her sons had not been very enthusiastic about my involvement in their affairs. Was that the reason for the radio silence? I resolved to give him another twenty-four hours after which, if I still hadn't heard from him, I would speak to Joy.

I was itching to know what was happening with the investigation into Goldie Barr's murder, but there were still no updates in the local newspapers. Jack had warned me to stay away from the investigation, and that would have been the sensible thing to do, but I'd never been a fan of sensible.

I could have called the police station and asked to speak to Big Mac, but the chances of him speaking to me were somewhere south of zero. Far better to try to confront him face to face, so after magicking myself back from Aunt Lucy's, I made my way to Washbridge police station.

The officer behind the reception desk glanced up from his computer. "Yes, how can I help you?"

"I'd like to speak to Detective McDonald."

"Is he expecting you?"

"No, but I have information about the Goldie Barr murder investigation."

"What's your name?"

"Jill Maxwell."

"Take a seat. I'll see if Detective McDonald can see you."

"Thanks."

The officer picked up the phone and spoke to Big Mac. "Sorry to disturb you, sir, but I have a woman here who says she has information about the Goldie Barr case. Maxwell. Jill Maxwell."

Although I couldn't hear the other side of the conversation, it was obvious from the officer's expression that Big Mac had made some comment about me. And nothing complimentary.

The officer finished on the call and said, "Detective McDonald will be down shortly."

"Thanks."

Shortly turned out to be thirty-five minutes later, but I didn't mind waiting if it meant that I would get to find out what was happening. The officer visibly jumped when Big Mac came charging through the door behind the desk.

Without so much as making eye contact with me, he snapped, "Maxwell! This way."

I jumped up and followed him back through the door he'd just come through. He led the way to one of the interview rooms and gestured that I should take a seat at one side of the table. He sat at the opposite side.

Before he could say anything, I jumped in first.

"What's happening on the Goldie Barr case, Detective?"

"You told my officer that you had information about the case. I hope you weren't lying, Maxwell."

"Absolutely not. I would never do that. I just thought we might share what we knew so far."

"That's not how this works. You said you have information relevant to the case. Do you, or don't you?"

"I do. Goldie confided in me a number of times before she was murdered."

"About what?"

"The first time, it was about the milk bottles. She told me that she thought someone had taken them into her house."

"Hold on. I thought you had *new* information. I already know about the incident you just mentioned. And the ones concerning the bowls and the beds."

"But don't you see it's those three incidents that will lead you to the murderer? If you can find out who meddled with the milk bottles, bowls and beds, you'll have your man."

"I disagree. My people spoke to Ms Barr about those incidents prior to her murder, and we concluded that they were all figments of her overactive imagination."

"And I suppose her murder was a figment of her imagination too, was it?" I thumped the desk, more in exasperation than in anger.

"That's enough. One more outburst like that and you'll be spending the night in a cell."

"But surely you have to revisit those incidents in light of her murder?"

"We don't, and for very good reason."

"What's that?"

"I shouldn't really be telling you this, but there'll be a press conference in the next couple of days, so you'll find out anyway."

"Tell me what?"

"A man has been charged with Goldie Barr's murder. And it has precisely nothing to do with those silly incidents you were just banging on about."

"What man? Who is he?"

"You'll have to wait for the press conference to find out along with everyone else." He stood up. "And I warn you that the next time you lie about having information related to one of our investigations, I will charge you with wasting police time."

After that, he showed me unceremoniously out of the building.

"Hello, stranger."

I turned around to find Daze standing there.

"Hey, there. What are you doing here? I thought you'd retired."

"I had, but after nine months I started to go stir crazy, so I asked if I could have my old job back."

"That's great."

"Not really." She frowned. "They said no."

"What? Why? You were the best rogue retriever by a country mile. No disrespect to Blaze."

"That's as maybe, but there's a new regime at RR HQ and they've introduced wholesale changes."

"What kind of changes?"

"Basically, everything has to be done strictly by the book now. They're more interested in crossing 'T's and dotting 'I's than they are in actually catching the bad guys."

"How's that working out?"

"Just as you'd expect. The number of reported incidents in the human world has tripled while the number of apprehensions has halved."

"If things are that bad, why wouldn't they welcome you back with open arms?"

"Because I wasn't known for playing by the book. They're worried I might make them look bad."

"That's ridiculous."

"Maybe, but they're not going to change their minds."

"So you're still retired, then?"

"Officially, yes."

"And unofficially?"

"Do you have time for a coffee?"

"Sure. Do you know anywhere around here?"

"I certainly do." She grinned. "This way."

She led the way down the road to the first junction and then took a sharp left.

"Where are we headed?" I said, trying to keep up with her.

"You'll see."

About twenty yards down the road, she turned into a narrow alley that appeared to be deserted. I could see that it was a dead end, and there didn't appear to be any shops down there, so I was confused as to where she was headed.

When she was just a few yards from the end of the alley, she stopped, and said, "Here we are."

Totally confused, I looked around, "Am I missing something?"

"I take it you've not been to the Crossover Coffee Bar before?"

"I've never even heard of it. Where is it?"

"Here." She pointed to the brick wall that formed the end of the alley.

"I don't—"

"Before I could finish my sentence, Daze pressed several bricks, each one of which glowed a different colour. After she'd finished, the wall turned into a doorway, above which was a sign with the word: **Crossover**.

"After you." Daze ushered me to go ahead.

I stepped inside and took the stairs down into what appeared to be the basement. At the bottom of the stairs was another doorway, next to which stood a tall werewolf wearing a tux.

"Hi, Albert," Daze said. "I've brought a guest. I hope that's okay."

"Of course." He smiled at me. "Any friend of Daze is welcome in the Crossover. I hope you don't mind my asking, but why is your face familiar to me?"

"This is Jill Maxwell," Daze said.

"Of course. I should have known. This is indeed an honour, Mrs Maxwell."

"Please call me Jill."

"If there's anything you need, Jill, please just ask."

"Thanks, I will."

I'd been in many coffee shops, but I'd never seen anything quite like this. It was clear that no expense had been spared.

"What do you think?" Daze said.

"It's amazing." As I continued to look around, it became obvious that there were sups of every kind in there. "I had no idea there was a sup-only coffee shop in Washbridge."

"There isn't."

I checked again, in case I'd missed any humans amongst the clientele, but there were none.

"I don't understand. There are no humans in here."

"That's right." She grinned, clearly enjoying my confusion. "And we aren't in Washbridge any longer."

"But I—where are we?"

"Candlefield of course."

"Now, I'm really confused."

"Come with me and I'll show you."

She led the way to the opposite side of the shop where there was another door. This one wasn't guarded by a doorman.

"Go outside and take a look," she said.

I stepped outside and found myself in the market square in Candlefield. I turned to Daze who had followed me outside.

"I've been here lots of times, but I've never seen this coffee shop before."

"That's because it only opened a couple of weeks ago. Come back inside and I'll get us a drink."

While Daze went to the counter to get the drinks, I took a seat in one of the many semi-circular booths that bordered the walls. As soon as she returned, I began to fire questions at her.

"How can there be entrances to this place in the human world and the sup world?"

"Because the coffee shop is connected to both of them. Hence the name."

"Hang on. Does that mean a human could use this to get to Candlefield?"

"No."

"But what if they knew the code that you used to make the entrance appear?"

"Even if they somehow got hold of the code, which is highly unlikely, the wall wouldn't respond to a human. Only sups can gain entry via the Washbridge entrance."

"What about travelling the other way? Can any sup use this as a shortcut to get to the human world?"

"No. Effectively, it's one way travel only. Any sup already in the human world can gain access to Candlefield, but not vice versa."

"Does that mean we can't go back?"

"No, we'll be okay because we came in that way, but anyone entering through the Candlefield entrance won't be permitted to exit via the Washbridge door."

"It's all rather confusing."

"Not really. The purpose of this place isn't to provide a tunnel between the two worlds. It's to provide a venue for sups who live in different worlds to meet and have a coffee. So for example, if a vampire, living in Candlefield, wants to meet up for coffee with a friend or relative who lives in the human world, they can arrange to meet here."

"I get it. I think."

"Remember, not all sups can magic themselves back and forth between the two worlds like you can. Before this place existed, they would have had to travel by conventional transport."

"That makes sense."

"Actually, I have arranged to meet someone here," Daze said.

"Sorry, you should have said. I'll drink up and—"

"There's no need to do that." She checked her watch. "He should be here any moment unless he's late again." She glanced over at the Candlefield entrance. "Here he is now."

"Blaze," I blurted out.

"Hello, stranger." He shook my hand. "How long has it been?"

"It must be three years."

"Sit with Jill," Daze said. "I'll go and get you a drink. Your usual, I assume?"

"Yes, please."

Blaze took a seat opposite me. He looked very smart in

what must have been a very expensive suit. A far cry from the catsuit he used to wear all the time.

"It's great to see you again, Blaze."

"Likewise. What do you think about this place?"

"It's fantastic, but I'm still trying to get my head around how it works."

"If you figure it out, let me know." He laughed.

"It's kind of freaking me out, seeing you and Daze dressed in suits."

"I still miss my catsuit."

Just then, Daze arrived with Blaze's drink.

"Come on, Daze," I said. "I'm on tenterhooks to know what you've been up to since you left the rogue retrievers."

"I'm not really supposed to tell anyone. It's top secret."

"That just makes me want to know more than ever."

"What do you think, Blaze?" she said. "Should I tell her?"

"Don't tease her." He turned to me and grinned. "You didn't really think bumping into Daze today was an accident, did you, Jill?"

"I *did*." I turned to Daze. "What's going on?"

"Sorry for the subterfuge," she said. "I couldn't resist it."

"So, what are you doing if you've not actually retired?"

"After I was rejected by the new regime at the rogue retrievers, I resigned myself to a long boring retirement, but then, out of the blue I was contacted by Edward Raise, better known as Erase. He was in overall charge of the rogue retrievers when I first became one. An amazing man who commanded the respect of everyone who worked for him. Unlike those pencil-pushers who are in charge now, Erase had walked the walk himself. He was a tough nut but always very fair. Unfortunately, he retired not long after I joined so I didn't get to work under him for long."

"He's kind of a folk hero to rogue retrievers," Blaze chipped in.

Daze continued, "Don't ask me how, but he had somehow heard that I'd applied to rejoin the rogue retrievers and that I'd been turned down. He asked if I'd meet with him. I didn't hesitate, but to be honest, I thought it would probably be just for a chat about the old days. Boy was I wrong. It turned out that Erase hadn't actually retired. He'd been recruited to head a new department, which was so secret that even today, you won't find any record of it in Candlefield."

"Sounds intriguing. What is it?"

"H-I-D-E. It stands for Human world: Intelligence, Detection and Extraction."

"And what do they do?"

"Every year, thousands of sups are apprehended in the human world for all manner of infringements, many of them quite trivial."

"We should know," Blaze said. "We arrested many of them."

Daze nodded. "HIDE isn't concerned with those. It's focussed on stopping the sups who are responsible for major crimes in the human world."

I jumped in. "I take it Erase asked you to join HIDE?"

"Correct, but I didn't agree immediately."

"Why not?"

"To be honest, I wasn't sure I was qualified to do the job."

"Are you kidding? You're the best rogue retriever there's ever been."

"Maybe. Maybe not, but the work at HIDE is next level. They deal with some horrible stuff and are up against some very smart criminals."

"But you agreed in the end?"

"I did, but only after they'd agreed that I could bring an assistant on board with me."

"So you recruited Blaze?"

"Yes, but only because my first choice turned me down." She laughed. "Just kidding. I wouldn't work with anyone else."

"Well, congratulations to you both, I guess. How's it going?"

"The work is really demanding," Daze said. "Like I said, we're dealing with some really smart criminals."

"What kind of crimes are you talking about?"

"All sorts," Blaze said. "For example, currently we're working on a nationwide fraud case based on crypto currency, but really it's any major crime committed in the human world by a sup."

"So how come you decided to *bump* into me today?"

"I've been wanting to make contact with you for some time," Daze said. "You're the one person I know with strong connections to both the human and sup worlds who has the sort of skills we might need from time to time."

"How come you didn't get in touch before?"

"As I said: HIDE doesn't officially exist. It took me a long time to persuade Erase to allow me to make contact with you. He's paranoid that word of the department might leak out."

"I would never do that."

"I know that, and in the end, I was able to persuade him to let me set up this meeting, to see what you thought."

"What exactly would you want me to do?"

"Our investigations inevitably span both worlds. We might need you to help with the human world part of that from time to time. I wouldn't expect it to be very often, but when something crops up, you will of course be well compensated. The department has a very *big* budget. What do you say? Are you in?"

"Would I get a smart suit like yours?"

"You could definitely do with a wardrobe upgrade." Blaze grinned.

"Cheek. Yeah, I'm in."

After what had turned out to be a quite extraordinary meeting with Daze and Blaze, I left the Crossover through the same entrance that I'd entered. Or at least, that's what I thought, but when I stepped out of the door, I wasn't in the same alley that I'd initially walked down with Daze. I turned to go back into the coffee bar, but the door had disappeared. When I got to the opposite end of the alley, I discovered I was actually on the high street, just a few doors down from Coffee Animal. Totally confused, I resolved to ask Daze to explain exactly how I was supposed to gain access to the Crossover in the future.

Chapter 5

"I don't understand you sometimes," Jack said in between mouthfuls of muesli. "No, I take that back. I don't understand you *any* of the time."

"I might know you'd take the police's side."

"I'm not taking anyone's side. Only yesterday, you were complaining that they weren't doing enough to find Goldie's murderer. Now, you're complaining that they've charged someone with her murder."

"I never said that. I just can't believe Big Mac doesn't think the incidents that preceded the murder were related to it."

"Perhaps they weren't. So what?"

"I don't buy it. Do you seriously expect me to believe that someone broke into her house on three separate occasions, but that had nothing to do with her murder?"

"It's possible. Can't you at least postpone judgement until you know more about the man they've charged?"

"It doesn't look like I have any choice."

"I'd better get to the store. Monty was a bit under the weather yesterday and I'm not sure if he'll make it in today."

"Don't forget to bring some custard creams back with you tonight."

"Money?"

"Take it out of the weekly shopping budget."

"We don't have a weekly shopping budget."

"Then we should start one. First item on the list is three packets of custard creams."

"You're a hopeless case." He gave me a kiss. "Take care out there."

I was just about to leave the house when my phone rang.

"Jill, it's Joy. I was just checking that Troy has been in touch to arrange your visit to the warehouse."

"I haven't heard from him yet."

"That boy will be the death of me. I'm sorry about this, Jill. Leave it with me; I'll light a fire under him."

"Okay."

The fire obviously had the desired effect because, before I got to the car, my phone rang again.

"Jill Maxwell speaking."

"This is Troy from Joy's Toys." The guy sounded as though he'd just woken up and was still half asleep. "My mother said I was to give you a call."

"I'd like to pay a visit to your warehouse, to see the toys that have been returned as faulty."

"I could just send you photos if you like."

"Thanks, but I'd rather see them in person. I'd also like to look around the warehouse."

"Okay. How about next week?"

"I'd rather do it today."

"Wednesday is my day to do the invoices."

"That's okay. I only need you to give me access to the warehouse and point me in the direction of the rejected toys."

"I'm not sure I'll have time today."

"Okay, I'll just give your mother a call and tell her I can't do any more work on the case."

"No!" He suddenly sounded much more awake. "Don't do that. I'll find time for you today, but can we make it mid-morning?"

"Sure." I figured it would probably take until then for him to wake up. "Can you tell me how to find the warehouse?"

"Do you know Dingle Lane?"

"I don't think so."

"How about Pringle Road?"

"Never heard of it."

"What about Single Street?"

"No." I was beginning to think he was taking the mickey. "Are you near to any landmarks I might know?"

"Do you know Big Sally's Launderette?"

Amazingly, I did. I'd walked past there with Aunt Lucy one day and the name had stuck with me.

"Yes, I do."

"That's on Single Street. You need to walk down as far as the launderette, then take the next left onto Pringle Road. At the end of that road, take a right onto Dingle Lane. We're halfway down there on the right."

"Okay, I'll be with you about ten-thirty."

It was obvious that Troy didn't appreciate my involvement in the company's affairs, but fortunately for me, he was terrified of his mother.

***

Jules was at her desk, and she did not look well.

"What's wrong, Jules? You look terrible."

"I feel it. I was up most of the night, being sick. I think it might have been something I ate."

"Why on earth did you come into the office?"

"I thought I might feel better after getting some fresh air, but if anything, I feel even worse."

"Then you'd better get off home. And don't bother with the bus. Call a taxi and I'll refund your fare."

"Thanks, Jill. Would you like me to call Mrs V? She said she'd be happy to cover any time I was off."

"Okay, but tell her not to bother if she already has something else planned."

"I'll try my best to get in tomorrow."

"You mustn't come back until you're fully recovered. Do you hear me?"

"Okay."

Winky was reading a book, but he lowered it before I could see the title.

"Something she ate." He scoffed.

"She's obviously not well."

"She was probably out on the pop last night."

"You're so cynical. I don't think Jules drinks alcohol."

"Right. And I never touch milk or salmon." He went back to his book, and this time I could see the title.

"Haunting for beginners?"

"I took it out of GT library yesterday."

"Why do you need a book on haunting? You're already haunting me, aren't you?"

"This isn't haunting. This is just hanging out. There's much more to haunting."

"Such as?"

"The whole point of a haunting is to give someone the heebie-jeebies."

"So, basically, it's all about scaring people."

"Yeah."

"That's a horrible, despicable thing to do to anyone."

"Do you really think so?"

"Yes, I do."

"Oh, okay. I was actually thinking about haunting the guy next door."

"Peter Petty?"

"Yeah. I thought a good haunting might persuade him to look for a new office."

"Actually, now I come to think about it, perhaps there is a time and place for haunting."

"You just said it was a terrible, despicable thing to do."

"Err, yeah, but I didn't know the context then. If it means we get to see the back of Peter Petty, then I'm all in favour of it. When are you going to start?"

"That all depends."

"On what?"

"On how long it takes me to absorb all the information in this book. There's a lot to take in."

"You'd better get studying, then."

"One thing I've discovered over the years is that I'm able to absorb information much quicker after I've eaten salmon."

"Red not pink?"

"Obviously."

Jules popped her head around the door. "I've spoken to Mrs V, Jill. She's getting Armi to run her into town."

"I hope you told her not to come if she already had plans."

"I did, and she said she'd be glad to get out of the house."

"Thanks. Now, call a taxi and get yourself home. And don't come back until you're feeling better."

"Okay, thanks."

Although I was pleased that Sylvia Silver had taken over my accounts, she could be a bit of a tyrant. She insisted that I email copies of all invoices, bills and receipts every week, and if I was late by even a day, she was on my case. I'd accumulated a number of receipts over the last week, so I spent the next half hour scanning them on my phone, and then I sent them to her by email. I'd no doubt she would get back to me to query some of them—she always did.

When it was time to visit Joy's Toy's warehouse, I magicked myself to Big Sally's Launderette on Single Street. From there, I took the next left onto Pringle Road. At the end of that road, I took a right onto Dingle Lane, from where I could see the warehouse on the opposite side of the road. The building was old and smaller than I'd expected; it was painted bright pink, which certainly made it stand out from all the other dull coloured buildings on the street.

The double doors were locked, so I pressed the bell and waited.

And waited.

After a couple of minutes, I tried the bell again, but with the same result. If Troy was deliberately messing me around, he would regret it big time. I was just about to try the bell one more time when one of the doors opened. The man who appeared in the doorway looked like he'd shaved with a blunt razor.

"Jill?"

"Yeah. Troy?"

"Sorry it took me a while to answer the door. I was on the phone to my mother. Come in, please."

After he'd locked the doors behind us, I followed him

inside.

"Are you here by yourself?" I asked.

"No, the others are on their break at the moment. Do you want to see the returns first?"

"Yes, please."

He weaved his way through the rows of shelving, filled with boxes of all shapes and sizes.

"The returns are over there, in the corner."

I hadn't expected there to be quite so many. The pile of returns was a couple of feet high and covered a sizeable area. I'd thought that maybe the issue would be restricted to one or two lines, but there was all manner of toys on the pile.

"Is it okay if I take a look at some of them?"

"Sure. I'll be in my office just over there." He pointed to a door just a short walk away. "Come and join me when you've seen everything you need to, and I'll organise a drink for us."

"Okay, thanks."

In amongst the returned toys were many of those that I'd seen in the toy shop: A toy train had one of its funnels missing—it appeared to have snapped off. A cuddly teddy had split open and was spilling out its stuffing, a jigsaw box had a sticker attached to it that read: two pieces missing.

I spent at least twenty minutes examining the different toys to see if I could find any kind of pattern, but there was nothing obvious. In fact, there were several instances where the same toy had been returned but with different faults. The scale of the problem was much bigger than I'd expected. While I'd been examining the defective toys, some of the other workers had returned from their break.

There were several different sups, but the majority of them appeared to be elves.

I found Troy at his desk, looking at his phone.

"Is tea okay?"

"Fine. Milk no sugar, please."

He walked across the room, filled a kettle at the small sink, and then took out two Joy's Toy's mugs.

"Thanks." I took a sip. How long have you run the warehouse?"

"It's almost six years now. Mum used to run both this and the shop before that."

"That can't have been easy."

"I don't know how she did it. Although, the volume of sales wasn't anything like it is today. What did you make of the rejects?"

"There's a lot more than I expected."

"It wasn't always like this. Up until recently, you could count the number of returns we'd get every month on the fingers of one hand."

"Something has obviously changed. What do you put it down to?"

"No idea."

"Come on. You must have some theory."

He shrugged, but there was something in his demeanour that told me he was holding something back.

"Come on, Troy. What do you think is going on?"

"Okay, I'll tell you, but it won't do any good."

"Try me."

"You know my brother, Roy, runs manufacturing, I assume?"

"Yes, your mother said."

"He's not been happy for a while."

"Any particular reason?"

"We had an offer to buy the business a few months ago, which he wanted to accept, but Mum and I voted against the sale. The three of us each hold equal shares."

"Are you saying you think your brother is somehow behind the increase in returns?"

"I'm not saying anything, just that these problems started not long after we rejected the sale."

"Could I see where all the toys are packaged?"

"Sure. I'll take you over there."

The packaging department was a hive of activity. Half a dozen elves were seated at a long bench where they manually wrapped toys of all shapes and sizes. Then they added handwritten labels to each parcel before putting them on a conveyor belt, which disappeared through a hole in the wall.

"What's on the other side of that wall?"

"The despatch department. That's where they sort out the packages for the vans. Would you like to see it?"

"Actually, I'd rather talk to some of the workers in here if that's okay with you?"

"No problem. I'll be back in my office when you're done."

I waited until Troy had left and then walked over to the elf who was seated at one end of the bench.

"Hi, do you mind if I interrupt you for a moment?"

"Be my guest. I'm due to go for my break anyway. Mind if I get my flask?"

"Not at all."

I followed him into a small room where he retrieved his backpack from a locker.

"Would you like a drink of tea?" He held up the flask.

"There's plenty."

"No, thanks. I've just had a drink with Troy. Sorry, I didn't catch your name."

"Toppo, at your service."

"I'm Jill. I'm here to try and find out why so many toys have been returned recently."

"Me and the guys figured as much. It's been getting ridiculous."

"Do you have any theories around what's behind it, Toppo?"

"Not a clue. None of us have."

"Troy hinted that he thought the problem might lie with manufacturing."

"He would say that." He grinned. "He and his brother don't get along. It's hardly surprising that he would try and put the blame on Roy."

"I take it you don't agree?"

"We see all the toys that leave this building, and there's been no discernible drop in quality as far as we can tell."

"Are you saying that the toys you're sending out are the same quality as they've always been?"

"Definitely. Better if anything."

"Am I to assume if I spoke to your work colleagues, they'd say the same thing?"

"Without a doubt, but don't take my word for it. Talk to them."

Toppo's confidence that his colleagues would share the same view proved to be correct. I spoke to each one of them and they all told me more or less the same thing.

"How did that go?" Troy asked when I returned to his office.

"Okay, thanks. Don't get up. I can see myself out."

"Will you be paying Roy a visit?"
"Definitely."

Chapter 6

My visit to Joy's Toy's warehouse had been useful, but the feedback I'd received was confusing. Troy seemed adamant that the quality of the toys being manufactured in the factory, run by his brother, had deteriorated. The elves in the despatch department, on the other hand, had all insisted that the quality of the toys being sent out was as good as ever.

Both of those things couldn't be true. Maybe my visit to the manufacturing unit would throw more light on the subject, but Roy was proving just as difficult to get hold of as his brother. Since leaving the warehouse, I'd called him twice, only to be left listening to endless hold music.

I magicked myself back to Washbridge, picked up a sandwich, and then headed to the office where I found Mrs V behind the desk.

"Thanks very much for stepping in like this, Mrs V. I hope I haven't spoiled your plans."

"Actually, you did me a favour. Armi wanted me to go with him to that awful cuckoo clock shop again. Honestly, Jill, if that man brings any more cuckoo clocks home, I won't be responsible for my actions. Would you like me to make you a drink?"

"No, thanks. I had one not long ago. Any calls?"

"A Mr Cane called wanting to buy some sugar. I told him that he must have the wrong number."

"Right. Thanks again for doing this."

I went through to my office.

"Winky! Where are you?"

He suddenly appeared on my desk.

"Where did you come from?"

"I was practising my haunting skills. That's called the deep invisible. It worked, didn't it?"

"If by that you mean that I couldn't see you, then yes, it did."

"Great. At this rate, I should be ready to go by tomorrow."

"That's good, but I have a bone to pick with you."

"What did I do now?"

"Mr Cane?"

"Oh that." He laughed. "Sorry, I just couldn't resist. It's been ages since the old bag lady was here."

"I thought we'd had this out some time ago, and that you'd promised there would be no more prank calls."

"I thought that only applied to Jules."

"It applies to whoever is working on reception. I don't want you wasting their time with your stupidity."

"Spoilsport."

I'd only been back at my desk for a few minutes when I heard the outer door open. Moments later, Mrs V popped her head around the door.

"It's your sister, Jill."

This was getting beyond a joke. Kathy was spending more time at my office than she did at her own home.

"You'd better show her in."

"I will, but could you come out here for a moment first? There seems to be some confusion."

Before I could ask what it was all about, she'd gone back through to the outer office, so I was forced to follow her.

"What seems to be the problem?" I asked the two of them.

"Your sister just asked me about my friend, Vinky."

Oh bum, and double bum.

"You told me Mrs V had a friend called Vinky," Kathy said. "But she's never heard of him."

"I've never heard of him," Mrs V confirmed.

The two of them looked to me for an explanation, so I obliged.

"Kathy, you really must get that hearing of yours checked."

"What are you talking about? You definitely told me that Vinky was a friend of Mrs V's, and that he liked to sit on your sofa; the one that makes those disgusting noises."

"What I actually said was that Vinky was a friend of Mrs *Fee*."

"Who on earth is Mrs *Fee*?" Kathy asked.

"She's one of the temps I had to use when Jules was on holiday. That was before Mrs V came back from Australia."

"And her name is Mrs Fee?"

"Yeah, Fiona Fee. She wasn't terribly good if I'm honest. She spent most of the time chatting on the phone and her friends were always popping around to the office, as though it was some kind of social club. I came back here on two separate occasions and found her and Vinky on my sofa. I was glad to see the back of her."

Ladies and gentlemen, that right there is the gold standard of lying. And it left both Kathy and Mrs V speechless.

"What did you want, anyway, Kathy?"

"Let's go through to your office and I'll tell you." She brushed past me, and once inside my office, closed the door.

"Why all the secrecy?" I said.

"I want to talk to you about the gallery opening party, but I didn't want Mrs V to hear in case she asked for a ticket."

"Why wouldn't you want Mrs V there?"

"It's a question of numbers. We're already at maximum capacity, so I didn't want to have to disappoint her."

"I'm sure she'd be devastated." Not. "So, what exactly did you want to tell me about the opening?"

"It's about Gregor, actually."

"Who?"

"Gregor Leggor. I told you about him."

"Is he the artist guy?"

"*Artist guy*? The man is a modern-day genius."

"What about him?"

"I need a favour."

"I don't like the sound of that. What kind of favour?"

"Gregor doesn't do hotels."

"What do you mean he *doesn't do them*?"

"He says they're soulless."

"Where's he going to stay—hold on—you're not going to ask what I think you're going to ask, are you?"

"It would only be for a few days."

"Why can't he stay at your place?"

"Obviously, I would have let him stay there, but I've already agreed for several VIP visitors to stay with us. Please, Jill, it would mean the world to me. And it's not like you don't have plenty of space now that Florence has moved out."

"She hasn't moved out! She's just at boarding school."

"Will you do it?"

"Is he a weirdo?"

"No, of course not."

"So, you've met him?"

"No, but I've read a lot about him."

"Great. How many nights would it be for?"

"Two. Three max."

"I'll have to check with Jack before I say yes."

"That's okay. I rang him before I came over here. He's all over the idea. He said it would be fascinating to have an artist stay with you."

"Are you telling me that you spoke to Jack before—"

"I'll let you have more details about Gregor's special requirements nearer the time."

"What kind of special requirements?"

"Thanks, Jill, you're the best." She practically sprinted out of the door.

"You let that sister of yours walk all over you," Winky said.

"Shut up."

"I hope you know what you've let yourself in for. That Leggor guy sounds like a bit of a nutter if you ask me."

"How would you know?"

"I read an article about him in Future Art magazine. I'll send you a link."

After reading said article, I came to the conclusion that Mr Leggor was a bona fide fruit and nut case.

It was with little expectation of success that I made another call to Joy's Toy's manufacturing unit, but to my surprise, it was answered on the first ring.

"Joy's Toy's Manufacturing. Shamus speaking."

"Oh hi. Would it be possible to speak to Roy?"

"Which Roy would that be? We have several."

"Joy's son."

"Ah, you want Big Roy. Who's calling, please?"

"My name is Jill Maxwell. I believe his mother has told him to expect a call from me."

"Hold the line, would you, please?"

"Sure."

Moments later, a different voice said, "This is Roy."

"Hi, I'd like to pay a visit to your manufacturing unit."

"No problem. When would you like to come over?"

"I'm pretty much tied up tomorrow. How about Friday?"

"Sure. Would you prefer the morning or afternoon?"

"Nine-thirty?"

"That's fine."

Roy provided me with directions and said that he looked forward to meeting me. My first impression of Roy was more favourable than of his brother, who had done his best to put off my visit.

I'd no sooner finished speaking to Roy than my phone rang again with an unknown number.

"Is that Jill Maxwell?" The male voice echoed as though the caller was on speaker phone.

"That's me."

"Do you live at the Old Watermill in Middle Tweaking?"

"Yes, I do. Who am I speaking to?"

"My name is Randal Bobsworth. I'm a planning officer at Washbridge City Council."

Oh bum!

"What can I do for you Mr Jobsworth?"

"It's *Bobs*worth."

"Sorry, that's what I meant. How can I help you?"

"We've received a report, Mrs Maxwell. About your fence."

"A fence?" I decided to act dumb.

Yes, yes, I know. Acting dumb shouldn't be difficult for me to do. You guys are so predictable.

"You may or may not be aware that the maximum height allowed for a fence is two metres. Anything higher than that requires planning permission."

"Yes, I seem to remember reading that somewhere. Luckily, all our fences are less than two metres in height."

"Not according to the person who submitted the report in front of me. He states that one of your fences is two metres and two centimetres in height."

"I assume the report is from a Mr Flatley."

"Unfortunately, I'm unable to confirm or deny that. Data Protection, you understand."

"Well, whoever submitted that report is wrong. The fence is definitely no more than two metres high. I'm really sorry that you've been troubled unnecessarily."

"It's really no trouble, Mrs Maxwell. This is my job, and I take it very seriously."

"I'm sure you do, but now you have the facts, you'll be able to close the case."

"I'm afraid it isn't that simple."

"Why not?"

"Think about it for a minute. We can't simply take your word that the fence is the requisite height, can we?"

"Are you calling me a liar?"

"Certainly not. That would be most unprofessional. No, what I'm saying is that we need to establish the facts, and the only way for us to do that is to send one of our operatives to measure the fence. That way, we'll know if we need to take any further action or not."

"The fence definitely isn't oversize, but just out of curiosity, what kind of action do you take in cases where a fence is over two metres high?"

"A penalty fine would be levied against the person in question."

"How big a fine?"

"That would depend upon a number of things: How much over the height limit the fence is, how long it has been standing, that kind of thing. It's rarely more than a thousand pounds."

"A *thousand*?"

"Yes, rarely more than that. And of course the person would be required to remove the offending fence. Or reduce its size where that's practical. Anyway, from what you've told me, you shouldn't need to worry about any of that."

"You said someone would come out to measure our fence. When will that happen?"

"I can't give you a precise date. It will depend on our Mr Measures' current workload, but it should definitely be within the week."

"A Mr Measures will be measuring our fence?"

"That is correct. Now, is there anything else you'd like to ask me?"

"No, thanks."

"More good news?" Winky said when I came off the phone.

"Stupid bureaucrats. I hate them all."

"Are you sure? You sound like you're on the *fence* about it." He began to roll around with laughter.

"Shut up and get back to your haunting studies."

To take my mind off the fence situation, I decided to do a search online for Gregor Leggor.

"What are those supposed to be?" I said to no one in particular.

"What are you looking at?" Winky jumped onto the desk.

"Paintings by Gregor Leggor. Just look at the state of these. What are they supposed to be?"

"Have you got them the right way up?"

"Who knows? They're rubbish. I could do better than that, blindfolded, with one hand tied behind my back. They're just splodges of colour thrown randomly on a canvas."

Winky pointed. "Look at the reviews, though."

In disbelief, I read the dozens of glowing reviews, which without exception praised Gregor for his amazing work.

"Either all these people are insane or I am." I sighed.

"Much as it pains me to say it, I don't think you're the one who's insane. Those paintings are complete rubbish. I wouldn't give you ten-pence for any of them."

"Look at this article. It says Gregor's latest work was sold for a quarter of a million."

"The world has gone crazy."

***

To my surprise, Jack was already home when I arrived back at the old watermill.

"Monty didn't come in this morning, but by midday, he was feeling better, so he said he'd take the late shift. It's meat and potato pie for dinner."

"Great." I sighed.

"What's up? I thought you'd be pleased that I'd got away early."

"I am. Sorry."

"Something is wrong. I can tell."

"I'm going to kill him."

"That could be any one of several people. You're going to have to narrow it down for me."

"Flat Head."

"You're not still going on about that fence, are you? I told you that nothing will come of it."

"That's where you're wrong. I had a call today from a Mr Randal Bobsworth in the planning department at Washbridge City Council."

"*Jobsworth*?"

"*Bobs*worth. But it might as well have been because he really is one."

"What did he say?"

"That they'd had a report about our oversize fence."

"What did you say?"

"What do you think I said? I told him that it wasn't over two metres high and that whoever had reported it was wrong."

"And?"

"And he said that they'd be sending someone around to measure it. And get this: if they find it's over two metres high, they'll impose a fine of up to a thousand pounds."

"A grand? That seems stiff."

"There's more. If it is oversize, they'll demand we remove the fence altogether."

"That's not good."

"It makes my blood boil. That fence has been there for

years, minding its own business, and causing precisely no harm to anyone. Then, Flat Head comes along and sticks his oar in for no reason other than to be a total—"

"I did warn you not to antagonise him."

"Oh, so now it's my fault, is it?"

"I didn't say that. I guess this means we're going to have to remove the fence."

"Are you crazy? Why would we do that?"

"If we remove it before they come out to measure it, at least we'll avoid the fine."

"Stuff that for a game of soldiers. That fence isn't going anywhere."

"But what about—"

"Don't you worry about the fence. There will be no fine and no pulling it down while I still have breath in my body."

"What are you going to do?"

"Best you don't know."

"You're probably right. I'd only worry."

"The only person who should be worrying right now is Flat Head."

"You're not going to do anything stupid, are you, Jill?"

"Me? No, of course not." Snigger.

Chapter 7

The previous evening, I'd been so wound up about the fence and Flat Head that I'd forgotten to tackle Jack about the Gregor Leggor situation, but that was about to change.

"I can't believe you agreed that Leggor guy could stay with us," I said while buttering my toast.

"Kathy told me she'd already asked you, and that you were happy about it provided that I was."

"She's so devious that sister of mine."

"I wonder who she gets that from."

"I am *not* devious," I objected. "You realise that she played us off against one another, don't you?"

"It looks that way. Still, it will be nice to have an intellectual in the house to talk to."

"You've got me."

"Yeah. Right." He grinned.

"Anyway, what makes you think he's an intellectual? He might be as thick as two short planks."

"I doubt it."

"One thing is for sure: the guy can't paint for toffee. I did a search online for his paintings. They're rubbish."

"I looked at them too. I found them quite challenging."

"*Challenging*? What does that mean?"

"I felt like the artist was challenging the viewer to interpret his work in a way that gave meaning to them."

"That sounds just like the kind of claptrap that Kathy would spout."

"We did talk about Leggor and his work."

"I knew it. All that rubbish about challenging the viewer to interpret the work is just a way of trying to distract you from the truth."

"Which is?"

"It's complete rubbish that any two-year-old could produce."

"I do hope you aren't going to say any of that to Gregor when he stays with us."

"I won't. Not unless he starts spouting on about what a genius he is."

Jack picked up the morning newspaper. "Did you know about this, Jill? They've named the person that they've arrested for Goldie's murder. It's her ex."

"Liam? I don't believe it." I grabbed the paper from him and read the article.

"I wonder why McDonald didn't tell you that it was Liam who was being charged."

"Because he hates my guts, but also because he probably knew I'd have told him that he'd made a mistake."

"You can't be sure of that."

"Goldie spoke to Liam, and she was convinced he wasn't involved with any of that nonsense before the murder. That's good enough for me."

"The police must have evidence, or they wouldn't have charged him."

"Hmm."

"I hope this means that you're going to drop this thing now."

"We'll see."

"Jill!"

"Okay, okay. I'll leave it alone. Happy now?"

"I would be if I believed you."

***

On my drive into the office, I couldn't get Goldie Barr out of my head. Although I'd told Jack that I would drop it, I simply couldn't believe that Liam was responsible for her murder. He was a cheat, who had dumped her for someone else, but he'd never been abusive to the best of my knowledge. More to the point, Goldie had said he was happy with his new partner, living in Newcastle. What did he have to gain from Goldie's death? It didn't make sense.

"Jill! Help!"

I looked up to see Peter Petty hurrying along the corridor.

"What's wrong, Peter?"

"In there." He pointed to the open door of his office.

"Is there someone in there?"

"No."

"I don't understand. What's the matter?"

"There's some*thing* in there."

It was only then that the penny dropped: This had to be Winky's doing.

"Would you like me to take a look?" I offered.

"Yes, please."

He stood behind me and practically pushed me towards the open door. I hesitated, purely for effect, then popped my head inside.

"Hello? Is anyone there?"

"Whooo, whooo, whooo." Came the response.

"Did you hear that?" Petty grabbed my arm tightly.

"Hear *what*?"

"That whooing sound."

"*Whooing*?" I gave him a confused look.

"Whooo, whooo, whooo."

"There it is again. You must have heard it this time."

"I think that's just the wind coming through the vent above the window. It is very windy outside."

"Are you sure?"

"Yeah, it's perfectly safe. Come and look."

Gingerly, he stepped inside and looked around. "Are you sure it was the wind?"

"Positive, but I think it's calming down out there, so you probably won't hear it again."

"I hope not."

"Are you okay now, Peter?"

"Yeah, I guess so. Thanks."

"It's good to be back behind this desk, Jill," Mrs V said.

"I see you've brought your knitting."

"You don't mind, do you?"

"Of course not. It's just like the good old days."

"Tea?"

"Yes, please."

Winky was chuckling to himself. "Did you see the state of that guy?"

"*Whooo, whooo, whooo*?" I mocked. "Is that seriously the best you could do?"

"That was only for starters. Just wait until he gets the full show."

"When will that be?"

"As soon as I've perfected my routine."

"I'm beginning to feel sorry for Petty. Maybe you should leave off him."

"Really?"

"No, not really. The sooner you drive that idiot out of

this building, the better."

***

The Beasley case was an unusual one. He was being blackmailed, by person or persons unknown, because he'd been recorded saying that he wished his mother was dead. Not long afterwards, his mother apparently fell down the basement steps and died. Beasley was the sole heir to her money and her house. Whoever was blackmailing him had threatened to take the recording of Beasley's unfortunate outburst to the police. In my opinion, if he hadn't killed his mother, which he insisted he hadn't, he needn't worry about someone giving the recording to the police because they'd see it for what it was.

He lived on a street with one of the worst names I'd ever encountered and, trust me, I'd come across a lot of bad ones. What kind of name was Turnip Shed Road? Had there really been a shed full of turnips there once upon a time? Somehow, I doubted it. I simply couldn't have lived on a street with that name. I would have petitioned the council to change it, and if that had failed, I would have been forced to move.

All the houses on Turnip Shed Road were detached and looked as though they'd been built in the fifties or sixties. It was obvious that they'd all been upgraded in recent years—all that was with the exception of number thirty-seven, which is where Mr Beasley lived. The walls were in desperate need of pointing, and all of the window frames looked rotten. Worst of all, though, was the garden, which was almost shoulder high with weeds. The net curtains at the downstairs windows, which had once been white, were now grey. Mr Beasley had not said if he intended to continue living in the house, but if he decided to sell, he would either have to spend a lot of money to renovate it or be prepared to sell at a price way below market value.

There was no doorbell, so I knocked on the door, which had also seen better days. I didn't have to wait long because Beasley opened the door almost immediately.

"Did you find your way here okay?"

"Yeah, no problem. What's with the name of the road?"

"Sorry?"

"It's rather unusual, isn't it?"

"Not as unusual as it used to be."

"They actually changed the name to this one?"

"Yes. Until ten years ago it was called Turnip Shed *Avenue*, but then they had the good sense to change it to Turnip Shed *Road*. Much better."

"*Right*? I was actually referring—never mind."

"Do come in."

I'd hoped that the interior of the house would be better than the exterior, but if the hall and living room were anything to go by, I was to be very disappointed. The décor, furniture and ornaments looked like they'd been bought at the same time as the house was built.

"I see you're still having trouble with your back, Mr Beasley."

"It's Bobby. And yes, it's particularly bad today. Take a seat, please."

I studied the sofa and two chairs and settled on the one with the fewest stains. It was as uncomfortable as it was disgusting.

"I believe you said that you lived here with your mother?"

"That's right." He picked up a framed photograph from the sideboard. "This is her."

"She looks like a lovely lady."

"She was."

"What will you do now?"

"What do you mean?"

"It's a very large house for just one person. Do you plan to sell it and move on?"

"Maybe, but it's a big step."

"You mentioned that your mother had taken out a life insurance policy."

"Yes, but I didn't know that until after she died. I found it when I was going through her papers."

"Are you the sole beneficiary?"

"Yes."

"May I ask how much the policy is for?"

"One-hundred thousand pounds."

"When you came to my office, you mentioned that you are to inherit her estate. Would you mind telling me how much that amounts to?"

"It's not been finalised yet, but there's about one-hundred thousand split between two bank accounts. And then there's the value of the house."

"What would you say it's worth?"

"I'm not sure, but an identical one across the road was sold two months ago for three hundred thousand."

"Obviously, this house would need a lot of work before it could fetch that kind of money, so let's say two-hundred and fifty-thousand pounds. That would give you a total inheritance, including the proceeds from the insurance policy, of close to half a million pounds. Would you agree?"

"I suppose so. Is that important?"

"It may not be, but if the police do decide to investigate, they'll definitely consider that to be a possible motive."

"I didn't kill her. I loved my Mother."

"I believe you, which is why my advice to you is still to report the blackmail to the police."

"I told you. I can't do that."

"Because of the recording?"

"That's right."

"Could I hear it?"

"Do you really need to? I've told you what's on it."

"I'd still like to hear it myself."

"Okay. Wait there and I'll go and get it."

He walked gingerly out of the room, and I could hear him go slowly upstairs. A few minutes later, he returned, holding an old-fashioned cassette player in one hand.

"It's on cassette?" I said.

"Yeah. I had to go to a second-hand shop to buy this player so that I could listen to it."

I expected him to press the play button, but he just stood there, staring at it.

"Bobby? Shall we listen to it?"

His hand was visibly trembling as he pressed play.

The voice on the tape was unmistakeably that of Mr Beasley, but he sounded much louder and brasher than I'd expected.

"I hate that old cow. I wish she was dead then I could have some fun. Why doesn't she just die?"

Beasley pressed the stop button, but he didn't speak,

nor did he turn to face me.

"That's actually a lot worse than I imagined," I said.

"I know." He sat down and finally managed to make eye contact with me. "I'm so ashamed."

"It sounds like you were drunk."

"I was or I would never have said that."

"Do you often get drunk?"

"Hardly ever. It was my birthday, and I went a bit wild. I was really sick that night. What do you think now you've heard it?"

"I don't think it changes anything. What you said was awful, but I doubt anyone would interpret it as an actual threat to kill your mother. Quite the opposite in fact. Someone who intended to commit murder would hardly be likely to broadcast their intentions for all to hear. Plus, it's pretty obvious to anyone that you were under the influence of drink."

"I still don't want to go to the police."

"I think that's a mistake, but obviously it's your call. Will you show me the basement where your mother fell?"

"Of course." He struggled to his feet, clearly relieved to move on from the tape. "This way."

The hallway was L-shaped, and the basement door was located opposite the kitchen. I tried it, but it was locked. Or so I thought.

"It's very stiff," Beasley said. "Let me do it."

I stepped aside and watched him put his shoulder to the door, which did the trick.

"Was your mother able to open that?"

"No, which is why it was always left ajar when she was alive." He reached inside and caught hold of the light-pull. "Watch your step. The stairs are quite narrow."

He wasn't kidding. The well-worn stone steps were barely wide enough for my delicate little feet. It didn't help that the low-wattage bulb was barely strong enough to light the steps. Thankfully, I made it down in one piece.

"This space is huge. What do you keep down here?"

"Just rubbish, really. And the model railway of course."

"Model railway?"

"It's over there in the far corner. Come and see."

He led the way across the stone floor to one of the dark corners. Only when I got closer could I see the large model railway that was spread across four wooden tables. Beasley clicked a switch that illuminated a series of lights above the layout.

It brought back memories (not all good) of one Mr Hosey.

"This is very impressive," I said out of politeness. "I take it this is your hobby."

"Mine? No. I have no interest in toy trains. This belonged to Mother. She spent more time down here than she did in the house."

"I see. What will happen to it now?"

"I haven't given it much thought. I've had too many other things on my mind."

"Of course."

"I did get an offer for it, though."

"Oh?"

"From Fred Pinstone. He's a member of the Washbridge model railway club that Mother used to attend. She never liked him. She always said he was devious."

"I take it you rejected his offer?"

"Yes. I'm sure he was trying to lowball me, but that's not why I turned it down. It was downright disrespectful.

Mother had only died a few days before."

"You said your mother used to go to the model railway club. Did she go anywhere else regularly? To see friends, maybe?"

"No, the only time she ever left the house was to go to that stupid club or to go shopping sometimes. I did the majority of that for her."

"I assume this Pinstone guy must have been down here for him to have seen this setup?"

"Yes, Mother would invite one of the members from the club to visit occasionally."

"Okay, I think I've seen everything I need to see down here. Could I see the letter that you received from the blackmailer?"

"Sure. It's in my bedside cabinet. I'll go and get it for you."

I returned to the living room while he went to get the letter. Having seen the basement, it was easy to see how Beasley's mother could have tripped. The sticky door, the narrow steps and the poor lighting were a lethal combination, particularly for someone of her age. On the other hand, she obviously spent a lot of time in the basement with her model railway, so she should have been used to getting up and down those steps.

"Here you are." Beasley handed me a single sheet of paper.

The letter had obviously been written on an old-fashioned typewriter, which had a faulty letter 't'.

"This says that you have to make the payment by two weeks on Friday or they'll pass the recording to the police."

"Don't you think I know that?" he snapped. "Sorry, I

just need to know you can find out who's behind it and stop them."

"I'm going to do my best. It says you're supposed to post the money to an address in Crewe. Does that address ring any bells?"

"No, I've never been to Crewe in my life."

"Okay. I'll get that address checked out. What about the envelope it came in?"

"It didn't."

"No envelope?"

"It was pushed through the letterbox just like that."

"It was hand delivered?"

"Yes. Is that important?"

"It could be. Can I hang on to it?"

"Sure."

"I think I've covered everything I need for now. If I think of anything else, I'll give you a call."

"Okay."

Chapter 8

I was on my way back to my office when I got a phone call from an unknown number.

"Is that Jill Maxwell?"

"Speaking."

"My name is Arnold Makepiece. I'm a lawyer, representing Mr Liam Locks. I believe you and he were neighbours before he moved to Newcastle."

"That's right."

"I'm not sure if you're aware, but Mr Locks has been charged with the murder of his estranged wife."

"Yes, I read it in the newspaper this morning."

"What was your reaction when you saw it?"

I hesitated. "I was a little surprised."

"My client didn't to it. He's innocent."

"You would say that, though, wouldn't you?"

"He has instructed me to ask you to go and talk to him."

"Me? Why does he want to talk to me?"

"Mr Locks said that you are a private investigator. He wants you to help prove his innocence. He's willing to pay, naturally."

"I'm not sure I should get involved. I'm too close to the victim."

"It's for that very reason that he wants you on the case. He told me that his wife had discussed with you her concerns that someone was stalking her prior to her murder. Is that true?"

"We didn't discuss stalking per se, but there were a number of incidents that unsettled Goldie."

"Will you at least speak to Mr Locks? No commitment. Just hear what he has to say."

"I suppose that couldn't do any harm. When?"

"That will depend on the authorities. I'll try to arrange something within the next few days. Can I call you?"

"Sure."

"Thank you, Mrs Maxwell. I'll convey the good news to Mr Locks."

When I arrived back at the office, there was a man, dressed in an expensive suit, standing at Mrs V's desk.

"Oh, she's here now," Mrs V said. "Jill, this is Mr Winkmore."

"Willy Winkmore." The man stepped forward and offered his hand. "I'm Client Liaison Manager here at Washbridge Central Point. I don't believe we've met."

"I don't believe we have."

"Might we go somewhere where we can talk in private?"

"Sure, come through to my office."

Thankfully, Mr Winkmore couldn't see Winky who had chosen that moment to wash his nether regions.

"Do you mind if I sit?" he asked, and before I could stop him, he'd taken a seat on the sofa.

Pretending not to have heard the unfortunate noise that had emanated from the furniture, I said, "Would you care for a drink, Mr Wink—err—"

"More. No, thank you. I have rather a lot on today, but an urgent matter has arisen."

"Oh?"

"Yes, in fact it was brought to my attention by your neighbour, Mr Petty."

"Oh. Look, if it's about the two-ply, I really don't—"

"*Two-ply*? No, your neighbour has suggested that there

may be some kind of paranormal activity in the building."

I glanced across at Winky who was sniggering to himself.

"What kind of paranormal activity?"

"I did try to press Mr Petty on that very point, but all he could tell me was that he has heard some strange noises and experienced an unexpected drop in temperature. Normally, I would have dismissed the matter out of hand, but the poor man was clearly traumatised. That's why I agreed to talk to the other occupants of offices on this floor, to see if anyone else had encountered anything similar."

"I've not seen or heard anything out of the ordinary. Has anyone else?"

"So far no, but I do have a couple more people to catch up with." He stood up. "I do appreciate you sparing me your time like this."

"My pleasure."

"It looks like our plan is working," Winky said after Winkmore had left.

"I'm having second thoughts about this. The poor man is clearly terrified."

"He will be when he sees ghost cat tomorrow."

"Maybe we should just forget the whole thing."

The door opened and Mrs V stepped into my office.

"A Mr Petty came around while you were out, Jill. He asked if you'd thought any more about being the media face of the two-ply campaign. I wasn't sure what he was talking about, but he assured me you would understand."

"Okay, thanks, Mrs V. I need you to look up an address in Crewe for me, please." I handed her the note I'd taken from the blackmail letter. "See if you can find out who or what is there, will you?"

"Will do."

As soon as she'd left my office, I turned to Winky. "Forget what I just said about taking it easy on Mr Petty. Full steam ahead with the haunting."

"You got it."

***

As I drove into Middle Tweaking, there was a squirrel on the road. That wasn't, in itself, so unusual because there are dozens if not hundreds of the cute little creatures in the village. What was different this time was that the squirrel was six feet tall, and it was blocking my way. For a moment, I thought it might be the work of a rogue witch or wizard, but then I spotted an equally tall hedgehog who waved to the squirrel, to warn it of my approach. The squirrel turned around, saw my car, and then stepped to the side of the road. After waving me past, it went and joined the hedgehog.

Intrigued, I parked outside the old watermill, but instead of going into the house, I waited for the squirrel and hedgehog.

"Hey, guys, are you here for the con at the hotel?"

"Yes, it's our first time here," said the hedgehog.

"What's the theme?"

"Woodland creatures. Do you live here in the village?"

"Yeah, right here."

"Nice house."

"Thanks."

"Do they hold many cons here?" the squirrel asked.

"This is the first one. The hotel was only recently

acquired by Cosplay Conventions International. I'd better get inside. I hope you have a good weekend."

"Thanks."

As Jack had had to work late in the store, I had made dinner.

"What do you think of the sausages?" I asked. "I wasn't sure if they were maybe a bit overcooked?"

"They're fine. I like my sausages black."

"Cheek. They aren't black."

"A badger came into the store just before I closed."

"I saw a squirrel and a hedgehog on the drive into the village."

"I think these cosplays are going to be good for Middle Tweaking."

"I doubt Flat Head would agree with you. As we speak, he's probably complaining to the environment agency that the village is being overrun by giant woodland creatures. By the way, I was contacted by Liam Locks' solicitor today."

"What did he want?"

"Apparently, Liam wants to hire me to prove his innocence."

"What did you say?"

"That I didn't think I should get involved because I was too close to Goldie, but the solicitor said Liam was adamant that he wanted me on the case."

"Are you going to do it?"

"I don't know. I've agreed to talk to Liam. I'll see how that goes before making a decision."

Jack stood up and picked up his plate.

"You haven't eaten all your sausages," I said.

"I'm full. It was Monty's birthday, and he bought cake for Kiki and me. It must have taken the edge off my appetite."

Jack was obviously lying, but I couldn't blame him for leaving the near charcoal sausages.

I'd just put my plate in the sink when there was a knock at the door.

"I'll get it," Jack offered.

From the kitchen, I could hear him speaking to a man whose voice I didn't recognise. Moments later, Jack walked back into the kitchen, accompanied by a short man with a pencil moustache.

"Jill, this is Mr Measures."

"Measures? From the planning department?"

"That is correct. Roland Measures." He took out an ID card and flashed it at me. "I believe you were expecting my visit."

"Well, yes, but your colleague Mr Jobsworth said—"

"*Bobsworth*."

"He said it would probably be a few days before you got in touch. Do you normally make visits at this time of day?"

"Actually, no. My normal hours are Monday to Friday, nine to five. However, two of my colleagues have recently left the job unexpectedly, so I've had to increase my hours in order to keep up with the workload."

"Why didn't you at least contact us to let us know that you'd be coming?"

"There's really no need for that because I can measure the fence without your assistance. I only knocked at the door out of courtesy, to let you know I was here."

Oh bum! If he measured the fence, he was bound to

declare it oversize and then we'd be stuck with a fine. Worse still, we'd be forced to take it down. If ever a cunning plan had been needed, this was it.

"You poor man, having to work such long hours," I said, drawing a puzzled look from Jack. "You must be exhausted."

"If I'm honest, it is beginning to take its toll."

"I'm not surprised. Are you eating properly?"

"I just have to grab a sandwich when I get the chance."

"Sandwiches? That won't be enough to sustain you. You look like a man who enjoys a good fry-up."

"It's true. I do. But it's been a long time since I've had one."

"Then we will remedy that situation immediately. Jack, make this man one of your famous fry-ups."

I'm not sure who looked more shocked: Jack or Mr Measures.

"I really don't have the time, Mrs Maxwell," Measures' objection was only half-hearted which gave me hope.

"Rubbish. Do you have any more visits to make today?"

"Actually, no this is the last one."

"There you are then. Jack, what are you waiting for? This poor man is ravenous."

"Okay," Measures said. "That's most generous of you. Perhaps I should take a look at the fence first, though."

"No, you stay right there. The fence will still be there after you've eaten your meal."

While Jack prepared the fry-up, I sneaked out of the kitchen and through to the lounge. I'd managed to buy a little time, but now came the difficult part: I needed to find a spell that would get me out of this situation. After bringing up the spell book app on my phone, I searched using the term 'fence', but the two spells it brought up related to the sport of fencing. I spent the next few minutes racking my brain to come up with any other search term that might prove fruitful, and then it struck me. I typed in the word: Measure.

That produced more than thirty different spells. I read through each one and I was beginning to think I'd lucked out again when I came across a spell called the 'measurement adjuster' spell. Eureka! This appeared to be exactly what I was looking for. If the blurb was to be believed, it would change the result obtained when measuring objects. It gave an example of measuring someone's waist. By casting the spell on the tape measure, the result could show the waist measurement to be inches less than it actually was. If I'd had more time, I might have dwelled on trying to understand the circumstances that had caused someone to come up with such a spell, but time was at a premium, so I couldn't afford to worry about that. I would just have to hope that the spell did exactly what it said on the tin.

By the time I returned to the kitchen, Mr Measures was mopping up the last of the tomato juice with a slice of fried bread. Jack gave me a quizzical look, but there was no way I could tell him what I was up to while Measures was in the room.

"That was delicious." Measures wiped his mouth with a handkerchief. "Thank you, Mr Maxwell."

"My pleasure." Jack picked up the empty plate.

"Well, I suppose I'd better get back to the job in hand." Measures stood up.

"Why not wait a few minutes," I said. "You don't want to get indigestion."

"No, I really must get started. Hilary will wonder where I've got to."

"Is Hilary your wife?"

"No, she's my chinchilla."

"Right."

"May I go out through this door?"

"Sure."

He opened the door onto the garden and stepped outside.

"What's going on?" Jack whispered.

"I'll tell you later." I followed Measures outside.

"There's really no need for you to come out here, Mrs Maxwell," Measures said. "It's rather muddy."

"I'd like to see you take the measurement if that's okay?"

"Of course."

Once we had reached the fence, he put his backpack down and took out a retractable tape measure.

"What make is that, Mr Measures?"

"Sorry?"

"The tape measure. I wondered what make it was. I've always had a keen interest in them."

"Really?"

"Yes, my father had quite a collection of them."

"It's a Ragmore."

"Of course. Only the best for the planning department, eh? May I?" I held out my hand.

"You want to see it?"

"If you don't mind."

"I can assure you it's accurate."

"I don't doubt that for a moment. After all, it is a Ragmore. Still, if I could just take a quick look."

"I suppose it wouldn't do any harm." He passed it to me.

While pretending to examine it, I quickly cast the spell, and then handed it back to him.

"Is it okay if I measure the fence now?"

"Of course. I'm eager to know the outcome." I turned back to Jack and gave him a thumbs up.

Moments later, Measures revealed the result. "Your fence is two metres and eight centimetres high, Mrs Maxwell. I'm sorry to inform you that means it is eight centimetres above regulations."

"What? It can't be."

"The tape measure doesn't lie, I'm afraid." He held out the tape to show me.

And then it hit me. The spell I'd used could increase or decrease the result and, like an idiot, I'd used the wrong version, with the result that the fence appeared to be even higher than it actually was.

I took the tape from Measures and pretended to stare at it in disbelief whilst actually recasting the spell—this time using the correct parameters.

"I'd like you to doublecheck it," I handed back the tape.

"But, Mrs Maxwell, you've seen the result for yourself."

"Yes, but it's important to account for operator error, don't you agree?"

"I can assure you that I've been doing this for several years, and I know what I'm doing."

"I don't doubt it, Mr Measures, but even the best of us can make the occasional error. Please, just measure the fence one more time."

"If you insist." He sighed.

He repeated the exercise, but this time he wasn't so

quick to announce the result. Instead, he just kept staring at the tape.

"Well?" I prompted him. "What's the verdict?"

"I don't understand it."

"How high is the fence?"

"Two metres exactly."

"That's what I've been trying to tell your people from the start."

"I think I'll try one more time."

"Of course. Best to be sure."

He measured the fence one last time, and then confirmed the result.

"It appears my first measure must have been incorrect. I apologise."

"No need. We all make mistakes. Do I take it this means there will be no penalty charge?"

"That's right. The fence is within the permitted height."

"And I won't need to take it down?"

"Certainly not."

"Thank you, Mr Measures."

"I'll be on my way. Thank you for your hospitality."

"How on earth did you manage that?" Jack asked when I walked back into the house. "I thought we were sunk after his first measure."

"Have I ever told you that you married a genius?"

"Many times."

Chapter 9

"I can't wait to bump into Flat Head," I said at breakfast.

"You're not going to gloat, are you, Jill?" Jack had chosen a new brand of muesli, and judging by his expression, he wasn't impressed.

"Of course I'm going to gloat. At every opportunity."

"Why not just take the victory?"

"Because the man is an obnoxious idiot. New muesli not hitting the mark?"

"I wish I'd stuck to my usual brand. This is a bit dry."

"*Dry*? Isn't that the definition of muesli? You can have some Chococandy Pops if you like?"

"I think I'll pass."

Not long after Jack had left to go to the store, I heard a fluttering sound. I thought for a moment the door to the garden must be open, and that a butterfly had flown in.

It wasn't a butterfly.

"Hiya."

The tiny voice caught me off guard, and it took me a moment to realise that it came from a tiny fairy who had landed on the kitchen table.

"Hello? Who are you?"

"My name is Sweetbell. Are you Jill?"

"I am."

"I'm here about Ringabell."

"Oh?"

"It doesn't sound as though you were expecting me."

"No. Should I be?"

"Your grandmother said that she'd tell you to expect me

this morning."

"Right. I'm afraid she didn't."

"In that case, I'm sorry to drop in on you like this. Is now a bad time?"

"For what, exactly?"

"Your grandmother was going to explain our predicament to you."

"I'm sorry, but you're going to have to back up a little. I hadn't even heard of Ringabell until my aunt mentioned it a couple of days ago, and my grandmother hasn't discussed it with me at all."

"Oh dear, this is all very embarrassing."

"Why don't you tell me exactly what it is my grandmother signed me up for?"

"Sure. I don't suppose I could have a drink of water, could I?"

"Of course."

Instinctively, I went to the cupboard to get a glass, but then realised what a stupid idea that was. The fairy could easily have drowned in one of those glasses. Then I remembered I had a couple of thimbles in a kitchen drawer, so I ran a little water into one of those and handed it to her.

"Hmm, that's better. Thank you." She put the thimble down. "I probably should start by explaining that I'm a sunlight fairy. You've probably never heard of us."

"I can't say that I have. Although, I am aware of *starlight* fairies."

"We're a close relation, but we like to think we're a little smarter." She blushed. "Just kidding. Some of my best friends are starlight fairies."

"Do you know Trixieball?"

"Of course. Everyone knows Trixieball."

"Sorry, I interrupted you."

"This is the first year that sunlight fairies have been invited to take part in the Ringabell parade. It's quite an honour, as you can imagine."

"Congratulations."

"Thanks. To be perfectly honest, we were only invited as a last-minute substitute for the marshmallow trolls who were forced to withdraw."

"I see."

"The centrepiece of our float was to have been the sunlight mace, which has belonged to the royal family for hundreds of years. Without that, we fear no one will pay any attention to our small float."

"What happened? Was the mace stolen?"

"No. Worse than that. Droopybell dropped it."

"*Droopybell*?"

"She's been the queen's lady-in-waiting for ever. She's lovely, but she's grown fragile with age. It was an accident, and as you can imagine, she's devastated."

"I take it that the mace was damaged?"

"Not damaged, exactly. The mace itself is still intact, but most of the jewels were dislodged."

"Can't you just fix them back in place?"

"It's not as simple as that. The head of the mace was covered in thousands of tiny jewels, laid out in the most elaborate pattern. Would you like to see a photo?"

"Sure."

She took out a photo that was a close-up of the head of the mace. "It was made hundreds of years ago by a master craftsman. We've been unable to find anyone who can recreate the intricate pattern."

"Does that matter?"

"Yes, it's essential the mace is restored to its original condition. Your grandmother heard what happened, came to see our queen, and told her that the only way the mace could be restored to its original condition would be by using magic. She also said the only witch powerful enough to do it was you."

"That was good of her, but this is the first I've heard of it."

"Oh dear. I'm really sorry."

"It isn't your fault. This is typical of my grandmother."

"Does this mean that you won't be able to help?"

"Not necessarily."

"Would it help to see the mace and the jewels?"

"It can't do any harm."

"When would you like to come and see it?"

"There's no time like the present."

"Great." She looked me up and down. "You'll need to do something about your size first, though."

"I mean, I know I've put on a few pounds recently, but—"

"No, I meant your height. Can you shrink yourself?"

"Oh right. Yeah, I can do that." I cast the 'shrink' spell and, moments later, I was the same size as Sweetbell.

"Great. Will you take my hand?"

I did as she said and the next thing I knew, we were both standing inside a magnificent hall. From the ceiling hung four huge crystal chandeliers. In the centre of the room was a long wooden table, polished within an inch of its life. On it, was a golden mace, and scattered across the table next to it were thousands of tiny jewels of all shapes, sizes and colours. Standing around the table were a number of sunlight fairies, one of whom stepped forward.

"Jill Maxwell," she said. "This is indeed an honour. I'm Queen Moonlight. I can't thank you enough for agreeing to do this."

"Actually, your highness," Sweetbell cut in. "Jill didn't know anything about it until I told her a few minutes ago."

"Oh?" The queen's smile dissolved. "Your grandmother gave me to believe—"

"My grandmother has a habit of getting carried away, I'm afraid."

"Does this mean you won't be able to help?"

"May I?" I gestured towards the table.

"Of course."

Close up, it looked even worse.

"It's all my fault," said one of the other fairies.

"That's enough, Droopybell," the queen said. "It was an accident. You're not to blame yourself."

"I can't help it." She was on the verge of tears. "Sunlight fairies have been waiting so long to be invited to participate in the Ringabell parade, and now I've ruined it."

"Sweetbell, would you take Droopybell to her room and stay with her until she's okay?"

"Of course, your majesty."

The queen waited until they'd left the room before saying, "Poor Droopybell has been like that ever since it happened. She was pinning all her hopes on you being able to help, but judging by the look on your face, I assume this is mission impossible?"

"It just may be."

"Oh well. I guess we'll just have to withdraw from the

parade."

"Don't do that just yet."

"Oh?"

"I'd be lying if I said I was optimistic, but there's no harm in leaving it with me for a little while. Let me see if I can find a spell that can help."

"That's very kind of you."

"You realise I can't make any promises."

"I just appreciate you trying."

"Okay. If you could get someone to put all the jewels in a bag, I'll take them and the mace back with me if that's okay."

"Of course."

***

After Grandma had given up the hotel, she'd moved into a small cottage, which was just a few doors away from the store. Too close for Jack's liking. I was due to pay a visit to the manufacturing unit of Joy's Toys but first I decided to go and see Grandma.

I found her in the front garden, sitting on the bench, with a cup of tea on the table at her side. Her eyes were shut, and I thought for a moment that she was asleep.

"I thought you'd forgotten where I lived," Grandma said. "There's tea in the pot if you'd like one."

"No, thanks. I can't stay."

"You need to have a word with that human of yours."

"His name is Jack. About what?"

"I phoned him fifteen minutes ago and asked him to bring me a loaf of bread, and it still isn't here."

"He and I have both told you several times that the

store doesn't offer a delivery service. If you want anything, you'll have to walk down there, just like everyone else."

"So inconsiderate."

"Talking of which, don't you think it was rather inconsiderate of you not to tell me that you'd volunteered me to help the sunlight fairies?"

"I did tell you."

"You most definitely did not."

"Are you sure?"

"I'm positive. The first I heard about it was when one of the fairies paid me a visit just now. What possessed you to tell them that I'd be able to repair the mace?"

"Can't you?"

"No, I can't."

"My bad. I thought you were so powerful that you could do anything." She scoffed.

"I've never claimed that."

"Did you tell the queen you couldn't help?"

"I said it was unlikely but that I'd see if I could come up with something."

"There you are, then. I don't see what you're so riled up about."

"I'd appreciate it if in future you'd refrain from volunteering me for anything without checking with me first."

"Okay, but what about my loaf?"

***

In contrast to Joy's Toys warehouse, which was housed in a tired old building in the centre of Candlefield, the manufacturing unit was based on a modern industrial park on the outskirts of the town.

The automatic glass doors opened with a pleasing whooshing sound at my approach. So pleasing in fact, that I stepped back outside just so I could hear them close and open again. It was only after my third exit and re-entry that I realised I was being watched by a vampire who was seated behind the reception desk.

"Can I help you?" she said. Judging by the look she gave me she clearly thought I'd lost my mind.

"Sorry. I got a little carried away there. I'm here to see Roy."

"Which one?"

"Big Roy?"

"Who shall I say is here to see him?"

"Me."

"No, I meant—"

"Sorry, just messing with you. My name is Jill Maxwell."

"Oh yes, he said to expect you. Would you take a seat while I give him a call?"

"Sure."

"Would you like a drink while you wait?"

"No, thanks, I'm good."

I'd barely had time to take a seat when a handsome man with perfect hair appeared and flashed me a smile.

"Jill, how lovely to meet you."

"Thanks for seeing me." I stood up and shook his hand.

"No problem. I'm as eager to get to the bottom of this problem as Mum is. Did someone offer you a drink?"

"They did, but I'm fine, thanks."

"Let's go through to my office."

Unlike his brother's ramshackle office, Roy's was all chrome, glass and leather. He took a seat at his desk, and I sat opposite him.

"Have you come up with any ideas about what might be going on, Jill?" he asked.

"Not yet, but I did find my visit to the warehouse quite useful. I was surprised at the sheer volume of toys that have been returned as faulty."

"Not as surprised as I am. Every toy that leaves these premises is perfect. What did Troy say?"

"He suggested it could be a manufacturing problem."

"I thought as much. That's utter nonsense of course."

"The elves in the despatch department didn't agree with him. They were adamant that the quality of the toys they send out hasn't changed."

"They're right. And if Troy was being honest, he'd say the same thing. The truth is, Jill, that he's jealous."

"Of?"

"He has always wanted to run manufacturing, but Mum didn't think he was up to it, so she put me in charge. He's never forgiven her or me."

"Are you saying you think he might have sabotaged the toys deliberately?"

"No. Troy might be jealous, but he's not a fool. If this problem continues, it could threaten the future of the company. Troy wouldn't risk that."

"Do you have any theories about what is happening?"

"I wish I could tell you that I did, but I don't have the faintest idea. The only thing I know for certain is that every toy that leaves this factory is perfect."

"How can you be so sure?"

"I could spend the next hour explaining why I'm so

confident, or I could just give you a tour of the factory, which would be a lot less boring."

"Sounds good."

"Great." He stood up and walked over to the metal cupboard at the other side of the office. From there, he took two white coats, one of which he put on. The other, he handed to me. "Sorry, it's probably a bit long for you."

It came down to my ankles.

"It's fine."

"Right, let's go."

As we made our way to the shopfloor, Roy explained that all of the toys were made by hand. The factory itself was divided into a number of sections, each of which was responsible for a different line of toys.

"We have one section for soft toys, one for board games, one for small wooden toys, and one for jigsaws."

"You have a section dedicated just to jigsaws?"

"Yes, most people are surprised to learn that jigsaws make up the biggest percentage of our sales."

"That is surprising. Do you think we could start in the soft toy department?"

"Sure, that's my favourite too."

I wasn't prepared for just how many people were employed in the soft toy department—there were hundreds of them.

"Wow, this is huge."

"Take a walk around."

The room echoed to the sound of scissors and sewing machines. There were sups of all kinds, making all manner of soft toys.

"This is incredible," I said.

"We like to think so. And, in case you haven't noticed,

every toy is unique."

"What do you mean?"

"Well, for example, we don't churn out thousands of identical teddy bears. These guys have free license to make each one as they see fit. Provided, of course, it still resembles a teddy bear."

"That must require a lot of training."

"It does. Everyone in here served a one-year apprenticeship before they were allowed to produce toys for sale."

"Amazing."

"What would you like to see next?"

"Jigsaws, I think."

"Sure, this way."

The jigsaw department was no less impressive. It was divided into three sections: artwork, printing and cutting.

"These pictures are amazing," I said. "They could be hanging in a gallery."

"We employ only the most talented artists."

"Please tell me not every jigsaw is unique."

"No." He smiled. "If they were, no one would be able to afford them. We do restrict the number of jigsaws produced from a single piece of artwork to one hundred, though."

After the pictures were printed onto a thin sheet of wood, they were sent through to the cutting section, where they were cut into the pieces that would form the jigsaw.

"What do you think, Jill?" Roy asked.

"Once again, it's all most impressive."

"Which department would you like to visit next?"

"Actually, I think I've seen enough of manufacturing.

What I'd really like to know is how you ensure that no faulty toys slip through."

"In that case, we should pay a visit to our quality control department. Ready?"

"Yeah, let's do it."

The quality control department was much smaller than the other two sections that I'd just visited, and notably much quieter.

"We have highly trained specialists who oversee the different sections. Over there, the soft toys are all checked." He pointed to the far corner of the room where a dozen inspectors appeared to be checking every soft toy by hand. "If they find so much as a loose stitch, the toy will be rejected." He pointed to the other side of the room where twice as many inspectors were at work. "That's where all the small wooden toys are checked, double-checked, and then checked again."

While he'd been talking, my attention had been drawn to a single desk in between the soft toy and small wooden toy inspection sections. Seated at that desk was an elderly woman.

"What's going on over there?" I pointed to the woman.

"That's Nancy. She's been with us ever since the business was founded."

"What's she doing, exactly?"

"She's an essential part of the quality control department. Nancy is single-handedly responsible for checking all of the jigsaws."

"Single-handedly? But you turn out hundreds of them."

"I know, and Nancy checks every one of them. Want to see?"

"Definitely."

He led the way to Nancy's desk.

"Nancy, this is Jill Maxwell."

She was clearly in some pain as she struggled to her feet. "I heard you were coming in today, Mrs Maxwell. This is such an honour."

"Please call me Jill. It's nice to meet you too, Nancy. Please sit down."

"Thanks, I don't mind if I do."

"I was just telling Jill that you are responsible for checking every jigsaw that leaves this building, isn't that right, Nancy?"

"It is, and I love doing it. It doesn't feel like work to me."

"Why don't you give Jill a demonstration."

"Of course. Would you like to pick one, Jill?" She pointed to the pile of jigsaws next to her desk.

"Any?"

"Yes, I have to check them all before the day is out."

There must have been at least thirty in the pile, from which I chose one with a picture of three cute kittens playing with a ball of wool.

"How about this one?" I handed it to Nancy.

"Nice choice. I do love kittens." She opened the box, emptied the pieces (1000 according to the label), and then set about putting the jigsaw together.

I'm not sure when I was last so flabbergasted. Her hands moved so quickly that they were little more than a blur. In no time at all, the edge pieces were all in place. In less than ten minutes, she'd completed the jigsaw.

"That's amazing," I said, still in shock.

"I thought you'd be impressed," Roy said. "There's nothing worse than buying a jigsaw, only to find one or more of the pieces is missing. Nancy makes sure our customers never have to suffer that disappointment."

"Thanks very much for showing me, Nancy. I can't tell you how impressive that is."

"Would you like to see me do another one?"

"No, thanks. My mind is already well and truly blown."

After leaving Nancy, Roy showed me back to reception.

"Any more questions for me before you leave, Jill?"

"No, I don't think so. I appreciate your time."

Chapter 10

Jules was back at her desk, and she was dropping sausage roll crumbs all over it.

"Sorry, Jill." She managed through a mouthful of the pastry. "I was starving."

"That's okay. Are you sure you should be back at work?"

"Yes, I feel fine now."

"You didn't happen to buy me a sausage roll, did you?"

"No, sorry. I had no idea when you'd be back. I can nip out and get you one if you like."

"No, it's okay. Any calls?"

"Only Mrs V checking that I'd made it into the office. I called her last night to say I was feeling better and would be back at work today. Oh, and she asked me to tell you that she'd checked that address in Crewe."

"Right?"

"She said there is no such address. It doesn't exist."

Winky looked as pale as a ghost. Yes, I do realise that he *is* a ghost, but contrary to the common misconception, ghosts aren't always pale in colour. In fact, if you could see Winky, you would barely notice any difference to when he was alive—except for the additional eye of course.

"What's wrong?" I said.

"This is all your fault."

"What is?"

"You were the one who told me I should haunt that Petty guy."

"Rubbish. It was your idea. What's happened?"

"He says he's going to hire himself an exorcist."

"No."

"Yes. I overheard him talking to someone in the corridor. He said the management of the building weren't taking his complaint seriously, so he was going to take action himself."

"You'd probably better kick the haunting idea into touch."

"You don't seem to understand the gravity of the situation."

"Enlighten me."

"It may have escaped your notice, but I'm a ghost. If Petty does bring in an exorcist, goodness knows what they might do to me."

"I see what you mean. That could be a little tricky."

"*Tricky*? It could be devastating. What if the exorcist banishes me to GT forever?"

"Every cloud." I grinned.

"This isn't funny!"

"Sorry. Did Petty actually say that he'd already found an exorcist?"

"No, just that he was going to look for one."

"It might not be too late then."

"What do you mean?"

"I'll explain later." I hurried out of the office. "I'm just going next door to see Mr Petty, Jules. I won't be long."

I could hear movement inside Petty's office, so I knocked and walked in. The poor man almost jumped out of his skin.

"You made me jump, Jill."

"Sorry, Peter. Can you spare me a minute?"

"I was just about to take my afternoon constitutional

around the park."

"This won't take long, I promise."

"Okay. Is it about the two-ply?"

"No, it's about the other matter you brought to my attention recently."

"You mean the evil spirit that's occupying this building, and more specifically my office?"

"That's the one. Having given the matter more thought, I've realised that I didn't take your concerns seriously enough."

"No one else has either."

"And for that, I can only apologise. Have there been any more—err—incidents?"

"A couple, yes, that's why I've decided to take matters into my own hands."

"What have you done?"

"I'm going to engage the services of an exorcist, to rid me of this malevolent spirit."

"That's an excellent idea. Have you actually found anyone yet?"

"Not yet."

"In that case, I might be able to help. I have some experience in these matters."

"Really?"

"Yes, in fact I've had to avail myself of the services of an exorcist on more than one occasion. The woman in question is called Portia Parkspirit, and I can recommend her very highly. Would you like me to contact Portia on your behalf?"

"That would be awfully kind of you."

"Think nothing of it. I'll give her a call and have her get in touch with you."

***

The novelty of being taught by 'the most powerful witch in the world' had quickly worn off for the pupils at CASS, and they now viewed me as just another teacher, which was both a blessing and a curse.

"Joseph!" I shouted. "If I have to tell you again, I will send you to see Mrs Littledo."

"But, Miss, I wasn't doing anything."

"You were using the 'rain' spell to make it rain on Sophie again."

"No, I wasn't. There must be a leaking pipe." He glanced up at the ceiling.

"The pipes are fine, but you won't be if you do it again. Understood?"

"Yes, Miss."

"Now, where was I?"

"You were talking about the internet, Miss," Kristen said.

"Why don't we have the internet in this world?" Rodney asked. "It sounds cool."

"That's a very good question and one I've asked myself many times. In fact, several years ago, I was part of a campaign to try to bring the internet to Candlefield, but we were unsuccessful."

"Do you think it will ever happen, Miss?" Sophie said.

"I honestly don't know. How many of you have used the internet in the human world?"

About one third of the pupils raised their hands. The majority of those were kids who, like Florence, had been raised in the human world. The others, I assumed, must have visited the human world at some time or other.

"What do you think of it?"

"It's cool," Marcy said. "You can do anything online. It's rubbish here without it."

"It's not all good, though," David said.

"Why do you say that?"

"There are some nasty people online. My parents stopped me going on social media."

Just then, the classroom door opened, and Ms Mousemore, Mrs Littledo's assistant, popped her head inside.

"I'm awfully sorry to interrupt your lesson, Mrs Maxwell, but I need to take Helen Peep to see the headmistress."

Helen Peep was one of the quietest, and best-behaved kids in the class, so I couldn't believe she was in any kind of trouble.

"Sure." I turned to Helen who looked terrified. "You'd better go with Ms Mousemore."

Helen picked up her satchel, made her way between the desks, and left with Ms Mousemore.

"Helen's in trouble! Helen's in trouble!" Joseph chanted.

"That's enough, Joseph. You had your hand up earlier. What do you think of the internet?"

"It's dope, Miss. I play Minecraft all the time when I'm at home."

"Anything else?"

"Call of Duty."

"I actually meant do you use the internet for anything besides games?"

"Nah."

At the end of the lesson, I gestured for Florence to come

by my desk.

"How are you?" I asked.

"Fine. What do they want Helen Peep for?"

"I've no idea. You didn't contribute much in class today."

"How could I? You and dad never let me go online."

"That's not true."

"It might as well be. You put so many blocks and filters on my computer that the only thing I could look at was stuff for little kids or educational resources."

"We were only looking out for you."

"It doesn't matter now, anyway." She shrugged. "It's not like I can use it here."

"The twins are having a relaunch party for Cuppy C tomorrow."

"I thought they'd dumped that name?"

"They did, but they realised it was a mistake, so now they've brought it back. Complete with super-duper new sign."

"I never did like the new name."

"They asked if you'd come to the party."

"Tomorrow?"

"Yeah."

"I can't. It's the third round of the netball knockout tournament. We're playing away at Biggins High."

"You never mentioned it before. Would you like me to come and support you?"

"Definitely not. Nobody's parents go to these games. Well, except for Jessie's, but her parents are super weird."

"Fair enough. I'll just have to eat your share of the cupcakes."

"I don't doubt it. I'd better get going because I've got

Mrs Goggins next, and she'll go ballistic if I'm late."

"Okay. See you next week."

***

"We've just had a visitor," Jack said when I arrived home.

"Who?"

"Mr Flatley. You've just missed him."

"What did that idiot want?"

"Apparently, he heard back from the planning department. They told him that his report had been investigated and that the fence was found to be within the permitted height limits."

"I wish I'd been here to see him. I bet he was steaming, wasn't he?"

"He was so red in the face that I thought his head was going to explode."

"Serves him right."

"He's not going to let it lie."

"What do you mean? The authorities have approved the fence, so there's nothing else he can do."

"He said he's going to lodge an appeal."

"Can he do that?"

"I've no idea, but he's out there now, measuring the fence again for himself."

"He's doing *what*?" I glanced outside and saw the man in question, kneeling next to our fence, with a tape measure in his hand. "What were you thinking? Why did you let him go out there?"

"I didn't want to cause a scene."

"*Scene*? I'll show you a *scene*." I stormed out of the door and across the lawn. "Hey, Flathead, what do you think you're doing?"

Flatley stood up. "I've asked you not to call me that."

"You're trespassing."

"No, I'm not. Your husband gave me permission to come out here."

"Well, I'm withdrawing that permission, and I'd like you to leave right now."

"You can't stop me going around to the other side of the fence and measuring it from there. That's on the public pathway."

"Why would you waste your time? The man from the planning department has already pronounced it legal."

"There's no way this fence is only two metres high. Look." He held the tape against the fence.

"I don't care what your cheapo tape measure says. Now, are you going to get out of my garden, or do I have to remove you by force?"

"I'll go, but like I told your husband, I intend to lodge an appeal."

"Knock yourself out."

I waited until he'd left the garden and then I went back inside.

"Don't ever let that imbecile on our property again."

"Has he gone?"

"Yes."

"Is he still planning on lodging an appeal?"

"He says so. It won't do any good, though, will it?"

"I don't know. I have no idea how these bureaucrats work."

"We had a bumper day at the store today," Jack said

over dinner.

"How come?"

"It was just one woodland creature after another."

"From the con, I assume."

"Yeah, there were dozens of them throughout the day."

"These conventions are going to be a great boon for the village."

"I agree." Jack nodded. "But I'm not sure all the residents share that view."

"Flat Head doesn't for one."

"It's not just him. The store was so busy with giant woodland creatures that some of our regular customers had to wait much longer than usual. I overheard a few of them complaining about all the *silly people in costumes*."

"They'll get used to it, and it's not like it'll be every day."

"There was one funny moment in the store today."

"Did one of Kiki's false eyelashes fall off?"

"Jill!"

"Sorry. What happened?"

"I'd just finished serving two field voles when I looked up and saw a lion standing there."

"A *lion*? Why would someone dress as a lion for a woodland creatures' convention?"

"I have no idea, and to be honest, I didn't like to ask."

Chapter 11

It was Saturday morning, and Jack had to work in the store, so I had the day to myself. I only had a small breakfast because it was the twins' relaunch party later, and I wanted to leave room for cake. Lots of it.

Two weeks from today, it would be Ringabell, and the sunlight fairies were relying on me to repair the mace that would be the centrepiece of their float. I'd done my best to manage their expectations, but I knew they would be devastated if I failed. If I was unsuccessful, they would most likely withdraw from the Ringabell parade.

I put the mace on the table and then emptied out the bag containing the jewels next to it. It was only then that I realised the magnitude of the task. When I'd last seen the jewels, I was sunlight fairy size. Back at full-size, the jewels appeared so small that they were barely distinguishable from one another. If I was going to restore the mace to its former glory, I would need to shrink myself again.

After making myself sunlight fairy size, I then had to somehow come up with a spell that would refix the jewels onto the mace in their original pattern. The obvious starting point was the 'take it back' spell, which was one of the first spells I had ever learned, way back when I first discovered I was a witch. In the early days of using that spell, I'd only been able to restore an object that had been changed or damaged within the last few minutes. As I'd grown more powerful and experienced, I'd managed to extend the window of time during which I could recover an object. Somehow, though, I doubted that the spell would work on the mace because it had been damaged so long ago. Still, nothing ventured, nothing gained, so I focussed on the mace and jewels, and cast the spell.

Nothing happened. Zilch. Nada.

The mace and jewels just lay there, taunting me.

I was not beaten yet, though, so I consulted the spell book app, which included a useful cross-reference between similar or related spells. One of them was titled 'take-it back extender', which sounded promising, but when I checked the details, it turned out to be no better than the one I'd come up with myself; it would only work on something damaged or changed within the last two days. The other links proved to be no more helpful.

It was all Grandma's fault that I was in this position, so I figured she could at least try to help me to find a solution. I took a walk across the village to her cottage, and en route, I came across two human-size badgers, a fox, a squirrel, and the lion that Jack had told me about.

Unlike Grandma, who had a habit of just walking into our house, I knocked on her door. She answered on the first knock. "If you've brought my loaf, you're too late. I got tired of waiting, so I had crackers instead."

"I haven't brought your loaf."

"What do you want, then?"

"Can I come in?"

"Must you? I was just about to cut my toenails."

"This will only take a few minutes."

"Come on, then, but don't expect a drink. I'm cutting back on tea and coffee."

"Why?"

"Too many hot drinks give me warts."

"Right? Shall we go through to the kitchen?"

"I thought this wasn't going to take long?"

"It won't, but I need to use your table."

"Okay, but make it quick."

Once inside the kitchen, I took the tiny mace out of my pocket and placed it on the kitchen table. Then I poured out the jewels next to it.

"What's all this?" Grandma said.

"That's the sunlight fairies' mace. The one you told them I would restore. And those are all the jewels that need refixing into the original pattern."

"That's not going to be easy."

"Tell me about it."

"How are you going to do it?"

"I don't have a clue."

"Have you tried tweaking the 'take-it back' spell?"

"That was my first thought, but I can't get it to work because it's so long since it was damaged."

"That's a shame. What will you do, then?"

"I thought I'd ask you for suggestions. That's why I'm here."

"Don't you think I have better things to do with my time than worry about some silly mace?"

"You were the one who approached the sunlight fairies and offered to help."

"Yes, but only in a moment of weakness."

"And what do you mean you don't have the time? Since you sold all of your businesses, what do you do with yourself all day, exactly?"

"Not that it's any of your business, but I'm involved with a number of charitable organisations."

"Well, you're going to have to find time to help me with this because I've drawn a blank."

"Alright, I'll give it some thought. Satisfied now?"

"I will be if you come up with something."

"If there's nothing else, I have toenails to attend to. Unless, of course, you'd like to clip them for me."

"Not a chance."

***

I was headed back to the old watermill when my phone rang.

"Mrs Maxwell? It's Arnold Makepiece, Liam Locks' lawyer."

"Hi."

"Would you by any chance be free on Monday morning?"

"Possibly. Why?"

"I've taken the liberty of arranging for you to meet with Liam at ten o'clock on Monday. Will you be able to make it then?"

"Where's he being held?"

"At Longdale Prison. It's about thirty—"

"It's okay. I know where it is. Yes, I can make that."

"Excellent, I'll meet you in the car park at nine-forty-five."

"I'll be there."

I'd just ended the call when I bumped into Old Mrs Johnson. She was a lovely old lady who had moved into the village a couple of years earlier, after her husband of forty years had died. She was a friendly soul who had quicky become one of my favourite neighbours.

"Good morning, Mrs Johnson, lovely day."

"Oh, hello, Jill, I didn't spot you there."

She seemed a little nervous, so I thought I should check

if she was okay.

"Is everything alright, Mrs Johnson?"

"I'm not sure it is, Jill. I haven't been sleeping too well recently, so I went to see Dr Fuller. He gave me some pills that he said would help."

"And did they?"

"Oh yes. I've been sleeping like a log since I started on them, but I'm a little concerned they may be having some side effects."

"What kind of side effects?"

"I think I'm seeing things." She glanced around.

"What kind of things?"

"You'll think I'm silly if I tell you."

"I won't. I promise."

"When I came out of my cottage earlier, I saw a hedgehog."

"There are quite a few of those in the village. We often get them in our garden."

"Yes, dear, but this one was six feet tall. And then, just now, when I came out of your store, I saw two giant rabbits. I think I'd better go back to Dr Fuller on Monday and tell him he'll need to change my prescription."

"You're not seeing things, Mrs Johnson. Those are people dressed up as woodland creatures."

"Are you sure? Why would anyone want to do that?"

"Do you remember the residents' meeting that was held the other week?"

"Which one was that, dear?"

"The one where the vicar talked about the change of ownership at the hotel."

"Oh yes. When Mrs Richardson walked out because they hadn't laid on any tea."

"That's the one."

"I'm sure she could have managed an hour without a cuppa."

"Yes, anyway, at that meeting, we talked about the hotel, and that it was going to be used for holding cosplay conventions. Do you remember that?"

"Vaguely, but I didn't really understand it if I'm honest."

"The people you saw dressed as woodland creatures are here for the first convention to be held at the hotel."

"Oh."

"Do you see?"

"Not really. Why would they want to dress up as rabbits and hedgehogs?"

It was a valid question.

"They just do it for fun, but it's all very harmless. Certainly, nothing to worry about."

"How often will there be conventions at the hotel?"

"I'm not sure. Maybe every weekend."

"Does that mean there'll be giant rabbits in the village every week?"

"No. The theme of each convention will be different, so for example, next weekend, you might see giant vegetables or giant fish in the village. But you really don't have anything to worry about."

"Okay. Thanks for putting my mind at ease. At least I won't have to trouble the doctor again. I'm sure I'll get used to it eventually."

***

It was a shame that Florence couldn't attend the

relaunch of Cuppy C, but I'd promised her that I'd make up for her absence by eating her share of the cake.

What? I know it's a sacrifice, but it's one I'm willing to make for my daughter.

I magicked myself over to the street where a large crowd was already gathered outside of Cuppy C. The twins had created an archway of pink and white balloons over the door, but that's not what had grabbed everyone's attention. Several people were pointing at the recently installed neon sign, and it only took a quick glance to reveal why. The capital letter at the beginning of the word Cuppy was not illuminated, so the sign appeared to read uppy C.

Through the window, I could see the twins remonstrating with a hapless vampire, who was wearing overalls with the words Candlefield Signs printed on the back. When the doors finally opened, there would be a mad rush to get to the cakes, so I decided to magic myself inside.

"I keep telling you that there's nothing I can do until Monday morning," the vampire said.

"And we keep telling you that today is our relaunch party," Amber snapped.

"I understand that and if there was something I could do, I would do it, but there isn't. All I can do is offer my sincere apologies. These things happen."

"That's just great." Pearl spotted me. "Have you seen it, Jill?"

"What's that?"

"The 'C'."

"Not since I was last at Candle Sands."

"This isn't funny, Jill! I meant the sign! The C isn't

working."

"Sorry."

I grabbed a lemon cupcake and was just about to take a bite when Amber snapped, "Put that down!"

"Just one."

"No, you can wait until the doors open like everyone else."

Clearly, she wasn't going to back down, so somewhat reluctantly, I replaced the cupcake.

"I'll be back first thing on Monday morning," the vampire said, as he headed for the rear exit.

"What a useless article he is." Pearl sighed.

"It seems to be a common trait with those in the signage business," I said. "Do you remember all the trouble I had with the sign at my old office? Mr Sid Song and that sign were almost the death of me."

Just then, an elderly witch knocked on the window and pointed to her watch.

"We should have opened two minutes ago," Amber said.

Pearl unlocked the doors, and while the twins had their backs to me, I grabbed the lemon cupcake and a small Victoria sponge cake, before the hordes could descend upon them.

If the success of the relaunch was to be judged on the number of people attending, then it was without a shadow of a doubt, a resounding success. I'd never seen the shop so busy since its first relaunch. Tables were at a premium, but I'd managed to snag one by the window. Much of the talk was about the return of the name Cuppy C, and the consensus was that it was the right move. A few people mentioned the faulty sign, but the majority were too busy stuffing their faces to be concerned about that.

I was just contemplating whether it was worth losing my seat to go and grab more cake when I spotted Aunt Lucy through the window. I was surprised that she was late to the party, and she looked a little flustered. When she caught sight of me, she gestured to my cup, and I gathered that she was asking if I wanted another drink. I had intended leaving, but it seemed rude to leave now, so I nodded. While she was getting the drinks, I managed to grab a free chair and drag it over to my table. It took her almost fifteen minutes to get served, but when she finally made it over to me, she was carrying a tray with two cups and a plate containing four cupcakes.

"It's manic in here." She passed me a coffee. "I wasn't sure if I should get you a cupcake or not. Have you already had one?"

"No, it was too crowded," I lied. "Thanks. I'll only have the one, though."

"Did you notice the C in the sign isn't working?" Aunt Lucy took a bite of her caramel cream cupcake.

"I did, but don't tell the twins you spotted it. They've been doing their nut about it."

"I thought Florence might have come with you."

"I did ask her, but she had an important netball match today."

"In that case, you'd better have the cupcake I grabbed for her."

"Go on, then. If you insist."

Chapter 12

We'd enjoyed a restful Sunday, during which Jack and I had taken a drive out into the countryside for a picnic. We'd been able to do that because the dynamic duo, AKA Monty and Kiki had run the store.

But Monday morning had come around only too quickly, and with it the realisation that I probably should have spent the weekend working on my cases.

"It's all your fault," I said to Jack over breakfast.

"What is? What did I do now?"

"You forced me to go on a picnic yesterday when you knew I should have been working."

"I don't remember having to force you. In fact, you were the one who suggested the picnic. That's why I called Kiki on Saturday evening to ask if she'd do an extra shift on Sunday."

"It's still your fault."

"Fine. Why don't we just agree that everything is my fault? It will avoid a lot of arguments."

"That's the best idea you've had in a long time."

"What have you got planned for this morning?" Jack asked, before finishing the last of his muesli by putting the bowl to his mouth and tipping it up.

"Do you have to do that? It's disgusting."

"I don't want any to go to waste."

"Gross. In answer to your question, I'm going to Longdale Prison to see Liam Locks."

***

I arrived at the prison with fifteen minutes to spare.

Having only spoken to Liam's lawyer on the phone, I had no idea what he looked like. A few minutes later, when a white Lexus with the number plate ARNLD 5 pulled into a space close to mine, I figured that must be my man. It took him longer than it should have to extract himself from the car because Arnold Makepiece was clearly a man who enjoyed his food.

"Jill?" As he approached, he brushed breadcrumbs from his jacket.

"Mr Makepiece, I presume."

"Arnold, please. Sorry for my appearance. I had to grab a snack on the way over here. Thank you for agreeing to do this."

"That's okay, but I hope you made it clear to Liam that I haven't yet agreed to take on his case."

"Absolutely. He knows it's up to him to convince you to do so, and he's eager to do just that."

"Good. How is he doing?"

"Not great, as you can imagine. Although he and Ms Locks were no longer together, he—"

"Barr. Goldie had reverted to using her maiden name."

"Quite. Anyway, Liam still had a soft spot for her, which is why he travelled down from Newcastle to see her. But it would be best if I allow him to tell you himself."

"Agreed."

As always, the formalities to gain access to the prison took longer than was strictly necessary, but eventually we were shown to a small, windowless room where we were told to await Liam.

Five minutes later, he arrived, accompanied by a prison guard. It was some time since I'd seen Liam, and the intervening months had not been kind to him. His brown hair was tinged with grey, not something I recalled seeing previously. He looked thinner too, although that might just have been the prison-issue clothing, which was at least two sizes too big for him. His eyes looked heavy as though he hadn't slept in some time.

"Jill, thank you for doing this." He welled up as he spoke.

"How are you holding up?"

"I'm not." He slumped onto the chair. "This is like a nightmare I can't wake up from. I didn't kill Goldie. I would never hurt her. You have to believe me."

"It doesn't matter what I believe. The police obviously think they have a case otherwise they wouldn't have charged you."

"They should be out there looking for the real killer."

"That's as maybe, but right now, they think they have their man. Why don't you talk me through everything that happened?"

"It all started when Goldie called me to ask if I'd been behind those pranks in her house."

"*Pranks*? Is that what she called them?"

"No. Sorry, I shouldn't have said *prank*. They had her pretty freaked out. I could tell that much just by talking to her. She said you'd told her to contact me, to see if I was behind them."

"That's right. I did."

"I had nothing to do with it. I told Goldie that, and I'm pretty sure she believed me. Look, what happened between me and her was one hundred percent my fault. I know that, but it doesn't mean I didn't still care for her. I would never have done anything to upset or hurt her."

"After you'd told her that you weren't the one who was doing those things. What then?"

"She rang me twice. If I'm honest, I didn't think much about it the first time. But then, when she called again, after the bed thing, I could tell she was absolutely freaking out. That's when I decided to go and see her. Lorraine wasn't very impressed I can tell you."

"*Lorraine*?"

"She and I live together now."

"Did you explain why you wanted to visit Goldie?"

"I did, but I'm pretty sure she thought I was lying. I went anyway. I wish now that I hadn't."

"When did you visit Goldie?"

"It was the same day that she was murdered."

"What happened?"

"Nothing much. She was surprised to see me."

"You didn't tell her you were coming?"

"No. It was a spur of the moment thing. When she saw me on the doorstep, she fell into my arms and sobbed. We went inside and I made her a cup of tea. When she'd recovered, she told me everything that had happened: the milk bottles, the bowls, the beds and the book. It was crazy stuff. I offered to go to the police with her, but she insisted it would be a waste of time because they'd already made it clear that they weren't taking it seriously."

"Hold on a minute, Liam. You said *book*. What book?"

"Goldie had found it in the hallway earlier that morning. She thought someone must have pushed it through the letterbox."

"What was it?"

"A kid's nursery rhyme book. One of those with the

thick pages."

"A board book?"

"Possibly. I'm not sure what they're called."

"Did you tell the police about the book?"

"Yeah, but they reckon there was no trace of it in the house."

"What did you do while you were at the house?"

"Mainly, I was just trying to calm Goldie down. I offered to stay with her for a couple of days—even though Lorraine would probably have killed me—but Goldie said she was going to stay with her mother. She'd already packed a case. I even offered to drive her there, but she wouldn't hear of it, so after a couple of hours, I left and went back to Newcastle. The next thing I heard was when I got a phone call that evening to tell me Goldie had been murdered."

"When did the police arrest you?"

"A few days later. When they turned up at my door, I assumed they were just going to ask me about my visit to see her. I couldn't believe it when they charged me with her murder."

I turned to Makepiece who had remained silent while Liam and I had been talking. "Do we know how Goldie was killed?"

"Blunt force trauma to the head."

"And the murder weapon?"

"An ornamental poker. It was found beside the body, apparently."

"They say my fingerprints and DNA are on it," Liam said. "But they would be because I'd lived in that house for years."

"Where was the poker usually kept?"

"On the fireplace. We bought it when we were in York several years ago."

"Do they have any other evidence against you?"

"No. It's purely circumstantial. If I hadn't gone to see her, I wouldn't be sitting here now. They can't convict me on the strength of that, can they?"

"Anything can happen once a case goes before a jury. The only surefire way of ensuring that doesn't happen is to find the real murderer."

"Can you do that, Jill?" There was a desperation in Liam's voice. "Will you help me?"

"I will but I want to make one thing clear: I'm not doing this for you. I'm doing it for Goldie. I owe it to her to bring her murderer to justice."

"Thanks, Jill. I can't tell you how much this means to me."

"I need you to think if there's anyone who might have wished Goldie ill."

"I've done nothing but that since they locked me up, but I've drawn a blank. You know what Goldie was like: She never had a bad word to say about anyone. I can't think of a single person who would have wanted to hurt her. It must have been a stranger. That sort of thing does happen, doesn't it?"

"Random murders? Yes, but in the vast majority of cases, the murderer is known to the victim. I know you said you can't think of anyone, but I want you to keep going over it, and if you come up with anyone—no matter how unlikely—tell Arnold, and he'll brief me."

"Okay, I will."

"What do you think?" Arnold asked as we walked back

to our cars.

"The evidence they have is paper-thin, but it wouldn't be the first time an innocent man has been convicted under similar circumstances."

***

It was time for my alter ego, Portia Parkspirit, to make an appearance. I didn't want to take the risk that Peter Petty might recognise me, so I used the 'doppelganger' spell to make me look like Kathy. Luckily, it would only be for a short period; poor old Kathy was stuck with that face permanently.

What? Of course I'm joking. Sheesh!

Suitably attired in exorcist chic, I knocked on Petty's door. He cracked the door open only wide enough to peek through the gap.

"Yes? Can I help you?"

"Mr Petty?"

"Yes. Do you have an appointment?"

"No, but I was asked to contact you by Jill Maxwell. She led me to believe it was urgent."

"Are you Porcelain Parkspirit?"

"It's actually Portia, but yes, I am."

He opened the door fully. "Do come in, Mrs Parkspirit."

"It's Ms, but you may call me Portia."

"I do appreciate you coming so promptly. Mrs Maxwell speaks very highly of you."

"Coming from a woman of her status, that is praise indeed. You're very lucky to have her as a neighbour."

"I guess so. I should tell you, Portia, that I have no experience of exorcisms."

"Very few people do. Perhaps you could tell me about the spirits that have been causing you distress."

"Right, yes, well, there's not much to tell really. Every now and then, there's this whooo, whooo, whooo sound."

"Are you sure it was three whooos?"

"I think so. Does it matter?"

"It's extremely important. The number of whooos will help me to narrow down the type of spirit that is causing you such distress. That, in turn, will ensure that I employ the appropriate measures to rid you of them. Might it have been two whooos? Or four?"

He thought about it for a moment. "No, it was definitely three."

"That's unfortunate."

"Why? What's wrong?"

"The three whooo spirits are the most difficult to eradicate."

"But you have to get rid of them."

"Fear not, Mr Petty. I said it was difficult, not that it was impossible. Now, I'm going to need you to leave me alone in here for about twenty minutes."

"Can't I stay and watch?"

"Definitely not. Trust me, you don't want to see what is about to happen. It could get very messy. Off you trot. And don't come back until twenty minutes have elapsed."

"Okay. Thank you."

I waited until I heard the lift doors open, and then I took a seat and put my feet up on his desk. I must have been more tired than I'd realised because I dozed off and only woke up when Petty knocked on the door.

"Portia? Is it safe to come in?"

I let him in. "It's perfectly safe now."

"Did you get rid of that awful thing?"

"As I feared, it wasn't easy, but in the end I prevailed."

"Thank you so much. Are you sure it won't come back?"

"Positive. You have nothing to fear, Mr Petty."

"I can't thank you enough. How much do I owe you?"

For a moment, I considered charging him for Portia's 'services', but in the end, I took pity on the poor man.

"Nothing. It was my pleasure to do this for my good friend, Jill. Perhaps you'll return the favour by helping her if ever she should need it."

"Absolutely. Tell me, is there somewhere I can leave a review for you?"

"It's kind of you to offer, but exorcism isn't the kind of thing that one can advertise. People tend to find me through word of mouth."

"Rest assured, Portia, I won't hesitate to recommend you to any of my friends or colleagues should the need arise."

Chapter 13

"I wish I could have been there to see his face," Winky said when I told him about the 'exorcism'.

"He bought it hook, line and sinker," I grinned. "But there's to be strictly no more haunting from now on."

"Aw. I thought I might give it another go in one of the offices on the floor below."

"Definitely not. Portia's appearance was a one-off. You'll have to find something else to amuse—"

Jules interrupted me mid-sentence. She didn't comment on the fact that I appeared to be talking to myself, but judging by her expression, she obviously thought I'd lost the plot.

"Your sister is here, Jill."

"Not again!"

"I heard that," Kathy shouted from the outer office. "This will only take a minute."

"You'd better show her in."

Kathy didn't wait to be asked. Instead, she stepped by Jules, and said, "That next door neighbour of yours is a bit weird, isn't he?"

"Mr Petty? Yeah. What did he do?"

"He was just coming out of his office as I stepped out of the lift. He called me Portia and said he was surprised to see me back again so soon. When I told him I wasn't Portia and that I didn't know what he was talking about, he smirked and said a nod is as good as a wink."

"I find it best to ignore him. Now, what do you want, Kathy?"

"Charming. Can't you just be pleased to see me?"

"I'm thrilled. What do you want?"

"It's about Gregor."

"Has he cancelled? Please tell me he's cancelled."

"Why would he cancel? This exhibition will be great for him."

"Has he decided to book a hotel instead?"

"No, I told you that he doesn't like hotels."

"What then?"

"You're going to need this." She opened her handbag, took out a sheet of paper, and handed it to me.

"Special dietary requirements?"

"Gregor has a very delicate digestive system. We can't afford for him to be ill while he's here."

"No meat. No dairy. No wheat. What does he eat?"

"It's all there. I've given you a list of the foods that are safe."

"I haven't heard of half of this stuff. Where am I supposed to buy it?"

"Fresh and Friendly should stock most of the things on there."

"I've never heard of them."

"Given the rubbish you eat, I'm not surprised. They're on Bridge Street."

"And is Gregor going to refund me?"

"No, and you mustn't ask him to."

"Someone better had because I don't imagine this lot will come cheap."

"Don't worry. I'll refund you for everything you buy. Just be sure to keep receipts so I can put it through the books."

"You're going to owe me big time for this."

"Oh, and I forgot to include a note that Gregor can only drink filtered water, so you'll have to buy one of those filter units. They aren't very expensive." She checked her watch. "I'd better get going because I have a meeting in twenty minutes."

"That sister of yours is taking the mickey," Winky said. "Let's have a look at that list."

"Here." I handed it to him.

"This lot is going to cost you a small fortune."

"I know. She'd better reimburse me."

***

When I'd visited Mr Beasley's house, he'd revealed that the ransom note had been hand-delivered. That snippet of information could prove to be crucial if I was to identify who posted the note through his door.

Although there were no CCTV cameras on Turnip Shed Road itself, I was hopeful that some of the residents might have installed their own personal system. To that end, I started by checking the properties on either side of Mr Beasley's, keeping a look out for any cameras or smart doorbells. There were none. Fortunately, I had more luck with the house on the opposite side of the road. Just above the upstairs' window was a small camera. Eureka!

I didn't think the house owner would be receptive to a request to view their CCTV footage from a total stranger, so I found a quiet spot, and magicked myself into a police officer's uniform. My first knock went unanswered, but after a second attempt, I heard someone shout, "Have some patience, will you? I was on the khazi." The door opened to reveal a man with a cigarette hanging from the corner of his mouth. His dirty vest was fighting a losing battle with his bulging stomach, and he had holes in both socks.

"Sorry to trouble you, *sir*."

"If it's about the lead from the church roof, I told your people I was at my brother's when it was nicked."

"No, this isn't about lead."

"Has that silly cow from next door been calling you lot again?"

"No, nothing like that. I noticed that you have a CCTV camera, and I was wondering if I might be able to take a look at the footage."

"No."

"It would only take a few minutes and it would—"

"The camera isn't real; it's one of them fake ones. The missus made me put it up before she ran off with my brother. She reckoned it would keep the thieves out. Didn't stop them nicking my bike, though. Talking of which, why haven't you lot found it yet? I told you who nicked it."

"I wouldn't know anything about that, sir, it's not really my department."

"Might have known. Too busy handing out speeding tickets, I suppose."

"Thank you for your time." I started to edge away from the door. "Have a good day."

"Some chance of that." He groaned. "The TV's on the blink again."

I was beginning to think this had been a wasted journey when I noticed the house, two doors down, had what looked like a brand-new camera mounted above the door. Hopefully, this one wouldn't be another dummy.

The woman who answered the door was holding a cute little Pomeranian.

"Hello, officer."

"Good day, madam. What an adorable little dog."

"This is Mitzi. Say hello to the nice officer, Mitzi."

Mitzi yawned.

"I'm sorry to trouble you, madam, but I noticed that you have a CCTV camera on the front of your house."

"I had it installed a few months ago after someone stole my lawnmower. I wouldn't have minded so much, but they took it while I was halfway through mowing the lawn. I'd just stepped inside to feed Mitzi and when I came back out, it had gone."

"That's terrible, but I'm actually investigating a serious incident that occurred across the road from your property, and I was wondering if your camera might have caught anything that could help."

"You're welcome to come and take a look, but you'll have to figure out how to work it yourself. I've read the manual a few times and I'm still no wiser."

"That's fine."

"My name is Petula by the way. Do come in. I'll log you onto the computer, and then I'll go and make us both a drink. Is tea okay?"

"That would be lovely. Thank you."

The CCTV software was pretty straightforward. All the footage was stored on the cloud, so I was quickly able to focus in on the day that the ransom note had been hand-delivered.

"Here you are, dear." Petula handed me a cup of tea. "Have you figured it out yet?"

"Yes, I think so."

"Is this about old Mrs Beasley?"

"I'm afraid I can't discuss the case."

"I understand. Sad affair. They say she fell down the basement steps, but I'm not so sure. It was her lad who got the house you know."

"Like I said: I'm not able to discuss the case."

"Sorry. I'll leave you to it. Give me a shout when you're done."

"I will, and thanks again for the tea."

Personal CCTV wasn't supposed to record the area outside your own property, but this system, in common with most I'd encountered, covered the front garden, the road and the opposite causeway. I began to view the footage, on fast-forward, from 5am on the day in question. At just after nine o'clock, the postman made his delivery to Beasley's house. After that, no one else approached the house until just after two o'clock when a woman pushed something through the letterbox. I could only see her from the back as she walked towards the house, but when she came back down the path, I had a much clearer view of her face. After freezing the frame, I was able to take a screenshot and email it to myself. It took another hour to view the rest of the footage for that day, and during that time, no one else approached the house.

"Petula, I've finished, thank you."

She came out of the kitchen.

"Did you get what you wanted, dear?"

"I hope so."

I now had a photo of the woman who I believed had delivered the ransom note to Mr Beasley, and I felt confident that he would be able to put a name to the face, so I hurried across the road to see him.

"I've no idea who that is," he said.

"Take a closer look."

He looked again at the photo, but then shook his head. "I've never seen her before in my life. Are you sure this is the person who put the ransom note through my letterbox?"

"If the note came on the day that you said it did, then yes, I'm pretty certain she was the one who delivered it. I've watched the CCTV footage, from the house across the road, and only two people came to your door during those twenty-four hours. One of them was the postman, but we know he didn't bring it because there was no address or stamp on the envelope. The other person was this woman."

"I don't understand."

"That makes two of us."

***

"Can you believe the nerve of that woman?" I said, as Jack prepared dinner.

"You're going to have to give me more than that. Which woman are we talking about?"

"That sister of mine." I took out the sheet of paper that Kathy had given me earlier that day. "Just look at this."

"Special dietary requirements? What's this about?"

"Our house guest, Mr Gregor Leggor, is apparently very fussy about what he will and won't eat."

"And drink. It says here he'll only drink filtered water. Still, he is an artist. It probably goes with the territory."

"You'll have to go and buy one of those water filter bottles from somewhere, Jack."

"Why me?"

"Because I've got to buy all this poncy food from this place with the stupid name."

"Fresh and Friendly? What's wrong with being friendly?"

"They can afford to be friendly with the prices they no doubt charge."

"I take it you haven't had a good day?"

"Not particularly. What about you?"

"Much quieter now the woodland creatures have all gone home. I did get some grief from your grandmother this afternoon, though."

"About what?"

"Apparently, the ingredients in her favourite minestrone soup have changed."

"How is that your fault?"

"It isn't, but that didn't stop her castigating me."

"You should ban her from the store."

"Oh yeah. Because I'm tired of living."

We were interrupted by a knock at the door.

"If that's Flat Head, I won't be responsible for my actions." I got to my feet.

"Sit down, Jill. Let me deal with it."

"Don't you dare let him in this house or into the garden."

"I won't, but you stay right there."

Somewhat reluctantly, I agreed, but only after he'd promised to leave the kitchen door ajar, so that I could listen in on his conversation. Jack thought he was tough, but too often he let people walk all over him.

It soon became clear that it wasn't Flat Head at the door. It was a man's voice but not one that I recognised. Whoever it was was softly spoken because despite my best efforts, I couldn't hear what was being discussed. After a few minutes, the door closed, and Jack came back through to the kitchen.

"Bad news," he said.

"What now? Who was it?"

"A man from the water authority. They need to do some emergency repairs, starting in one hour, which means we won't have any water."

"For how long?"

"He couldn't be sure, but he said it was unlikely to be restored before midday tomorrow."

"Well that's just dandy."

"He advised filling the bath, so we have water to flush the toilet. And they're setting up a water collection station in the grounds of the vicarage. We can collect as many bottles of water as we want."

"What about my shower in the morning?"

"You won't be able to have one. You'll just have to use a flannel."

"This day just gets better and better."

Chapter 14

I had hoped that the water might be restored by the next morning, but when I tried the tap in the bathroom, all it managed was a groan and a few pathetic drops. Jack might be happy to wash himself down with a flannel, but I needed a shower to set me up for the day ahead. It was quite some time since I'd last used the 'rain' spell, but just like riding a bike, it soon came back to me. Although, on reflection, that's probably not the best analogy to use, seeing as I'd never really mastered the art of bike riding. Anyway, I digress. I soon had a dark rain cloud hovering over the bath, and I was just about to step into it when I realised the rainwater would be stone cold.

Time to consult the spell book, methinks.

I had hoped that there might be a version of the spell that would produce warm rain, but no such luck. Fortunately, though, I found a solution by reading the comments attached to the 'rain' spell's listing. A number of people had suggested that the problem of the water temperature could be overcome by combining the 'rain' and the 'sunlight' spells. The latter was a new one to me, but it turned out to be quite straightforward and did the trick nicely. It wasn't exactly hot, but it took the edge off sufficiently to make it bearable.

"Jill! Are you in there?" Jack called from out on the landing.

"Yeah, I won't be long."

"Is the water back on?"

"No."

"I thought I could hear the shower." He pushed the door open and stepped inside.

"Do you mind?"

"What's going on?" He stared at the rain cloud and the mini sun.

"I'm not getting washed with a flannel."

"Are you sure it's safe?"

"Course it is. Now get out and close the door. There's a draught."

"I'll get in with you."

"No, you won't. There isn't room."

"Don't be daft."

Before I could stop him, he'd thrown off his pyjamas and climbed into the bath beside me.

"This is cozy." He grinned.

"Don't go getting any ideas. I've got a busy day ahead of me."

"Can you turn the temperature up a little?"

"No, I can't. You should think yourself lucky you don't have to use the flannel."

I washed myself as quickly as I could, climbed out of the bath, grabbed a towel and headed out of the bathroom. Before I went into the bedroom to get dried and dressed, I had one more thing to do.

"Hey!" Jack screeched from inside the bathroom. "That little sun thingy has disappeared, and the water is freezing."

Snigger.

By the time Jack caught up with me, I'd almost finished my bowl of cereal.

"You did that on purpose," he said.

"No, I didn't," I lied. "That spell has a time limit. You took too long in the shower, like you always do." I put the empty bowl in the sink and gave him a peck on the lips.

"Gotta run. See you tonight."

***

I'd only taken a couple of steps into my office before I stopped dead in my tracks. Winky was purring loudly because someone was tickling him under his chin. And that someone was Florence.

"This daughter of yours is a little treasure," Winky said.

"Florence? What are you doing here? What's wrong? Are you okay?" I rushed over and put my arms around her.

"I'm fine, Mum. Honestly."

"Why aren't you at school?"

"I need your help with something."

"What?"

"A little more to the right," Winky said.

"Leave him alone and come and sit over here."

"Don't stop!" Winky objected.

"What's going on?" I asked once Florence and I were seated on the sofa.

"Does your sofa always make that noise?" She giggled.

"Never mind that. You said you needed my help. Have you got yourself into some kind of trouble at CASS?"

"No, nothing like that. It's Helen Peep."

"What's the matter with her?"

"It's her father. He's been murdered."

"That's terrible. I'm so sorry."

"That's why she was called out of class last week, but we only found out what happened when she came in to school today."

"How is she?"

"She's a mess."

"She shouldn't have returned to school yet. It's too soon."

"She hasn't started lessons again. She only came in to talk to me."

"Why you? Are you close friends?"

"Not particularly. It's because you're my mum."

"I don't understand."

"Helen and her mother live here in the human world, and her mum is convinced that the murderer is a sup, so the human police don't stand a chance of catching the killer. Helen's mum asked if you'd help to find the murderer."

"Me? I can't."

"She said that she'd be able to pay you."

"It's not the money. I'm already snowed under with work."

"Please, Mum. I can't go back and tell Helen no. They're both clinging on by a thread."

"Okay, I'll speak to her mother."

"Thanks, you're the best." She took a small scrap of paper from her pocket and handed it to me. "This is her mother's phone number. I told Helen that you'd give her mother a call today."

"Did you now?" I grinned. "Go on. You'd better get back to school before you get in trouble."

"Okay. See you, soon. Thanks."

And with that, she disappeared.

"Why don't you scratch my chin like Florence does?" Winky said.

"Because you're a mangy old flea bag."

"Cheek. What does Florence want to be when she grows

up?"

"I don't actually know. We've never discussed it."

"Do you think she'll join the family business?"

"Definitely not. I want something better for her than this."

"I actually meant that store of yours. Obviously, she wouldn't want to join this no-mark outfit."

"You are this close to being on the wrong end of an exorcism."

I figured I might as well give Helen Peep's mother a call while it was still fresh in my mind. She answered on the first ring.

"Mrs Peep?"

"Who's that?"

"This is Jill Maxwell. Florence's mother. I believe you're expecting my call."

"Oh, thank you, Mrs Maxwell. I was hoping you might get in touch, but I wasn't expecting it to be so soon."

"Please call me Jill."

"I'm Mandy. I assume Florence told you what happened to my husband?"

"She told me Helen's father was murdered."

"That's right. I still can't believe he's gone." She sobbed. "Sorry, I'm not usually like this."

"Don't be silly. Would it help if I came over there?"

"That would be great. When could you come?"

"No time like the present. Why don't you give me your address and I'll magic myself straight over there."

One minute later, I was seated on the sofa next to her. As soon as I appeared, it was as though a dam had burst, and she broke down in a flood of tears. I figured there was no point in asking questions until she'd composed herself, so I waited patiently.

"I'm sorry about this, Jill. I've tried to hold it together for Helen's sake, but it's not easy. I've never known pain like this."

"It's okay. Take your time. Shall I make us both a drink?"

"I'll do it."

"No, you stay right there. Tea?"

"Yes, please."

By the time I'd made the tea, Mandy had managed to compose herself.

"Where's Helen?" I asked. "At CASS?"

"No, she's not ready to go back yet. She's upstairs in her bedroom. She was always Daddy's girl."

"Do you feel up to telling me what happened?"

"I'll try." She took a deep breath. "Where do you want me to start?"

"How did your husband die?"

"I was at work. He was here alone. I found him in the kitchen when I came home." Mandy hesitated and appeared to zone out for a moment, then she said, "There was blood everywhere."

"How was he killed?"

"He had sustained several blows to his head."

"Has the murder weapon been found?"

"I don't believe so."

"Was anything stolen?"

"Nothing. The police keep telling me that it was probably a burglary gone wrong. They reckon he must have disturbed the thief who then turned on him."

"It's possible, I suppose."

"I don't think so because when I arrived home, the door

was locked."

"Could someone have got in another way?"

"I don't see how because he was paranoid about keeping all the doors and windows locked, and there was no sign of damage to any of them."

"Is there any reason that he was like that? Had you been burgled before?"

"No. He wasn't always so paranoid. That only started quite recently."

"Do you know why?"

"A few weird things had happened. I didn't pay them much heed, but they seemed to freak him out."

"What kind of *weird* things?"

"The first time was when a toy sheep appeared on the stairs."

"I take it that it wasn't Helen's?"

"No, none of us had ever seen it before."

"Do you think someone came into the house and left it there?"

"They must have done, but I can't imagine why."

"And that freaked out your husband?"

"Not straight away. It was after the crook turned up in the kitchen that he changed."

"There was a burglar in your kitchen?"

"No." She managed a weak smile. "Not that kind of *crook*. Someone had put a shepherd's crook on the kitchen table. It totally freaked Beau out."

"*Beau*? Was that your husband's name?"

"Yeah. He got a lot of stick for that growing up, as you can imagine."

"I bet. Helen told Florence that you thought his murderer might be a sup. What makes you think that?"

"For the reason I mentioned before: whoever killed Beau somehow managed to get into the house even though all the doors and windows were locked."

"Your husband could have let them in."

"I doubt it, but even if he did, how did they manage to lock the door on their way out? The key was still in Beau's pocket. I believe that someone magicked themselves inside the house, like you did just now."

"That makes sense, I guess. Do you think I could take a look around?"

"Of course. Do you want me to come with you?"

"No, you stay there. It won't take me long."

I wanted to check all the windows and doors. Sure enough, they were all locked, and there was no sign of damage to any of them. The house had three bedrooms, the smallest of which was obviously being used for storage. It was full of all the usual rubbish, and I was just about to go back downstairs when I noticed something leaning against the wall in one corner of the room: A shepherd's crook.

When Mandy had told me her husband's name, I had immediately made the connection to Goldie's murder. I didn't say anything to Mandy, though, because I thought she would think I was crazy. As soon as I'd left her house, I called Daze, but it was Blaze who answered.

"Hey, Jill."

"Hi. I thought I'd rung Daze's number."

"You did. She's in a meeting with our boss, and he hates being interrupted by phone calls. Can I help?"

"I'm not sure. Is there any chance I could grab a few minutes with you two?"

"Sure, but it'll have to be this afternoon. Daze is likely to be tied up in this meeting for the next few hours."

"That's fine."

"How about two o'clock in Cuppy C, or whatever the twins are calling it this week."

"Sounds good. I'll see you both then."

"We'll be there."

Chapter 15

Although I'd visited both the warehouse and the manufacturing unit of Joy's Toys, I didn't feel like I'd made any progress, so I'd requested another meeting with Joy herself. Clearly keen to get to the bottom of the problem she'd said I could go straight over there, so I magicked myself to the shop.

"Hello, again," Leaf said.

"Hi. Joy is expecting me."

"She's in her office. She said you should go straight through."

Taking Leaf at her word, I walked straight into Joy's office, only to find her in conversation with a wizard who was wearing a horrible purple suit.

"Oh, sorry." I stood in the doorway. "Leaf said I should come through."

"It's okay, Jill. This is James."

The wizard stood up, flashed me a smile and shook my hand. "It's an honour to meet you, Jill."

"Nice to meet you too. I can come back later if you like, Joy."

"There's really no need," James said. "I was just leaving. See you soon, Joy."

"Bye, James." She waited until he was out of the door, and then said, "What have you got for me, Jill?"

"Not very much, to be honest. The manufacturing process is very impressive, and the quality control is obviously very tight."

"So you think the problem is with warehousing, then?"

"No. As far as I can see, the storage systems appear to be well designed, and the despatch department personnel convinced me that the toys are in good working order when they leave for the shops."

"Where does that leave us?"

"Back at square one, I'm afraid, which is why I requested this meeting. It occurred to me that instead of trying to identify *how* the toys are being damaged, it might be better to figure out who is behind it."

"Okay, but I've been racking my brain about that since it started, and so far, I've been unable to come up with anyone."

"Troy told me that there had recently been an offer to buy your business."

"That's right. In fact, it was James who made the offer."

"*James*? The man who was just here?"

"That's right. He's the owner of James' Games."

"Is that why he was here today? Was he trying to persuade you to change your mind?"

"No, he's a regular visitor. His family and mine have been friends for a very long time. Obviously, he was disappointed when we rejected his offer, but he understands it's just business. Today was just a social call."

"What about Roy?"

"What about him?"

"I believe he was keen to sell."

"I'm not sure I'd say he was keen, exactly, but he did vote to accept the offer."

"And when he was out voted?"

"You're surely not suggesting Roy might be behind the increase in returns, are you? Because I refuse to believe either of my boys would do anything like this."

"I'm not suggesting anything of the kind, but he must

have been disappointed when you and Troy rejected James' offer."

"He was, but he accepted the decision with good grace."

"Fair enough. Can you tell me more about where the rejected toys turned up?"

"How do you mean?"

"Well, for example, how many of them were found here in this shop?"

"None."

"Not a single one?"

"No, they all turned up in other shops that we supply. In fact, the majority of them were discovered in just five shops."

"And how many shops do you supply altogether?"

"I'm not sure, but it must be almost a hundred."

"Interesting. Would you let me have the details of the five shops where most of the faulty toys came to light."

"Of course. I'll get Leaf to draw up the list and let you have it."

"Great. And, unless you have any strong objections, I'd like to speak to James."

"I don't have any objections, but I think it would be a waste of your time. James has been super supportive since this problem arose. He really is a gentleman."

***

The 'C' in the Cuppy C sign was still not lighting up.

"They've not sorted out your sign yet, then," I said to Amber.

"That bunch are useless. They promised us that it would be sorted by this morning, but then they called a few minutes ago to say it's going to be Friday now."

"Maybe you should just change the name again." I grinned. "uppy C has a certain ring to it."

"I'm glad you find it funny," Pearl snapped.

"Sheesh, I was only joking."

"It's not a joking matter."

Clearly, I'd hit a nerve.

"Sorry. Can I get a caramel latte and one of those?" I pointed to the delicious looking cupcakes in the display cabinet below the counter.

"We're all out of cupcakes," Pearl said.

"What about those?"

"They've been reserved."

"Oh, come on. I've said I'm sorry. Give me one of those cupcakes."

"Shall we let her have one?" Amber asked her sister.

"Maybe. But only if she begs."

"I'm not begging."

"Fair enough." The twins both turned their backs on me.

"Okay, okay. I'm begging. Please let me have a cupcake."

"Pretty please?"

"You're enjoying this, aren't you?"

"Do you want a cupcake or not?"

"Pretty please can I have a cupcake?"

"Of course you can, Jill. We'll bring it over with your drink." She nodded to a corner table where Daze and Blaze were seated. I hadn't noticed them when I'd walked in.

"Having a spot of bother, Jill?" Blaze grinned.

"I was only joking around with them."

"I don't think they saw the funny side," Daze said. "Blaze said it sounded urgent when you called earlier."

"Your coffee and cupcake, *madam*." Amber put them on the table. "Enjoy!"

One bite confirmed that the humiliation of having to beg for the cupcake had been worthwhile.

"You guys said that you were focussing on major crimes committed by sups in the human world."

"That's right."

"Would you consider a serial killer to be a major crime?"

"Obviously," Daze said. "It doesn't get much more serious than that. Why? Are you saying that there's a serial killing sup on the loose?"

"I'm not sure, but I think it's possible."

"Tell us more."

I did, but judging by their expressions, they weren't convinced.

"It's a bit far-fetched, isn't it?" Blaze said. "A serial killer who chooses his victims because they have nursery rhyme character names?"

"It's not just their names, though, is it? Someone left a nursery rhyme book in Goldie's house."

"Was one left at Beau Peep's house too?"

"Not as far as I know, but someone did leave a toy sheep and a shepherd's crook in his house prior to his murder." I could see Daze and Blaze still weren't buying it, so I made one final plea. "All I'm asking is that you check through your unsolved murder files and see if there are any others that fit this pattern. If there are none, I'll abandon this theory. What do you say?"

"We're really pushed at the moment," Daze said.

"Fair enough. I just thought—"

"I was going to say that we're busy, but we owe you plenty of favours, so I'm prepared to put Blaze onto this for one day."

"Me?" Blaze didn't look thrilled at the prospect.

"Yes, you can take tomorrow to trawl through all the open murder cases and see what, if anything, you come up with. If you draw a blank, then that's an end to it. Okay?"

He turned to me. "Okay, but I wouldn't do it for anyone else."

"Thanks, guys."

***

I magicked myself back to Bridge Street in Washbridge where Fresh and Friendly were located. I must have walked past that shop a hundred times, but it had never registered with me.

"Good afternoon, madam." An over-excited young woman, with a nose ring and purple hair, came bounding over to me as soon as I'd stepped foot in the door. "Welcome to Fresh and Friendly. I'm Chrysalis."

I handed her the list that Kathy had given me. "I need to buy this lot."

Her face lit up the moment she saw it. "Gregor Leggor?"

"You've heard of him?"

"Of course I have. He's a hero of mine. His work speaks to every generation, don't you think?"

"I—err—"

"Are you like his personal assistant or something?"

"Nothing like that. He's just going to be staying with us for a few days."

"Amazeballs! You're so lucky. I've got a couple of tickets to see his work next weekend."

"That's great. Now, do you have any of this stuff?"

She studied the list for a moment. "Yes, we can do everything on here. Would you like me to gather it together for you, or would you prefer to do it yourself?"

"I'm happy for you to do it."

"This is such an honour. Just wait until I tell Rhoo that I was helping you to shop for Gregor Leggor."

"You have a kangaroo?"

"No, silly. He's my partner."

"Right."

"Why don't you grab a seat and look at our magazine while I put this lot together?"

"Sure."

I only managed to get through a couple of pages of the magazine, and that was more than enough. It was a long time since I'd seen such pretentious rubbish in print.

"That's everything." Chrysalis appeared with two baskets full of—err—something. "Will you be paying by cash or card?"

"Better make it card."

"Great. That'll be one-hundred and sixteen pounds and twenty-four pence, please."

"How much?"

"One-hundred and sixteen pounds and twenty-four pence. It would have been more, but the lentils are on special offer."

***

Thankfully, the water supply had been restored by the time I got home.

"How much?" Jack almost choked on his steak and kidney pie.

"One-hundred and twenty quid near enough. That sister of mine had better reimburse me or there'll be hell to pay. And get this: the young woman in Fresh and Friendly knew who Gregor Leggor is. In fact, she's something of a fangirl."

"I did tell you that he's famous. When exactly is he arriving?"

"I don't know. Kathy didn't say. The exhibition starts on Saturday, so I assume he'll arrive some time on Friday."

"One of us ought to stay at home that day to be here when he arrives."

"Don't look at me. I'm too busy. You'll have to get *Lashes* to cover for you while you take time off."

"Her name is Kiki, and she has already booked this Friday as a day's holiday."

"Going on a long drunken weekend hen party, I assume?"

"She's actually going to visit her grandmother who had a bad fall."

"Oh. What about Mr Ivers?"

"Monty has already agreed to work the weekend. I can't ask him."

"Great. I'd better call Kathy to find out what time Leggor is going to get here." I made the call and she answered on the first ring.

"Jill? I can't talk right now because I'm expecting a call from the caterers."

"I just want to know what time Gregor is going to arrive."

"He said he'd be with you about seven. Sorry, got to go."

"It's okay," I said to Jack. "He won't be here until seven in the evening. One of us is bound to be back by then."

"Good. You seem pretty stressed, Jill. Are you okay?"

"I just can't catch a break with any of the cases I'm working on at the moment. Every time I think I've got a lead it fizzles out."

"You'll work it out. You always do."

"I'm not so sure. Take the Beasley case, for example."

"The guy who is being blackmailed?"

"That's the one. I thought I was onto something when I realised that the blackmail note had been delivered by hand. Then, when I checked CCTV from the house opposite and saw a woman go to his door on the day the note was delivered, I really thought I'd cracked it."

"But?"

"But when I showed Beasley a still image of the woman, he didn't recognise her."

"Was she on the CCTV footage?"

"I've just said she was. Weren't you listening?"

"I meant the footage from inside the pub. Didn't you say that was where the recording had been made?"

"I'm an idiot." I sighed. "I didn't think to check if there was CCTV in the pub."

"It's just as well you're married to a genius, isn't it?"

Chapter 16

The next morning, as I walked to the car, someone called out my name. To my dismay, it was my least favourite resident of Middle Tweaking.

And, surprisingly, I don't mean Grandma.

"What do you want, Mr Flatley? I'm just on my way to work."

"I thought you should know that I've registered an appeal about the decision regarding your fence."

"Why would you do that? You measured it yourself and saw that it's only two metres high."

"You tricked me."

"How?"

"I don't know, but I went back and measured it again the next day, and just like I said originally, it's two centimetres too high."

"Nonsense."

"We'll see what the planning department have to say."

"I guess we will." I got into my car and drove away.

That man was really starting to get on my nerves.

***

Jules looked troubled about something.

"Are you okay, Jules?"

"That Petty guy was around here again."

"What did he want this time?"

"He reckons my typing is too loud. He said it's disturbing his line of thought."

"I hope you told him to do one."

"I said I'd try to type quieter."

"You will do no such thing. There's nothing wrong with the way you type. If he comes around here again, send him through to see me."

"Okay. Would you like tea?"

"Yes, please, but don't make too much noise stirring it." I grinned.

"I'm flashing," Winky said.

"You'd better not be. I won't have lewd behaviour in this office."

"I meant I'm flashing on and off. Watch." He pointed to his abdomen.

"I have no idea what you're talking about. Have you been sniffing the catnip again?"

"Just keep watching."

I was about to tell him to stop wasting my time when his tummy lit up.

"What's that?" I said.

Before I could answer, the light in his tummy began to flash red.

"See, what did I tell you?"

"What is it?" I said.

"How should I know?"

"Did you swallow a flashlight?"

"Of course. That's it. How could I have forgotten? No, of course I didn't. It just started a couple of hours ago."

"Maybe it'll stop again."

"Is that the best you can come up with? I might be dying."

"You're already dead."

Just then, Jules walked in with my cup of tea.

"What's that red flashing light, Jill?"

Somehow, and don't ask me how, Jules could see the flashing red light, even though she couldn't see Winky.

"I—err—I'm not sure. I think it must be something to do with the new Wi-Fi."

"Should it flash red like that?"

"Probably not. I'll get someone to check it."

Once Jules was out of the office, Winky started on at me again.

"You have to do something."

"Like what?"

"I don't know. Call someone."

"Like who? A vet? What am I supposed to tell them? That my invisible ghost cat has started to flash red?"

"This isn't a joking matter."

"Okay, okay. Let me think. I know. I'll give Mad a call. She might have come across this before."

"Hurry up. I might explode at any moment."

"Stop being so melodramatic. It's only a light." I took out my phone and rang Mad.

"I'm sorry to bother you, Mad, but I have a flashing cat situation."

"A what?"

I explained as best I could while Mad listened without interrupting. When I'd finished, there was only silence on the line.

"Mad? Are you still there?"

"Sorry, Jill, I'm here. I've never heard of anything like that. Is he still doing it?"

I quickly checked. "Yes, but he's flashing green now. I was hoping you might have some idea what's causing it."

"Sorry, no, but I can make some enquiries if you like."

"Would you? That'd be great."

"I'll get back to you as soon as I can."

"Well?" Winky demanded as soon as I'd finished on the call.

"She has no idea what it is, but she's going to ask around."

"What am I supposed to do in the meantime?"

"Pretend to be a traffic light?"

***

Beasley's local pub was called The Elephant and Donut. As if the name wasn't bad enough, the sign hanging above the door depicted an elephant holding a donut in its trunk. When I arrived there, at a little after ten o'clock, the doors were locked.

"They don't open until eleven," shouted a man who was walking by, pushing a wheelbarrow. "After a hair of the dog?"

"I'm not here for a drink."

"I'll believe you. Thousands wouldn't. Try around the back. Kenny won't be far away."

"Okay, thanks."

I walked around to the rear of the building where I could hear sounds coming from the other side of the tall wall and gate.

"Hello!" I shouted. "Anyone there?"

"Who's that?" Came back a man's voice.

"My name is Jill Maxwell. Are you the owner?"

"I'm the landlord if that will do."

"Sure. Is there any chance I could have a quick word?"

He didn't respond, but moments later, a key turned in a lock, and he pulled open one of the gates. The man, who had the physique of a bodybuilder, was wearing shorts and a white vest. Behind him were several piles of casks.

"Yes, love, what can I do for you?"

"I'm sorry to interrupt you."

"No problem. I'm ready for a break. Are you selling something?"

"No, nothing like that. I'm a private investigator."

"Really? I would have had you down as a model, but then I bet you get bored of men telling you how beautiful you are."

Oh boy.

"Do you by any chance have CCTV in the pub?"

"I do as it happens. Why? Were you thinking that you and I might make a movie together." He gave me a wink.

"I'm working on a case, and it would help my investigation if I was able to view your CCTV."

"I see. And what would be in it for me if I was to let you see it?"

"I can't pay you."

"I wasn't thinking of money. Just a little quid pro quo." He reached out and tried to stroke my cheek.

This guy was starting to creep me out, so I decided to cut the pleasantries.

"You look tired," I said.

"Me? I'm never—"

He didn't get to finish the sentence because the 'sleep' spell had despatched him to the land of Nod. After locking the gates, I stepped over sleeping beauty, and made my way into the pub. It took me a few minutes, but I eventually found the CCTV control unit in a small office behind the bar. A few more minutes and I'd teed up the footage from the evening when Beasley had been in the pub on his birthday. The pub had two separate rooms. In the larger of the two, I spotted Beasley, who was seated at a table all by himself. He cut quite a sad, pathetic figure. Over the next couple of hours of the footage, he put away a fair amount of alcohol, and even though there was no sound, it was obvious that he was the worse for wear.

I rewound and replayed the footage several times, and eventually spotted something interesting at the table in the booth behind Beasley. A woman was holding her phone above her head, and it struck me that she might be recording Beasley's rantings. The more I studied the footage, the more I became convinced that's exactly what she was doing. While she was holding the phone aloft, her arm was obscuring her face, but when she eventually lowered it, I managed to get a good look at her: It was the same woman I'd seen at Beasley's house on the day that the blackmail note had been delivered. Beasley had already told me that he didn't recognise her, but there was someone not a million miles away who might be able to put a name to the face.

The landlord looked so peaceful, lying spark out on the ground, that it seemed a shame to disturb him, but needs must, so I reversed the 'sleep' spell. He opened his eyes and looked around, clearly confused to find himself on the ground. "What happened?"

"You said you were feeling faint, so you lay down. Are you feeling okay now?"

"I—err—I guess so." He got uneasily to his feet. "Who did you say you were again?"

"My name is Jill. I was hoping you might know who this is." I held out my phone on which was a screenshot I'd taken of the woman from the CCTV. The resolution of the image wasn't great, so I wasn't over optimistic, but I could see in his eyes that he recognised her immediately.

"That's Gaby. She and her husband Fred are regulars."

"And you're sure it's her?"

"Yeah. That was the night of Pat's birthday do."

"Don't you mean Bobby?"

"Who's Bobby?"

"It doesn't matter. I don't suppose you know Gaby and Fred's surname, do you?"

"Yeah, it's Pinstone."

"Are you sure?"

"Course, I am. Now, why don't we go inside and chat?"

"Thanks, but I'm in a hurry."

Pinstone? Why did that name ring a bell?

***

Leaf at Joy's Toys had given me the contact details of the five shops that had returned the majority of the faulty toys. I was hoping that by talking to the owners of those shops, it might throw some light on who or what was behind the problem.

I started by paying a visit to Russell's Puzzles. The tiny frontage belied the size of the shop that covered three floors. There were no soft toys or train sets to be seen. Instead, as the name suggested, it was packed with all kinds of puzzles; the vast majority of which were jigsaws.

There was no one behind the counter and there didn't appear to be anyone on the shopfloor, so I pressed the small bell. Moments later, an elderly gentleman appeared on the stairs. He was moving rather gingerly, and I was a little concerned he might trip and fall, but he made it down unscathed.

"Sorry to keep you waiting." He wiped his brow. "I was on the top floor."

"That's okay. Are you here alone?"

"Yes, it's just me during the week. My wife helps out at the weekend. I'm Russell, by the way."

"Nice to meet you, Russell. I'm Jill. I take it this is your shop?"

"It is, but not for much longer."

"Oh?"

"You probably noticed that I'm not so sprightly these days."

"I wouldn't say—"

"It's okay. I'm ready to put my feet up."

"Who will take over after you retire?"

"No one, I'm afraid. Gaye and I never had kids."

"Couldn't you sell it?"

"Possibly, but I wouldn't get much for it and I'm not sure I can be bothered with all the hassle. Anyway, I'm sure you didn't come here to hear my life story. What can I do for you? Have you seen a puzzle you like?"

I was about to tell him that I wasn't there to buy anything, but after all the effort it had taken for him just to get down the stairs, I didn't have the heart.

"I'm looking for a jigsaw for my husband."

"Birthday?"

"No, just a little surprise."

"How lovely. He's very lucky to have such a loving wife."

"That's what I keep telling him."

"Any idea on subject matter for the jigsaw?"

"Not really."

"Does he have any particular interests?"

"He's a keen ten-pin bowler."

"Follow me." He led the way down the shop and stopped in front of a section headed: Sports and Pastimes. "There are a few jigsaws here on the theme of ten-pin bowling. Why don't you take a look and see if anything catches your eye? I'll be over at the counter."

"Okay, thanks."

"Good choice," Russell said when I placed one of the jigsaws on the counter. "Is your husband a cat person?"

"Not particularly, but I thought he'd find it amusing."

The image on the box was of three cats playing ten-pin bowling.

"Would you like it gift-wrapped?"

"No, it's okay. I'll take it as it is."

"As you wish. Anything else I can help you with today?"

"Can I be honest with you, Russell?"

"Of course."

"I didn't actually come here today to buy a jigsaw."

"Oh?"

"My name is Jill Maxwell. I'm a private investigator. Joy of Joy's Toys has hired me to try and find out what has caused the sudden increase in the number of faulty toys coming out of her factory. I assume you're aware of the issues she's been having?"

"I certainly am. A private investigator, eh? I never would have guessed. Does that mean you don't want the jigsaw?"

"No, I think Jack—that's my husband—will love it. Do you mind if I ask you about the problems you've been having with the jigsaws from Joy's Toys?"

"Of course not. Joy is a lovely lady. I've purchased jigsaws from Joy for years and I don't remember a single problem until quite recently. The first time someone brought a jigsaw back and said there was a piece missing, I automatically assumed they must have lost it themselves. I didn't say that to them, obviously. I simply replaced the jigsaw. But then it happened again and again. Joy was horrified when I spoke to her, and she promised to try and sort out the problem. I can't help but wonder if they've made some changes in the factory."

"I don't think it's that," I said. "I've looked around the factory and their processes are as tight as they ever were. Do you know Nancy who works at Joy's Toys?"

"Is she the lady who checks every jigsaw by hand?"

"That's right. She's amazing."

"It did occur to me that she might have retired, which could explain the issues they've been having."

"No, she still works there. I'm in the process of visiting the shops which have incurred the highest number of rejects. Yours is the first one I've been to so far."

"What are you hoping to find?"

"Honestly? I have no idea. I guess I'm just hoping that some kind of pattern might arise. Is there anything different you've noticed about the jigsaws you've received lately? Apart from the increase in the number of rejects, obviously."

"Not really. They're packaged the same way and delivered by the same van as they always have been. It's quite a mystery."

"Oh well. Thanks for your time, anyway."

"There is one thing, Jill."

"Yes?"

"It's probably nothing."

"Tell me, anyway."

"After we'd encountered a few jigsaws with missing pieces, one of my best customers placed an order for a jigsaw that I didn't have in stock. This old lady buys two or three jigsaws every month, so I wanted to make sure she didn't encounter the missing piece problem. When I received her jigsaw from Joy's Toys, I personally assembled it, to be sure all the pieces were there. And they were."

"You clearly care about your customers."

"That's true, but here's the kicker. Three days after the customer had collected the jigsaw, she returned it because one of the pieces was missing."

"How could that be if you'd checked it yourself?"

"I wish I knew."

"I'd better pay you for this." I took out my purse.

"There's no need. It's on the house."

"I can't allow you to do that."

"I insist. Call it my contribution to helping you resolve Joy's problems."

"That's very generous."

"Not really. Joy let me have this particular jigsaw and a dozen others free of charge, by way of apology for the problems we'd experienced. I told her it wasn't necessary, but she insisted I take them away with me."

"You went to see her?"

"Yes, at her invitation. I could tell then how upset she was."

"Thank you again for the jigsaw, Russell. And for your help."

"My pleasure. I hope you get to the bottom of it."

Chapter 17

"Any messages, Jules?"

"No, the phone hasn't rung yet today. Are you sure it's okay for me to knit?"

"It's fine, but I would like you to make me a coffee, please."

"Coming right up."

"How's it hanging, Flash?" I laughed.

"This isn't a laughing matter," Winky snapped.

"Sorry. It seems to be flashing faster than before."

"It is. Has that friend of yours got back to you yet?"

"Not yet."

"What am I supposed to do until she does? And don't say pretend to be a traffic light."

"How about you hire yourself out as a disco light?"

"I'll remember this the next time you're ill."

"You aren't ill. You're just—err—flashing."

"That Wi-Fi is still flashing," Jules said, as she handed me my coffee. "Do you want me to call maintenance?"

"Nah, it's fine. I seem to be able to get online okay. I'm sure it will sort itself out. Eventually."

"*Eventually*?" Winky said, once Jules was out of the room.

"Shush, I have to make an important call."

"What could be more important than my flashing?"

Ignoring his whingeing, I rang Mr Beasley.

"Bobby? It's Jill Maxwell."

"Do you have news for me?"

"Kind of. I've discovered that the address in Crewe, where you're supposed to send the money, doesn't exist."

"That makes no sense."

"I know, but more importantly, I think I may know who made that recording."

"Who?"

"The woman whose photo I showed you the other day; the one who came to your door the day the blackmail letter was delivered."

"But I told you I don't know who she is."

"I know, but I've managed to find out her name. It's Gaby Pinstone."

"*Pinstone*?"

"Does that ring a bell?"

"Yes, it does. Don't you remember I told you that Fred Pinstone had offered to buy Mum's model railway, but I turned him down."

"Of course. I knew I knew that name from somewhere."

"What does this mean?"

"It means I need to have a word with the Pinstones."

"Do you think they're behind the blackmail?"

"It's too early to say."

"Will you keep me posted?"

"Of course."

***

After grabbing a sandwich, I magicked myself to Candlefield. The next toy shop on my list to visit was Dudley's Cuddlies, which was right next to the bridge on River Street. The shop front boasted a super wide window, which was jammed full of cuddly toys of all shapes, sizes and colours.

"Hi," I said to the young woman behind one of the three counters. "Would it be possible to speak to Dudley?"

"Who?"

"Dudley."

"We don't have a Dudley working here."

"I assumed the shop owner was called Dudley."

"Oh, right. Sorry. He died ages ago; long before I started here."

"Who owns the shop now?"

"Teddy Hare."

"Teddy *Bear*?"

"No. It's *Hare*. Like a big rabbit. I don't mean *he's* like a big rabbit. I mean—"

"It's okay. I know what you meant. Is Teddy here?"

"Yes, but I'm not sure if he'll be able to see you. What's your name, please?"

"Jill Maxwell. Please tell him it's in connection with the faulty toys from Joy's Toys."

"Okay." She picked up the handset and pressed a button. "Mr Hare? It's Angela. There's a woman here called Jill Maxwell. She wondered if you could spare her a minute. It's about the faulty toys from Joy's Toys. Okay. Yes. Right."

"He says he'll be down in a couple of minutes and that I'm to ask if you'd like a drink."

"I'm okay, thanks."

Teddy Hare was a little too tall for his own body, and he almost tripped as he crossed the salesfloor to greet me.

"Nice to meet you, Jill. Joy called to say that you might be dropping in sometime."

"Is now convenient for a chat?"

"Absolutely. I'm happy to do anything I can to help."

"That's great. I take it that you specialise in cuddly toys."

"It's all we do, Jill. When I started this business, twenty years ago now, I decided to focus on one area and what could be better than cuddly toys? Do you have children?"

"A girl, but she's a little old for cuddly toys now."

"You're never too old for a cuddly toy." He grinned. "Don't tell me you don't still have a favourite cuddly toy because I won't believe you."

"I used to have one, but it got lost when we moved house."

"Name?"

"Sorry?"

"The name of the cuddly toy that you lost?"

"Bronnie. She was a little bear."

"I'm sure Bronnie has found a new home."

"I hope so."

"So, Jill, how can I help, exactly?"

"Can you tell me about your experience with the faulty toys?"

"Sure. If you'd told me six months ago that I'd have any problems with the toys that Joy's supplied, I would have laughed at the idea. In almost twenty years, we never had to reject a single one of Joy's toys."

"When did that change?"

"It all started with an octopus called Legs. About three days after we sold it, the lady who had purchased it brought it back because one of its legs had become unattached, and the stuffing was coming out. I was shocked, I can tell you, but I assumed it was a one-off. Obviously, I offered a refund, but the lady took another octopus instead. I returned the faulty one to Joy who was distraught and full of apologies. I told her not to worry and that I knew it was a one-off. She gave me a full refund of course. I thought no more about it until a couple of weeks later when a man came into the shop with a teddy bear whose head had split open. He was less polite—in fact, he was quite rude. I managed to calm him down by giving him a replacement plus a five-pound voucher for his next purchase. I was much more surprised that time because that particular teddy bear has been one of our best-sellers—we've sold thousands of them over the years. Since then, we've had several more rejects, to the point where I'm seriously thinking we might have to find a new supplier. It's not something I want to do, but I can't afford to keep upsetting my customers."

"Do you check the toys when they're delivered?"

"Of course. It used to be no more than a cursory check because I never felt it was necessary. Now, though, I insist that every toy from Joy's Toys is checked thoroughly before it goes onto the shelf."

"Have you found any faulty toys that way?"

"Not a single one. That's the weird thing."

"What do you mean?"

"The latest toy to be returned was a toy seal. We'd only recently started stocking those, so I know for a fact that every one of them on the shelf had been checked and double-checked on delivery, and yet about four days ago, one was returned because it had split open."

"That is strange."

"Have you got any idea what's going on, Jill?"

"Not yet."

"I heard that James of James' Games had made a bid to buy Joy out, and I was beginning to wonder if that distraction has caused her to take her eye off the ball."

"I don't think it's that. It's clear to me that Joy is as

passionate about the business as she's always been, and all of this is really upsetting her. Anyway, thanks for your time, Teddy."

"Wait there for a minute, would you?" He disappeared to the other side of the shop. When he returned, he had his hands behind his back. "This is for you." He handed me a teddy bear. "I realise you'll never be able to replace Bronnie, but hopefully this little guy will make her loss less painful."

"Thanks. That's very kind."

"His name is Humphrey."

***

"Has she got back to you yet?" Winky said, as soon as I walked into the office.

"Who?"

"That friend of yours. The one who's supposed to be sorting out this flashing."

"No, Mad hasn't got back to me yet."

"Call her again."

"There's no need. She'll call me as soon as she has an answer. Why don't you do something to take your mind off it?"

"Like what?"

I held out the jigsaw that I'd bought from Russell's Puzzles. "You could do this if you like."

"Did you buy that for me?"

"No, it's for Jack, but it won't matter if he doesn't get it for a few days."

"How many pieces is it?"

"Err, five hundred."

"That won't take me more than an hour."

"Yeah, right. I'd like to see you do it that quickly."

"Give it here, then."

Instead of handing it to him, I opened the box and poured the pieces onto the coffee table.

"Good luck."

"Hello! I'll need the cover. I might be good, but I can't do it without the picture."

"Sorry. There you go."

It was time to give Joy an update—not that there was much to report, so I gave her a call.

"Joy, it's Jill Maxwell."

"Hi, Jill. Russell called me earlier to say you'd been to see him."

"Yes, I've been to Dudley's Cuddlies too."

"Did you learn anything of interest?"

"Not really, but both of them expressed their surprise at this turn of events."

"What about James? Have you spoken to him yet?"

"Not yet, but I will soon. The main reason for my call is to ask how the toys are delivered to the other toy shops. Do you sub-contract the deliveries or do you have your own van?"

"We do all our own deliveries, and we have three vans."

"Would you happen to know if the same delivery van services all of the shops on the list that Leaf gave me?"

"Not off the top of my head, but I can check and get back to you."

"That would be great. Thanks."

"Done," Winky said.

"Don't be ridic—" I stared in disbelief at the completed jigsaw.

"How did you manage that?"

"I told you it wouldn't take me long."

"It's only been about ninety minutes."

"As long as that?" He sighed. "Shows I'm out of practice."

He wasn't as fast as Nancy, who worked in the quality control department at Joy's toys, but it was still phenomenally fast.

"I'm impressed."

"I'd probably have been faster if this stupid flashing wasn't so distracting. Can't you check in with your friend? Please."

"Okay." I called Mad. "Hey, I'm sorry to pester you, but Winky is driving me crazy. I don't suppose you've had any luck with this flashing problem, have you?"

"I'm just waiting on a call back from an old friend of mine who I think will be able to help. It's going to be tomorrow morning, though, I'm afraid."

"That's okay. Thanks, Mad."

"Well?" Winky said.

"She thinks she may have found someone who'll be able to help, but it's going to be tomorrow morning."

"How am I supposed to sleep tonight with this thing flashing all the time?"

"Sorry, that's the best I can do."

***

Jack arrived home at exactly the same time as I did. I'd

just got out of the car when he came walking down the road.

"You've finished early," I said.

"Monty has a dentist appointment tomorrow morning, so I said I'd go in early if he locked up tonight."

"That's good. I was just thinking that I could eat a fry-up for dinner."

"Were you planning on making it?"

"Me? Of course not. You're the fry-up expert, Jack. I can't hold a candle to you."

"I might have known." He unlocked the door. "What's that in your hand?"

"It's a present for you." I handed him the jigsaw.

"Thanks. What did I do to deserve this?"

"I saw it in the shop, and I thought you might like it. Do you?"

"Yeah, but it looks difficult."

"It can't be that difficult, Winky did it in under two hours."

"Winky? I thought you bought it for me?"

"I did but I had to do something to take his mind off the flashing."

"*Flashing*?"

"It's not what you think. Can't you just appreciate the gift?"

"I do. Sorry." As he leaned in to give me a kiss, he caught a sight of the teddy bear in my bag.

"What's that?"

"This is Humphrey. The guy in the toy shop gave him to me to replace my little Bronnie."

"Who's *Bronnie*?"

"The little bear I've had all my life but who I lost when

we moved house."

"I don't remember that. Did you mention it at the time?"

"No, because there was no such bear. I just made it up to get the guy onside. Now, how about that fry-up?"

Jack had just started to make dinner when there was a knock at the door.

"I'll get it." I jumped up from the table. If it was Flat Head again, he would be spending the rest of the evening as a cockroach.

It wasn't him; it was a man whose hair looked like a sweep's brush that had just been hit by lightning. Dressed all in green, he was holding a large green suitcase.

"Whatever you're selling, we don't need any." I made to close the door.

"Wait."

"I've told you. We don't buy anything at the door."

"I'm not selling anything. Are you Jill? Jill Maxwell?"

"Yes?"

"I'm Gregor Leggor. I believe your sister, Kathy, has arranged for me to stay with you for a few days."

"Mr Leggor? We weren't expecting you until Friday evening."

"I'm so sorry. I thought—never mind. I'm sure I'll be able to find a hotel until then."

"You don't need to do that." Although, nothing would have pleased me more than to have sent him away, Kathy would have skinned me alive. "Do come in, Mr Leggor."

"Thanks."

As he stepped inside, I saw him sniff the air.

"Sorry about the aroma. My husband is just making

dinner."

"It smells like bacon."

Judging by the list of Gregor's preferred foods, which Kathy had given me, I assumed that he would not go within a mile of a slice of bacon.

"Jack is making a fry-up, but don't worry, Kathy gave me a list of the food you like, and I managed to get all of it. Would you like to unpack? By the time you've finished, Jack and I should have eaten, and you'll be able to—"

"I don't suppose there's enough for three, is there?"

"Sorry?"

"The fry-up. I realise it's rather rude of me to ask, but I'd kill for a good fry-up."

"Really?"

"If there's not enough, I'll understand."

"No, I'm sure there'll be enough. Leave your suitcase in the hall and let's go and see Jack."

Jack was watching the pans when we entered the kitchen.

"What were they selling?" He asked without looking around.

"Nothing. Gregor Leggor is here."

"Oh?" Jack turned around and saw our guest. "I didn't realise you were coming today."

"I told your wife that I can get a hotel for a couple of days."

"I said that wasn't necessary," I said. "Gregor wondered if there would be enough food for him to join us for the fry-up."

"I was under the impression that you liked—err—more wholesome food. Jill bought a load of stuff from Fresh and Friendly. Are you sure you wouldn't prefer that?"

"Definitely not. A couple of years ago, in an interview for a magazine, I made the mistake of telling a journalist that I was something of a health freak. I'm not really sure why I said it, but ever since then, I've had to keep up the pretence. When I walked through your door, just now, and smelled the bacon, I had to ask if I could partake."

"Absolutely. Grab a seat. It shouldn't be long."

Gregor barely said a word over dinner; he was too busy tucking into Jack's award-winning fry-up. The man ate like someone who had not had a proper meal in a long time.

"That was absolutely delicious," he said. "Thank you so much."

"Our pleasure."

"Could I ask you both a small favour?"

"Sure."

"I'd appreciate it if you kept this to yourself, and definitely don't mention it to your sister. I need to keep up appearances for the benefit of my fans."

"No problem. We won't tell a soul."

"Why don't I show you to your room," Jack said. "You could probably do with an early night after your journey."

"Actually, I couldn't help but notice your jigsaw."

"Jill bought it for me today."

"I love jigsaws, but it's ages since I did one. I don't suppose you'd allow me to help you do it, would you?"

"Absolutely. I'll take your suitcase upstairs and then we can make a start on it."

"What about you, Jill?" Gregor said. "Will you join us?"

"Thanks, but I've got one or two things I need to do."

Much more interesting things like watching paint dry.

I'd not long since turned out the light, and I was just drifting off to sleep when…

"Oi!

The voice made me jump. Had I been dreaming? I switched on the light, but there was nothing to see. It must have been Jack or Gregor getting over-excited by the jigsaw, sad as that was. I was just about to turn off the light when it happened again.

"Oi, you!"

There was definitely someone or something in the bedroom. This wouldn't be the first time that some small creature had seen fit to enter my house uninvited.

"Who's there? Where are you?"

"Down here."

"Down where?" I looked over the side of the bed, but I couldn't see anything apart from the teddy bear. Perhaps someone was hiding underneath Humphrey. I picked up the bear, but there was no one there.

"Do you mind? Stop shaking me about."

Only then, did I realise the voice was coming from the teddy bear. I was so shocked that I dropped it back onto the floor.

"Ouch, that hurt."

"Sorry." Why was I apologising to an inanimate object?

"Pick me up."

I grabbed the bear again and put it onto the bed. "Who are you?"

"You know who I am. I'm Humphrey, but I prefer Humph."

"What are you?"

"What do you mean, what am I? I'm a teddy bear,

obviously."

"Are you a wizard? Or a shapeshifter?"

"I'm not a wizard, and I have no idea what that other thing is."

"If you aren't a wizard or a shapeshifter, what are you?"

"How many times do I have to tell you? I'm a teddy bear."

"How come you can talk?"

"What kind of question is that? How come *you* can talk?"

"I just can."

"Ditto."

"Did someone cast a spell on you? Was it my grandmother?"

"What's with your obsession with magic. No one has done anything to me. This is how I've always been."

"Can the other teddy bears in the shop talk?"

"No, it's just me as far as I can tell."

"How come you didn't talk on the way home or when I brought you into the house?"

"I wanted to get my bearings first. Get the lay of the land."

"And have you?"

"Yeah, I've already figured out that I'm going to have to keep an eye on you."

"What do you mean?"

"You're devious."

"I am *not* devious."

"So what was that tale you spun about your poor little Bronnie?"

"Oh, err—never mind about that. Can you walk too?"

"Of course I can't walk. I'm a teddy bear."

"Right. Well, I want to go to sleep, so I'm going to need you to be quiet now."

"Suits me." I picked him up and was about to put him back onto the floor. "What are you doing?"

"Putting you on the floor."

"Why can't I sleep on the bed with you? That's what we teddy bears do."

"No chance."

"Why not?"

"Because you can talk."

"That seems rather unfair."

"Tough. Now be quiet and go to sleep."

Chapter 18

"Jill! Wake up!"

"What time is it?"

"Six o'clock."

"Why are you waking me up in the middle of the night?"

"The teddy bear is talking to me."

"Go back to sleep."

He shook me. "I'm serious: the bear just spoke to me."

"I have a name," Humphrey said from somewhere under the bed.

"Did you hear that?" Jack said.

"Hang on a minute. Can *you* hear him?"

"What do you think I've been trying to tell you for the last five minutes?"

That was a strange and unexpected development. Not that a talking teddy bear wasn't already strange, but I'd assumed only I would be able to hear him.

"Did you know he could talk?" Jack asked.

"Not until I came to bed last night."

"Why didn't you warn me?"

"Because you were busy with the jigsaw."

"What are we going to do about it?"

"What do you want me to do about it?"

"I don't know. Can't you do something magical?"

"Perhaps I could use the 'Stop the teddy bear talking' spell."

"Yeah."

"If there was such a thing, but there isn't."

"You'll have to take it back to the shop."

"Less of the '*it*'," Humphrey said. "And I'm not going

back to that shop. Do you have any idea what it's like to be stuck upside down in a mountain of soft toys. Uncomfortable, that's what it is."

Jack rubbed his head. "I need some tablets."

"Are you ill?"

"No, I—err—"

"Are you hungover?"

"A bit, maybe."

"What must Gregor think? He's teetotal."

"That man is definitely not teetotal. He drank me under the table. I really do need those tablets."

"Okay."

I gave him the water and painkillers, and I was about to head downstairs when Humphrey shouted, "You aren't going to leave me up here, are you?"

"Yes." I turned to Jack. "Don't let him talk you into taking him downstairs. We can't afford to let Gregor see him."

"Do you think he'll be able to hear the bear talk too?"

"I don't see why not. If you can hear him, my guess is everyone will be able to."

"Okay, I'll leave him up here."

Gregor was seated at the kitchen table, and he looked as fresh as a daisy.

"Hmm, these are delicious." He spooned a heap of Strawberrycandy Pops into his mouth.

My memory might not be the best, but I was pretty sure that there were no Strawberrycandy Pops on Kathy's list of Gregor's preferred foods.

"How are you feeling, Gregor?"

"Me? Absolutely great, thanks, Jill. I slept like a log."

"I only ask because Jack is feeling a little under the weather."

"That's my fault, I'm afraid." He grinned. "I was the one who persuaded him to open that second bottle. Did Jack tell you that we finished the jigsaw?"

"Really?"

"Yeah, except for that one missing piece. Go see for yourself."

The completed jigsaw, minus one piece, was on the coffee table.

"What do you think, Jill?" Gregor had followed me into the lounge.

"Very impressive. Particularly, given the amount of wine you two managed to put away between you." I nodded to the two empty wine bottles.

"Jack got quite emotional when he realised there was a piece missing."

"That would be the wine."

We were interrupted by a knock at the door, which turned out to be Kathy.

"I just popped over to see if Gregor had settled in okay."

"Why didn't you tell me he was coming yesterday?"

"I did. Where is he?"

"In the lounge."

I followed her inside, just in time to see her look of horror when she registered the two empty wine bottles on the coffee table.

"Gregor, I'm so sorry," she said. "I thought my sister had more sense than to drink in front of a teetotaller. I hope you aren't too traumatised."

"I'm fine, thanks, Kathy," he reassured her.

Jack, who looked like death warmed up, appeared at the door. "Good morning, everyone."

"You look terrible," Kathy said. "Are you ill?"

"No, I'm fine."

"Are you sure? I don't want Gregor coming down with the lurgy, ahead of the exhibition."

"I'm positive. It's just—err—" he glanced at the empty wine bottles.

"I might have known." Kathy tutted. "I hope they are at least feeding you properly, Gregor. I gave Jill a list of your preferred foods."

"Oh yes." He nodded. "In fact, last night Jack made me his famous—err—." Oh no. We were so dead. "Salad. It was quite delicious."

"Thank goodness for that." Kathy sighed with relief. "I was worried they might have taken you to the local chippy. I thought I would drive you into town. There's a lovely little restaurant near the gallery where we can grab breakfast, and then we can go over the plans for the weekend."

"Sounds good. Let me just brush my teeth and I'll be with you in five."

As soon as he'd disappeared upstairs, Kathy turned her glare on Jack and me.

"What were you thinking? Getting drunk in front of Gregor?"

"Don't look at me." I shrugged. "I had an early night."

There's nothing quite like throwing your husband under the bus. Snigger.

"Jack?" Kathy snapped.

"I really have to get going," Jack said. "I should have opened the store half an hour ago."

Frustrated at his quick exit, Kathy turned her attention back to me. "How could you let this happen, Jill?"

"What's the problem? You've seen Gregor. He's perfectly fine. It's obvious that he didn't have any wine."

"If that's true, and that husband of yours drank both of those bottles, I'd say he has a serious problem."

"Ready when you are," Gregor shouted.

"You haven't heard the last of this." Was Kathy's parting remark.

By now, it was quite obvious that the fry-up eating, wine-drinking Gregor Leggor had very little in common with his public persona. And to be honest, I preferred the version we had seen. In addition to being a talented artist (allegedly), he was clearly something of a whizz with jigsaws. Okay, he wasn't at the same standard as Nancy (or Winky), but it was no mean feat to have completed that jigsaw in a few hours. I knew for sure that he must have done the lion's share of the puzzle because I'd seen Jack struggle with jigsaws when he was sober. After a few glasses of wine, he would have been next to useless.

I was trying to decide whether to leave the jigsaw on the coffee table, or to break it up and put it back in the box, when it occurred to me that what had happened last night was exactly the same thing as had happened with the other faulty toys. They had all been perfectly fine when they arrived at their respective toy shops, and even at the point when they were sold, but then they suddenly developed faults after they'd been taken home by the customer. I felt like that might be significant, but I wasn't exactly sure why. I was still mulling it over when I got a call from Joy.

"Jill, I've checked the van deliveries as you requested, and the toy shops that have had all the problems are all serviced by the same van."

"Interesting."

"I simply can't believe Mickey is responsible."

"*Mickey*?"

"Mickey Michaels. He's the driver of that van. He's been with us for years. And besides, how would he do it?"

"I don't know that he did, but I would like to talk to him. Can you tell me how I can get in touch with him, please."

Once Joy had given me the information, I ended the call. No sooner had I done so than my phone rang again.

"Jill, it's Blaze."

"Hi."

"It turns out you might be onto something after all."

"With the nursery rhymes, you mean?"

"Yeah. Daze would like the three of us to meet."

"Sure. When?"

"She's having her eyes tested this morning. How about this afternoon? At Uppy C."

"Don't let the twins hear you call it that." I laughed. "Sure, I'll see you then."

***

When I arrived at the office, Mad was talking to Jules.

"What time do you call this?" Mad tapped her watch and grinned.

"I had a bit of a jigsaw/teddy bear situation. Do you want a drink?"

"No, thanks. I can't stop.

"Come through."

As soon as she stepped into my office, Mad caught sight of Winky and burst out laughing.

"It's not funny!" Winky snapped. "I've barely had a wink of sleep."

"Sorry," Mad said. "It must be *blinking* annoying."

That sent us both into tears of laughter.

Judging by his expression, though, Winky was not amused. "Have you come up with a cure?"

"Sort of," Mad said.

"What does that mean?" Winky's patience was growing thin.

"I spoke to Gloria Betternow."

"Who's she when she's at home?"

"Winky, let Mad speak."

"As I was saying, I spoke to Gloria who is GT's leading authority on afflictions that can affect ghost cats, who live in the human world."

"And?" Winky snapped again.

"She gave me this prescription for you." Mad took the paper from her bag.

"Couldn't you have got the medicine for me?" Winky said.

"The pharmacist wouldn't give it to me. You have to collect it in person."

"Give it here." He snatched the prescription from her and disappeared.

"Sorry about that, Mad. That was beyond rude."

"It's okay. I'd probably be short tempered too if I was flashing all day long. I just hope it works."

"Me too or my life won't be worth living."

***

It was time that I had a few words with Fred and Gaby Pinstone, who I suspected of being behind the blackmail attempt on Bobby Beasley. For once lady fortune smiled down upon me because, just as I had parked a few doors down from their house, I saw them walking up the road. Judging by the number of bags they were carrying between them, they had just done their weekly shop. Once they were inside the house, I gave them ten minutes, to allow them time to put away their groceries.

It was Fred Pinstone who answered the door.

"Yes?"

"Mr Pinstone?"

"Yes, what do you want?"

"My name is Jill Maxwell. I represent Bobby Beasley. I wonder if you might spare me a few minutes?"

To my surprise, his face lit up. "Is it about the railway set?"

I hadn't anticipated that response, but he clearly thought I was there to discuss his offer to buy Beasley's mother's railway set.

"It might be better if we talked inside."

"Of course. Come on in. Gaby, we have a visitor."

His wife came out of the kitchen.

"This is—err," Fred said. "Sorry, I've forgotten your name."

"Jill Maxwell."

"Mrs Maxwell is here to talk about Beasley's model railway."

"Oh? Would you care for a cup of tea?"

"I'm fine, thanks."

"Let's go through to the parlour," Fred said.

The 'parlour' turned out to be the front room, which was already tiny, but made to seem even smaller by the model railway that occupied one-third of the space in there.

"Has Beasley changed his mind?" Fred asked. "It was a fair offer."

"Actually, I'm not here to discuss the sale of the model railway."

"Oh?" Fred's face fell. "What do you want, then?"

"I'm a private investigator. In the course of my investigations, it has come to my attention that you were both in the Elephant and Donut on the evening of the eighth, at about eight-thirty."

"We were there for Pat's birthday," Gaby said.

"What's this about?" Fred demanded.

"Someone is trying to blackmail Mr Beasley."

"About what?"

"I'd rather not get into that just now."

"What do you want with us?" Fred asked.

"I recently viewed CCTV footage from the day that the blackmail note was delivered to Mr Beasley's house."

"So?"

"It was delivered by hand, and the only person to visit Mr Beasley's house on that day was you, Gaby."

"Me?"

"We're not blackmailers if that's what you're insinuating," Fred said. "You're barking up the wrong tree."

"Have you ever been to Mr Beasley's house, Gaby?"

"Err—I—"

"You don't have to tell her anything, Gaby." Fred stood

up.

"Actually, I have, but only the once."

"What for?" I asked.

"Fred asked me to deliver the offer for Beasley's mother's model railway."

"Did you speak to Beasley?"

"No, I just put the offer through his letterbox and then left."

"Do you remember what date that would have been?"

She thought about it for a minute and then confirmed the date. It was the same day as I'd seen her visit the house on the CCTV footage. Was she telling the truth? Beasley hadn't mentioned that the offer from the Pinstones had arrived on the same day as the blackmail note, but I guessed it was possible.

"If you aren't here to discuss the sale of the model railway, I'm going to have to ask you to leave," Fred said.

Gaby's revelation had caught me off guard, and I didn't feel I had anything to gain by pressing them any further. At least, not until I'd had the chance to check with Beasley to confirm that the offer from the Pinstones and the blackmail note had arrived on the same day.

As soon as I was back in my car, I gave him a call.

"It's Jill Maxwell. Did you receive the Pinstone's offer to buy your mother's model railway on the same day as you received the blackmail note?"

"Yes, I did."

"Why didn't you tell me that before?"

"I didn't think it was important. Is it?"

"I don't know. Are you absolutely sure that they both arrived on the same day? I need you to be certain."

"I'm positive. I'd gone into town to buy some food for

Hammy and when I got back the blackmail note and the offer from the Pinstones were both on the mat in the hall."

"Who's Hammy? Was someone else staying with you that day?"

"No, Hammy is my hamster."

"Right. Okay, thanks."

Oh bum, and multiple more bums! I'd felt sure that the Pinstones were behind the blackmail attempt, but that theory had now been blown out of the water.

Chapter 19

Daze and Blaze were already seated at a table when I arrived at Cuppy C.

"Sorry, guys, am I late?"

"No, we were early," Daze said. "We thought we'd wait for you before we ordered."

"That way, you'd pay," Blaze quipped.

"That's *not* what I meant." Daze shot him a look.

"It's okay," I said. "I'll get them with my discount."

"You get a discount?" Blaze said.

"There has to be some compensation for being related to those two."

"I heard what you just said about us," Amber said when I was at the counter.

"I was only joking. You know I love you guys. Where's Pearl?"

"L is under the weather, so Pearl has taken the day off to be with her."

"Nothing serious, I hope?"

"Nah, it's just a bit of a cold. Pearl coddles her too much if you ask me."

"Like you don't do the same thing with Lily." I grinned.

"You're right. By the way, did you notice that the 'C' in the sign is working again?"

"That's good. No more Uppy C, then?"

"No, thank goodness."

I ordered for the three of us, and then took the drinks over to Daze and Blaze.

"No cake?" Blaze frowned.

"You don't need any cake," Daze said. "You need exercise. Lots of it."

"Rubbish. I'm in tiptop physical shape."

"Hmm."

Eager to know what they'd discovered, I cut short the discussion about Blaze's waistline. "So, guys, what did you find out?"

"Blaze did all the legwork, so I'll let him tell you." Daze took a sip of her coffee.

Blaze didn't need asking twice. "When you told us your theory about a possible serial killer, I thought you were crazy. And, after spending hours looking through all the open murder cases, I was even more sure you were, but then I came across the case of King Cole."

"As in Old King Cole?"

"Precisely. Obviously, it was the name that caught my attention first, but when I read the notes, it was clear that there were similarities to the more recent cases that you'd told us about."

"Such as?"

"Prior to his murder, the victim had reported there had been a number of break-ins at his property."

"Sounds familiar. Did he live with anyone?"

"No, he was single and lived there alone."

"That's a pity. Still, I might be able to get something out of the police."

"I doubt it," Blaze said. "The guy in charge of the case is a Detective Meanstreak. He's a hard ass who's unlikely to cooperate with any outsiders."

"Great."

"I did have an idea, though," Daze said.

"Oh boy." Blaze rolled his eyes.

"What does that mean?" Daze fixed him with a glare.

"Nothing."

"Come on, Blaze, you obviously have something to say on the subject."

"I think your idea is crazy, but I've already told you that."

"Hey, guys, I'm prepared to listen to any idea at this point," I said.

"Okay." Daze turned briefly to Blaze. "I don't want to hear a peep out of you until I've finished." After Blaze had made a show of zipping his lips, she continued, "For reasons we don't yet understand, the killer appears to be targeting people with names that are related to nursery rhyme characters. Right?"

"Correct."

"But here's something you may not know: the three murders all took place within a fifty-mile radius of Washbridge."

"Interesting."

"If that pattern continues, it's a pretty safe bet that his next victim will also have a name related to a nursery rhyme character, and they'll live in the same area. Right?"

"I guess."

"Here's my suggestion: We contact everyone who lives in that area whose name could be in any way related to a nursery rhyme character."

Blaze must have seen the look on my face because he said, "See, Jill, what did I tell you?"

"And I told you to stay quiet!" Daze almost took his head off.

"Sorry."

"I know it sounds crazy," Daze said. "But if your hunch about the nursery rhyme connection is right, there may be other people out there who are at grave risk. If we contact all the people who meet these criteria, we may be able to save them, as well as bring the murderer to justice."

"Okay, I can see that," I said. "But it's a mammoth task. And even if we were able to get in touch with these people, what would we say to them?"

"The good thing about the department we now work for is that it has a near unlimited budget."

"And yet, they still won't let me have a car," Blaze moaned.

"Be quiet." Daze snapped at him. "As I was saying, we can throw a lot of resources at this. We'll call everyone who lives in a fifty-mile radius of Washbridge whose name has any possible connection to a nursery rhyme character."

"And say what?"

"I'll get our people to pose as the police and say there has been a spate of break-ins in the area, and to ask if they've seen anything suspicious. If anyone has been marked out as the killer's next victim, they may have experienced some of the weird goings on that Goldie and Beau encountered prior to their murders."

"And if anyone has?"

"Then, we'll have potentially identified our killer's next victim. What do you think, Jill?"

"It's got to be worth a shot. It's not like I have any other bright ideas."

"Great. In that case, I'll put things in motion."

***

Joy had assured me that James of James' Games was an old family friend and that, although his bid to buy her company had been rejected, he wasn't the kind of person to hold a grudge, and that he certainly wasn't the type to sabotage her business. Joy might well have been correct, but I was troubled by the fact that the number of faulty toys had increased exponentially since his offer had been rejected. That was too much of a coincidence for my liking, so I owed it to the investigation to at least speak to the man.

I'd called his company and spoken to his PA who had promised to speak to James and get back to me within twenty-four hours. In the event, she called back within the hour to say that James could spare me some time that same afternoon if I was free.

"Nice to see you again, Jill." Still dressed in the horrible purple suit, he greeted me with a firm handshake.

"Thanks for seeing me at such short notice."

"No problem at all. Like I told Joy when I was last with her: if there's anything I can do to help, she has only to ask. I hate to see her so upset. She cares deeply about her business. Have you made any progress with your investigations?"

"Not really."

"May I speak candidly, Jill?"

"Absolutely."

"This is difficult for me to say because I consider Joy a close friend—" He hesitated.

"Go on."

"Joy's Toys is a business with an incredible history, but I've felt for a long time that it's stuck in the past."

"What do you mean?"

"Have you seen the manufacturing operation?"

"I have. It's very impressive."

"But very labour-intensive. There's virtually no automation in that factory."

"Surely, that's the whole appeal of the toys being produced."

"Maybe, but wherever sups are involved in the process, errors can creep in."

"I take it that you use robots in your factory."

"Absolutely. Eighty percent of the manufacturing process has been automated so far, and we're working on making that one hundred percent. I've tried to persuade Joy that it's time she upgraded her factory, but she's very much stuck in her ways."

"If you don't rate her manufacturing process, why did you want to buy the business?"

"Joy's Toys is a very valuable brand. Although, if the current crop of returns continues, that may quickly be diminished. And, as for the manufacturing process, we would have automated that in short order. Roy understands that his factory requires a complete overhaul, which is why he voted to accept my offer."

"Had you and he discussed what would happen if your bid succeeded?"

"Yes, and he'd agreed to stay on to oversee the automation."

"You must have been disappointed when your offer was rejected."

"Of course, but it didn't come as any great surprise. Joy and Troy were always going to vote no."

"And now?"

"Sorry?"

"What will you do now your offer has been rejected?"

"There's nothing much I can do unless either Joy or

Troy change their mind about selling."

"Do you have any theories who or what might be behind the issues Joy is experiencing?"

"I know Joy thinks that it's some kind of sabotage, but personally, I think the explanation is much simpler: sup error."

"Maybe."

"Would you like to take a look around our factory, Jill? I'll be glad to give you a personal tour."

"That's very kind, but I have another meeting in half an hour," I lied. "But thanks for your time."

James was a likeable enough guy and, clearly, he was someone that Joy trusted. Apart from his obsession with automation, I couldn't fault him because he'd seemed genuinely concerned for the predicament that Joy found herself in.

***

When I arrived home that evening, I was met at the door by Gregor.

"Gregor? I wasn't expecting you to be back yet."

"I know she's your sister, Jill, but Kathy is a bit full on. By mid-afternoon, I was exhausted from all the interviews she'd set up for me, so I told her I had a migraine, and made my escape."

"I know what you mean." I chuckled. "Kathy gives me a migraine too. How did it go today?"

"Really well, actually. Kathy might be a bit full on, but she's done a first-class job organising the exhibition and the marketing. Will you and Jack be coming to the official opening?"

"Art isn't really my thing, but Jack seems keen."

Talk of the devil: Jack walked in.

"Hey, you two. What's for dinner?"

"Nothing yet. I've only just got home," I said.

"I have a suggestion," Gregor said.

"No offence, but I can't eat any of that stuff on your list."

"That's not what I had in mind. Yesterday, you mentioned the chippy. It's ages since I had fish and chips. Do you reckon we could get some?"

"Sounds good to me," Jack said. "The nearest chippy is a few miles away, though. I've been saying for years that someone should open one here in the village."

"Do they sell mushy peas?"

"Of course," I said. "What about Kathy, though?"

"What about her?"

"She'll kill us if she thinks we've been feeding you fish and chips."

"I won't tell her if you don't." Gregor grinned.

"Jill, why don't you and Gregor go and get the chips?" Jack said.

"What are you going to do?"

"Nip back to the store and pick up a couple of bottles of wine. We finished the last one yesterday."

Chapter 20

The next morning, when I came downstairs, I had a nasty shock waiting for me.

"What's he doing down here?" I shouted at Jack. "I told you not to bring that teddy bear downstairs."

In response, Jack had the temerity to shush me, and then say, "Gregor will hear you."

"Do you mind not talking about me like I'm not here?" Humphrey had the nerve to interject.

"I'm not talking to you. I'm talking to my husband."

"He promised he wouldn't talk to Gregor if I brought him downstairs," Jack said.

"And you believed him?"

"I don't lie," Humphrey insisted.

"It's not a question of lying. You just don't know when to stay quiet. It took me ages to get off to sleep last night because every time I began to nod off, you started jabbering again."

"That was no excuse for slinging me in the spare room."

"I didn't *sling* you in there, and it was the only way I was ever going to get to sleep."

Just then, we all heard footsteps on the stairs.

"It's Gregor," Jack said.

"Don't you dare speak to him," I warned Humphrey. "Or it's back to the store with you."

Thankfully, Humphrey kept his word, and we managed to get through breakfast without any awkward talking bear incidents.

***

When I walked into my office, Winky was still flashing.

"I'm still flashing!"

"I can see that. Did you get the prescription filled?"

"Yeah."

"Didn't the medicine work?"

"I don't know if it works or not."

"What do you mean?"

"See for yourself." He handed me a large pot.

"Can't you open it?"

"Of course I can open it. Do you think I'm stupid?"

"There's no need to get crabby with me. What's the problem, then?"

"Open it and you'll see."

I popped open the top to reveal half a dozen large red and green tablets.

"Now do you understand?" Winky said.

"Not really."

"Look how big they are. How am I supposed to swallow those?"

He had a point. I wouldn't have fancied tackling those big boys and I was much bigger than Winky.

"Didn't they have the same medicine in liquid form?"

"I asked that, but they said it was only available as tablets."

"You'll just have to take them, then."

"I can't. I tried one and I almost choked to death."

"Aren't you already dead?"

"Yes, yes, but I don't want to risk dying again. Can't you just use magic?"

"To do what?"

"I don't know. You're supposed to be the world's best witch. Surely, you can come up with something."

"Okay, let me think. How about I use the 'shrink' spell to make the tablets smaller?"

"Sounds good. Go for it."

I cast the spell and shrank the tablets to a quarter of their normal size. "There you go."

"Brilliant." He took one of the tablets and washed it down with water.

"Did the pharmacist say how long it would take to stop you flashing?"

"She said I had to take four a day for the next three days, and that should sort it out. It better had. I'm not sure how much more of this I can take."

Just then, Jules came through to my office. It was obvious, even before she spoke, that something had upset her.

"Look what he's given me." She held up a large square of what looked like felt.

"*Who* gave you it?"

"Mr Petty. He said I had to put it under my keyboard so that it isn't so noisy."

"It isn't noisy, anyway. If I can't hear it in here, how can he hear it? The man is an idiot. Give me that thing."

I took the felt pad from her and headed next door. Normally, I would have knocked before going in, but I wasn't in the mood for niceties. I was already regretting letting Portia Parkspirit 'exorcise' the evil spirit that had been haunting him.

"Jill?" Petty looked up from his desk. "I didn't hear you knock."

"That's because I didn't. I just came to return this." I threw the square of felt onto his desk.

"Is it the wrong size? I can get—"

"It isn't the wrong size. Jules doesn't need it. Her typing makes barely any sound."

"That's easy for you to say, but you don't have my sensitive ears."

"You're right I don't, but you know what I would do if I did?"

"What?"

"I'd buy myself some earplugs."

***

In the time it had taken me to have it out with Petty, a visitor had arrived at my office. A visitor in the shape of my sister.

"I have a bone to pick with you, Jill."

"Oh good because I've been having such a great morning, and I was hoping that someone would come along and spoil it. You'd better come through." Once we were in my office, I continued, "Go on, then. Spit it out."

"Gregor told me that you won't be coming to the opening of his exhibition tomorrow."

"I'm really busy."

"He said you told him it wasn't really your thing."

"Yeah, well that too."

"You promised, Jill. You know how important this opening day is to me."

"I know, but who's going to miss me?"

"Me for one. Gregor for two. He sounded really disappointed when he told me."

"He did?"

"Yeah, he seems to really like you and Jack, although goodness knows why."

"What does that mean?"

"He told me how you twisted his arm to have fish and chips yesterday. And after all the trouble I had gone to, to draw up that list."

Twisted his arm? That was rich. I was tempted to throw Gregor under the bus by telling Kathy the truth: that he'd been the one who had insisted we have fish and chips, but call me a big softy, I didn't have the heart.

"I'll come to the opening if there's cake."

"I told you I can't have cake in case anyone messes up the pictures."

"You don't have to get cake for everyone. Just for me."

"You can't be serious."

"I'm deadly serious. Cake or I'm a no-show."

"Okay. I'll buy you a bun or something, but you have to promise to eat it out the back where no one can see you, and where you won't be able to ruin any of the exhibits."

"Deal."

"What's that flashing?" Kathy looked over to where Winky was sitting on my desk.

"It's something to do with the Wi-Fi, apparently. It's on the blink."

"Make sure Gregor gets an early night tonight. He needs to be on top form tomorrow morning."

"No problem. I'll make sure he's tucked up in bed by eight o'clock."

"Bye, then."

"Kathy."

"Yeah?"

"Make sure it's a really big bun."

"Are you really going to go to the opening?" Winky said after she'd left.

"Looks like it."

***

Mr Beasley had left a message with Jules, asking me to call him, but every time I tried, my call went to voicemail. I thought he might return my call, but when a couple of hours had passed by, and I still hadn't heard from him, I decided to pop over to his house.

When I arrived there, he answered the door, with a paintbrush in his hand.

"Jill? I wasn't expecting you."

"You asked my PA to get me to call you, but I couldn't get hold of you."

"Sorry, I've had the radio on."

"I take it you're decorating."

"Just a bit of touching up here and there. Come in."

"I assume your back is feeling better."

"Not really." He sighed. "But we have to soldier on, don't we?"

"What did you call about?"

"It's just that I'm getting really nervous. The deadline to pay the blackmail money is a week tomorrow, and I'm not sure what I should do."

"Just sit tight and do nothing."

"Do you have any idea at all who might be behind this yet?"

"I had suspected it might be Gaby Pinstone because she came to your door the day the blackmail note was delivered, and she and her husband, Fred, were in the pub when you had your outburst."

"How do you know?"

"Because I've seen the CCTV from the pub. They were sitting close to where you were. Apparently, they were there for someone else's birthday celebration."

"That would be Pat."

"You know her?"

"It's a he. He's been our postman for years."

"Postman Pat?"

"Yeah, he gets a lot of stick about that."

"I don't suppose you know where Pat lives do you?"

"On Westbridge Road, I believe. Why?"

"I have to go."

"But we haven't discussed the case yet. What am I going to do about the deadline?"

"Don't worry about it. It's all going to be okay."

Westbridge Road was a couple of miles away, so it took me no time at all to drive there. I had no idea which was his house, so I asked an old woman who was painting her fence.

"I'm sorry to interrupt you."

"No bother, dear. Any excuse to take a break from this."

"I'm looking for someone who lives on this street. His name is Pat, and I believe he's a postman. Do you happen to know which is his house?"

"Sure do. That's Pat Connor's place over there. Number seventy-three."

"Great, thanks."

It was late morning, so I was pretty confident that Pat would still be out on his rounds, but I rang the doorbell, just in case. There was no response, and a quick look through the windows, on the front of the house, showed no sign of life. The back of the house had a tall fence on all sides (possibly too tall—perhaps I should have reported it), and I was confident that no one could see me, so I magicked myself inside. The hallway and living room were full of framed photographs of the same woman, taken across the years. In what appeared to be the most recent photo, the woman had clearly lost weight and looked a shadow of her younger self.

I found nothing of interest downstairs, so I made my way upstairs where the smallest of the three bedrooms had been converted into a simple office. On the desk was a manual typewriter, which had a defective letter 't', just like the blackmail note sent to Beasley.

As soon as Beasley had mentioned that Pat was the postman, everything had clicked into place. Pat had been seated with the Pinstones, which meant he was close enough to Beasley to record his outburst. And, as the postman for that street, he had been able to deliver the blackmail note as part of his normal delivery run.

It was time to have a talk to postman Pat, and I didn't have long to wait because he returned home less than an hour later. After letting himself in, he made his way into the kitchen where he found me at the table, drinking a cup of tea.

"Would you like one?" I said. "The water's still hot."

"Who are you? How did you get in?"

"Why don't you take a seat, Pat? Is it okay to call you Pat?"

"I'm going to call the police."

"Why don't you do that? When they get here, you can tell them about your blackmail activities."

The colour drained from his face, and he slumped into the chair.

"I don't know what you're talking about," he said, rather unconvincingly.

"Don't let's waste each other's time with silly lies. You and I both know that you're trying to blackmail Bobby Beasley."

To my surprise, he began to cry. Not just a little sob; the man was wailing uncontrollably.

"Please don't tell the police. I can't go to prison. It will kill me."

"Let's not get ahead of ourselves. Why don't you tell me all about it?"

"What do you want to know?" He blew his nose.

"Let's start with why you made the recording in the first place."

"Because I could hear those terrible things he was saying about his poor mother."

"I agree that what he said wasn't nice, but why is it any business of yours?"

"I lost my mother just over a year ago. She was a wonderful woman. I still miss her every day."

"I'm sorry to hear that."

"I was devastated. I haven't been out since, except for work of course. I'm a postman."

"Yeah, your uniform kind of gave that away."

"Yes, of course. Anyway, some friends persuaded me to go to the local pub with them, to celebrate my birthday."

"The Pinstones?"

"Yeah."

"And you saw Bobby Beasley there?"

"Yeah, he was by himself."

"Did you speak to him?"

"No, he was already steaming when I got there, and he

only got worse as the night went on."

"Why did you decide to record what he was saying?"

"I was angry."

"Why? Because he was disturbing your celebrations?"

"No, I didn't care about that. I'm still grieving for my mum, and that idiot was shouting about how much he hated his mother, and saying how he wished she was dead."

"But what did you intend to do with the recording?"

"I was going to play it for his mother, to let her know what her horrible, selfish son was really like."

"Did you?"

"No. By the next day, I'd realised it was a stupid idea. The only thing it would have achieved would have been to upset his mother, and I didn't want to do that."

"But you didn't erase it?"

"No, I forgot all about it until—" He hesitated.

"Until you heard that Beasley's mother had died."

"That's right."

"Did you think he'd killed her?"

"I thought it was a possibility."

"Why didn't you take your suspicions and the recording to the police? Why blackmail him?"

"I thought it was a good way of proving he'd done it."

"I don't understand."

"If he was innocent, he wouldn't pay up. Why would he? He would have nothing to fear from the recording. But, if he was guilty, I figured he'd pay the money."

"So you sent him the blackmail letter?"

"Yeah. I copied the recording onto a cassette tape and sent that and the letter to him."

"Then what? What if he had paid up?"

"Then I would have gone to the police."

It was all kinds of messed up, but I sort of followed his logic.

"I can tell you that he has no intention of paying. That's why he hired me to find out who was behind this."

"How did you know it was me?"

"It wasn't difficult. Only two people went to his door the day the ransom note was delivered. When I eliminated the other person from my enquiries, that left only you. There is one thing I don't understand, though."

"What's that?"

"Beasley is supposed to send the cash to an address in Crewe, but I've checked and there's no such address. If he'd decided to pay up, how were you going to get the money?"

"Beasley always posts his letters in the post box at the end of his street. As part of my round, I empty that box. I've checked it every day, to see if there is a letter for that Crewe address."

"And if there had been one?"

"Then I would have handed that to the police too. What happens now?"

"That depends on Beasley."

"Are you going to tell him I was the one blackmailing him?"

"I have no choice, but I'll explain what drove you to do it. It'll be up to him if he wants to go to the police."

"Please tell him I'm sorry."

"I will, but first you need to give me all copies of the tape."

"I only have one."

"Get it."

He walked over to a cupboard, and retrieved a cassette, which he handed to me.

"Are you sure this is the only copy?"

"I promise."

"What about the original recording?"

"That was on my phone. I've deleted it."

"Show me."

He handed me his phone, and I crushed it into a million pieces.

"Hey, I needed that."

"Buy a new one."

By the time I left, Pat was a gibbering wreck, terrified that Beasley would report him to the police. Based upon what Beasley had told me, I doubted that would happen, but I didn't tell Pat that because I figured it would do him no harm to stew for a while.

Chapter 21

Beasley was clearly surprised to see me back at his door so soon.

"Jill? Did you forget something?"

"No, I came to tell you I've found out who is blackmailing you."

"Who is it?"

"Your postman."

"Pat?"

"That's right."

"Are you sure it's him?"

"I'm positive. Can I come inside?"

"Yeah. Go through to the living room while I clean off this paint."

He joined me a few minutes later, and although he'd cleaned his hands, his head was still covered in spots of paint.

"You'd better tell me what you know," he said.

He sat in silence while I explained what I'd discovered. When I'd finished, he said, "He was going to play the tape to Mum?"

"Yes, but he changed his mind because he didn't want to upset her."

"He shouldn't have tried to blackmail me."

"You're right, but it doesn't sound like it was ever about the money. It was more of a test. If you'd paid up, he would have taken that as a sign you were guilty, and he would have handed the tape to the police."

"I didn't murder Mum."

"I know, and so does Pat now. I believe him when he says he's sorry for what he did, and you have to remember his state of mind after losing his own mother."

"It's no excuse for all the stress and worry he's put me through."

"You're right, which is why you still have the option of going to the police if you want to."

"I've already told you that I'm not going to do that."

"That's your call. If it's any consolation, I don't think Pat is an evil person. He just did something very stupid."

"I guess that's that, then."

"Not quite." I handed him the cassette. "This is the only other copy."

"Are you sure?"

"Yeah."

"Thanks, Jill, I feel like a great weight has been lifted off my shoulders."

"My pleasure."

***

Mickey Michaels, the driver who delivered to the shops that had encountered the majority of faulty toys, was a werewolf with a thing for buttercups. Mickey's jacket and trousers were resplendent in their buttercup print. Even his shoes had them printed on the sides. We'd agreed to meet at a small café, called Polly's Pot, which was a couple of streets from Joy's Toys.

"Does Joy think I had something to do with it?" he asked nervously while sipping his camomile tea.

"No, I'm sure she doesn't. In fact, she had nothing but good things to say about you."

"That's a relief. I can't afford to lose this job because our first baby is due in just under a month."

"Congratulations."

"Thanks. Have you been in here before?"

"No, but it seems nice."

"It is. Polly is lovely, but she's down with the flu at the moment."

"Can I ask you a few questions about your deliveries?"

"Sure. Ask away."

"How many days do you make deliveries?"

"Five days: Monday to Friday."

"And do you deliver to the same shops every day?"

"I only make a delivery to those stores that placed an order the day before. On Mondays, I deliver all the toys that were ordered by the shops over the weekend."

"How often do you deliver to each shop?"

"It varies. Some shops place orders most days; others only place an order once a week, so I visit them much less frequently."

"I assume that means you don't follow the same route every day?"

"That's right. It depends which shops I'm delivering to on a particular day."

"And how long does it usually take?"

"First, I have to pack the van. That can take up to an hour. I usually leave the warehouse about 10am, and I'm normally back there by four."

"Is that you done?"

"No. All the drivers have to clean their vans at the end of each day, ready for the next day's deliveries. Joy is adamant that the vans look their best at all times."

"And what time do you normally get away?"

"Around 5pm."

"What about breaks? For lunch etc."

"I always grab my breakfast at Kat's."

"Where's that?"

"Haven't you heard of Kat's? You're missing out. It's a roadside diner on Eatmore Road. Her breakfasts are to die for, and the prices are very reasonable."

"Where do you park the van when you go into the diner?"

"In the car park around the back. There's no parking on the front."

"Can you see the van from inside the diner?"

"No, but I always make sure it's locked."

"What about lunch?"

"I always bring a packed lunch, which I eat in the van. I don't need much because I always have a huge breakfast."

"Any other breaks?"

"Only to go to the loo, but there again, I always make sure the van is locked."

"Do you have any theories about what might be happening to the toys, Mickey?"

"Absolutely none. I check and double-check every package I deliver for any sign of damage, but there never is any. I don't understand what's happening. What about you, Jill, do you have any idea what's going on?"

"Not yet, but there's no getting away from the fact that all the faulty toys were delivered by your van."

***

Not long after I'd finished talking to Mickey, I got a call from Daze.

"Jill, I think we may have a hit."

"Already? I thought it would take much longer."

"Me too, and I don't want to get your hopes up too high because this could prove to be nothing. Blaze and I are in Cuppy C. Have you got a minute to join us?"

"Sure, I'll be straight over."

Daze and Blaze already had drinks, so I wasn't going to bother with one, but before I could join them, Amber called after me. "Did you forget something?"

"Sorry?"

"This isn't your personal office. If you want to use our premises, you'll need to at least buy a drink."

"Very funny."

"I'm not joking, Jill."

Judging by her expression, she wasn't.

"Okay, I'll have a caramel latte, please. Will you bring it over?"

"Have you forgotten something?"

"I said *please*."

"I meant paying for it."

"Oh yeah, sorry." I made the payment then joined Blaze and Daze at their table. "What's up with Amber? She's like a bear with a sore backside."

"Look around," Daze said. "I think the twins are fed up with people using this place as their office."

Until Daze had mentioned it, I hadn't really noticed, but when I looked around, several of the tables were occupied with sups working on their laptops.

"That guy over there has been nursing the same drink since mid-morning," Blaze said.

"How do you know? Have you been in since then too?"

"No, Pearl told us."

"They should tell him he has to buy another drink," I said. "Amber was quick enough to tell me. Now, what have you got for me?"

"We've had our people calling everyone, who lives in a fifty-mile radius of Washbridge, with a name that has a connection to a nursery rhyme figure. They pretended to be the police and said they were following up on the report of a break-in. Needless to say, most of the people had no idea what the caller was talking about because they hadn't had a break-in, which immediately eliminated them. But then, one of our callers spoke to a man called Robert Shafto."

"As in Bobby Shafto's gone to sea?"

"Exactly. He was surprised to get the call because he hadn't actually been in contact with the police, but he had experienced two break-ins over the last two weeks."

"Why hadn't he contacted the police himself?"

"That's where it gets interesting. He didn't contact them because there was no forced entry, and nothing was stolen."

"How can he even be sure there was a break-in, then?"

"Whoever did it, left something behind each time: the first time it was a comb; the second time it was a silver buckle."

"That's sounds just like what happened to Goldie."

"That's what we thought."

"If it's the same person, then Robert Shafto could be in extreme danger. The next break-in could result in his murder."

"Which is why we need you to persuade him to move out."

"Why haven't you done that already?"

"What are we supposed to tell him? That someone is murdering people who have nursery rhyme character names, and we believe he's going to be the next victim?"

"Why not? That's exactly what's happening."

"Because it sounds crazy."

"It's not going to sound any less crazy coming from me, is it?"

The two of them just shrugged.

"We did our bit by finding him," Blaze said. "I'm sure you'll come up with something."

"It sounds like I don't have any choice."

"If you manage to get him out of the house, I thought the three of us could take turns in house-sitting, to wait for our murderer to show up," Daze said. "If you can get Bobby out of there today, Blaze will stay in the house tonight."

"I have a date tonight," he objected.

"Cancel it. I'll take tomorrow night, and then Jill can take Monday."

"What if the murderer is still a no-show after Monday?"

"We'll cycle through again until he shows his face. What do you say?"

"You'd better give me his address."

***

After magicking myself back to Washbridge, I drove to Robert Shafto's address. As soon as he answered the door, and before I had the chance to introduce myself, he snapped, "About time, too."

"Sorry?"

"Aren't you here about the leccy?"

"*Leccy*?"

"Electricity. What are you? Stupid? It's been off since six

o'clock last night."

"I'm not here about the electricity."

"Who are you, then?"

"I'm Detective Maxwell. Washbridge police."

"What do you want?"

"I believe you spoke to one of my colleagues on the phone. You told them about a couple of break-ins."

"Nothing was stolen."

"Even so, Bobby, I—"

"Don't call me that. I go by Rob."

"Sorry, I was about to say that we believe you may be in danger."

"Because some nutter left a comb and a buckle in my house? That's cobblers. I wish I'd never mentioned it now. It was probably just one of my daft mates who did it. It's just the kind of thing they would do. They're always taking the mickey out of me because of my name. I blame my stupid parents."

"Surely, you must be concerned that someone gained access to your house?"

"The only thing I'm concerned about right now is getting the power back on. I can't even make a cup of tea."

"Couldn't you just boil some water?"

"Genius. Why didn't I think of that? Oh yeah, because I don't have gas. That's why. So unless you can fix it, I've got nothing else to say to you." And to emphasise his point, he closed the door in my face.

What was I supposed to do now? I couldn't force the man to leave against his wishes. It was time to call in the cavalry, so I rang my old buddy, Edna the surveillance fairy.

"Edna speaking."

"Edna, it's Jill Maxwell. Are you free at the moment?"

"I could be. Depends."

"On what?"

"On whether you're willing to pay my new rates."

"You can't possibly have put up your prices again. It's not five minutes since you raised them."

"Have you seen what's happened to the cost of living lately?"

"How many custard creams are you going to charge me this time?"

"I've gone off custard creams."

"What? You can't be off custard creams. That's not possible."

"Chocolate digestives are now my payment of choice. Dark chocolate not milk. Five packets per day. That's the large packets, obviously."

"Okay, I agree, but I need you to start immediately."

"No problem." The words were no sooner out of her mouth than she appeared on my shoulder.

"I've told you not to do that."

"What's your problem?"

"You're no lightweight."

"You'd better watch what you're saying, or you'll have to find someone else to do your surveillance."

"Sorry."

"What's the job this time?"

"See that house over there?"

"The one with the green door?"

"Yeah. A Mr Robert Shafto lives there."

"Bobby Shafto?"

"He goes by Rob."

"I bet he does."

"Anyway, I need you to keep an eye on it and contact me straight away if someone comes to the house."

"Who?"

"Anyone. It doesn't matter who. Just give me a call straight away."

"Fair enough. How long do you want me to do this for?"

"I don't know. It could be a few days."

"In that case, I'll have to bring in Clem to share the shifts."

"Clem?"

"She and I work together occasionally."

"Fair enough."

"She'll want paying in Jammy Dodgers."

"I'm already paying you. Why do I have to pay her too?"

"It's the only way you'll get twenty-four-hour cover."

"Okay, okay. Just do it, and make sure you or Clem let me know the minute anyone comes to the house."

After agreeing the terms of the deal with Edna, I called Daze to update her.

"I guess you won't be needing Blaze and me, then?"

"No. Shafto is adamant that he isn't moving out, so I'm going to have to rely on Edna to keep watch. I'll keep you posted."

Chapter 22

"Kathy is going to kill us," I snapped at Jack.

It was seven-thirty on Saturday morning, and Gregor was still sound asleep in bed.

"It's not our fault," Jack said.

"It certainly isn't *my* fault. I wasn't the one who kept him up drinking until the early hours."

"Neither did I. I came to bed at just after eleven, and he wasn't drunk then. He must have opened another bottle after I'd left him."

"You should never have left him alone."

"He wasn't alone," Humphrey chipped in. "I was with him."

"Oh great. Please tell me you didn't speak to him."

"Maybe the odd word or two."

"This is a disaster. You shouldn't have allowed it to happen, Jack."

"What was I supposed to do? Drag Gregor upstairs to bed?"

"If necessary, yes. Kathy said he had to be at the gallery by nine-thirty. If he isn't there, we're toast."

"She can't blame us because Gregor decided to get drunk."

"Do you want to bet? Go upstairs and get him up."

"How am I supposed to do that?"

"I don't care. Drag him into the shower and then dress him if you have to. I'll make some strong coffee."

Thirty minutes later, Jack helped Gregor down the stairs and deposited him onto one of the chairs in the kitchen.

"My head hurts." Gregor rubbed his forehead.

"I don't care. Drink this." I put a mug of black coffee on

the table in front of him.

"I don't think I can."

"Try!"

"Do you have any painkillers?"

"Jack, go and get him some paracetamol."

"I don't think I can go to the opening," Gregor said.

"You're going even if I have—"

Before I could finish the sentence, he'd dashed over to the sink and thrown up. After which, he slumped down onto the kitchen floor.

"Is he alright?" Jack said when he returned with the tablets.

"Does he look alright?"

He looked the polar opposite of alright. He was as white as a sheet, and he was snoring.

"Do you think I should call Kathy and tell her?" Jack said.

"Only if you're tired of living."

"He can't turn up looking like this."

"You think?"

"You'll have to do it," Jack blurted out.

"Do what?"

"You'll have to be Gregor."

"I can't."

"Yes, you can. You've done it loads of times. What's the name of that spell you use to make you look like someone else?"

"The 'doppelganger' spell, but just looking like him isn't going to be enough."

"You know how he talks, and you've seen his mannerisms."

"That's not the problem either. People will expect me to

talk about the paintings, and I don't know the first thing about them."

"Knowing nothing about a subject has never stopped you talking about it before."

"Careful. You're on very thin ice."

"Do you have a better idea?"

Unfortunately, I didn't, so I cast the 'doppelganger' spell to make me look like Gregor.

"You'd better get him out of those clothes," I said.

Jack extricated Gregor from his suit, which fortunately he hadn't thrown up all over. Once I had slipped it on, I turned to Jack.

"What do you think?"

"Perfect. You even sound like him. It's a bit creepy if I'm honest. What shall I do with Gregor?"

"We'll take him upstairs and put him on the bed. I'll leave him a note on the bedside table, to tell him to get to the gallery as soon as he's sobered up. Hopefully, I can blag my way through until then."

Jack drove him and me into town and pulled up outside the gallery where Kathy was waiting on the pavement.

She opened the car door. "I was beginning to worry."

"You didn't think I'd let you down, did you?" I said in my best Gregor voice.

"I knew *you* wouldn't be late, Gregor, but I was worried that sister of mine might have delayed you."

"Not at all. Jill has been the perfect host."

"Where is she, anyway? She promised that she'd come."

"She's a bit under the weather," Jack said. "But she said she'll try to make it in a bit later."

"She better had. You can park just down the street, Jack. Gregor, you come with me, and I'll go through the running order with you."

"Perfect. I don't suppose I could get a cup of tea, could I?"

"Of course. Green? I know that's your favourite."

"Actually, I'd prefer regular tea if that's okay with you?"

"No problem."

"I'm also feeling a little dithery. I don't suppose you have anything sugary, do you?"

"What kind of thing?"

"A bun, maybe."

"There's a cake shop just down the street. I could send someone down there if you like."

"That would be lovely. Something strawberry-flavoured, maybe."

"Right. I'll get straight on it."

A few minutes later, I was enjoying a strawberry cupcake, washed down with a cup of tea.

"How are you feeling now?" Kathy asked.

"Fine. That cupcake seems to have done the trick."

"Great. Are you ready for me to go through the running order?"

"Sure."

"The doors open in just over twenty-minutes. I'll welcome everyone, then I'll introduce you and you can say a few words about the exhibition."

"I'd rather not."

"Sorry, I don't understand."

"I prefer not to talk about my work before people have had a chance to see it for themselves. That way, they don't have preconceived ideas about what they should take from each piece."

"But I assume you'll be happy to talk to the patrons and answer their questions as they look around the exhibits?"

"Of course."

I was hoping that Gregor would have recovered sufficiently to make an appearance by then.

The doors opened on time, and to Kathy's obvious delight, a couple of dozen people were already waiting outside. She wasted no time in climbing onto a chair and calling for silence.

"Welcome everyone to the opening of Gallery K. This is a very exciting day for me, and I'm delighted that I was able to persuade Gregor Leggor to be our first exhibitor. I'm sure I don't need to tell you that he has established himself as one of the most innovative and exciting artists of his generation. I had hoped he might say a few words at this juncture, but he's adamant that he prefers not to discuss his work until you've had time to absorb it for yourself. He will be with us all day, though, so if you have anything you'd like to discuss with him, please don't be shy to approach him. That's right, isn't it, Gregor?"

I smiled and nodded.

The guests began to move around the gallery, taking in the artwork. I'd seen photos of his work online, but they didn't do justice to how bad they actually were. They really did look like a three-year old had just randomly splashed paint onto the canvas.

"Excuse me, Mr Leggor."

I turned around to see a middle-aged woman with pink hair and more jewellery than you could shake a stick at.

"Yes?"

"I just love this piece." She pointed to the large painting on the wall next to us. Essentially, it was a white canvas onto which someone appeared to have splashed blue paint diagonally from the bottom left corner to the top right corner.

"Er, thank you."

"I'm a little confused by the name, though." She pointed to the small plaque below the painting that read: Destiny Red.

My immediate thought was that Kathy had mixed the name plaques up, but before I could say as much, the woman continued, "It's about the starkness of life alone, isn't it?"

"Starkness? Err, yes, that's right."

"I knew it. Absolute genius."

"Thank you."

"How's it going, Gregor?" Jack appeared at my shoulder.

"The people in here are all nuts," I whispered. "Have you looked around? These paintings are all rubbish."

"Shush! Someone might hear you."

Just then, Kathy came floating over. "Is everything okay, Gregor?"

"Everything is fine."

"I've already had three people interested in purchasing pieces."

"That's terrific." They must need their heads looking at.

"Any word on Jill, Jack?" Kathy said.

"I'm sure she won't be long."

"She'd better not be. Don't monopolise Gregor. He needs to circulate."

I was doing my level best to steer clear of the art-lovers, but as I moved from one section of the exhibition to another, I ran straight into a rotund man with a penchant for velvet.

"Mr Leggor, I was hoping to grab a word with you. I'm Freddie Flintrock of the Cambridgeshire Flintrocks."

"Right. Hi."

"I believe you spoke to my brother Barnaby last month in Paris."

"Err, I—"

"He told me your work was exceptional, but it's even better than he said."

"Thank you."

"Custard."

"Sorry?"

"Custard," he repeated, and pointed to the painting on the opposite wall. Essentially, it was just a yellow square. "I've fallen in love with it."

"Right."

"Kathy is being rather coy about the price. I thought maybe you'd be able to give me some idea."

"The price?" I glanced again at the painting. I wouldn't have given you ten pence for it.

"Freddie!" Kathy suddenly butted in. "What have I told you about talking prices?"

"Sorry, Kathy, but I simply must have Custard."

"Then you can discuss it with me later."

"Very well, but don't let anyone else steal it away from me."

"No more negotiating, Gregor, please," Kathy said after Freddie had moved away. "If anyone tries to talk price with you, send them over to see me."

"Okay, will do."

Over the next two hours, more people arrived at the gallery—all of them, apparently, excited to view random coloured splashes of paint. Despite doing my best to keep my distance, I'd already had to endure two agonising discussions on the merits of Gregor's masterpieces. The most difficult part of which was keeping a straight face while listening to people spout nonsense.

When someone tapped on my shoulder from behind, I assumed I was in for another mind-numbing conversation, but it was Jack.

"Gregor's here!"

"Where?"

"Over there by the door."

"What on earth is he wearing?"

"It looks like one of my suits; it's a couple of sizes too big for him."

"We can't let Kathy see him. Go and grab him and take him into the back."

"What shall I say to him?"

"Anything. Just get him out of here before Kathy sees him. I'll change back into myself and bring his suit through to you. Go on! Quick!"

I watched as Jack grabbed a confused looking Gregor by the arm and led him into the back. I then headed into the loo where I reversed the 'doppelganger' spell. With Gregor's suit under my arm, I headed towards the back room.

"Jill, I'm so sorry about this morning," Gregor said.

"Don't worry about that now. Just get changed into this." I handed him his suit.

"Where did you find that? I looked everywhere for it."

"Never mind. Just put it on, get out there, and mix with your fans."

"That was a close call," Jack said after Gregor had gone

to mingle with his adoring fans.

"I need a drink."

I'd no sooner stepped back into the gallery than Kathy homed in on me.

"Nice of you to make an appearance at last."

"Sorry I'm late."

"You knew how important this was to me."

"I'm here now, aren't I? It looks like it's going well."

"It's amazing. I've already negotiated the sale of one piece for over half a mill."

"Amazeballs."

"Why do you always have to be so childish?"

Chapter 23

Sunday, which was the final day of Gregor's exhibition, went much more smoothly. That was due, in no small part, to the fact that we'd ensured he didn't have a drop to drink on Saturday night. Jack and I didn't attend the second day, but Gregor told us that he'd sold another two pieces, which made a total sales of almost two million. I didn't know what Kathy's commission would be, but even if it was only one percent, that added up to a nice chunk of change for only two days' work.

Gregor, who was heading to the USA later that day, joined Jack and me for breakfast on Monday morning.

"I'll miss your fry-ups, Jack," he said.

"We'll miss you. Are you likely to exhibit at Kathy's gallery again?"

"Not in the foreseeable. I'm fully booked for the next twelve months. I only managed it this time because I had a last-minute cancellation in Venice." He turned to me. "And thanks again, Jill, for having me here. I know I've been a lot of trouble."

"It was our pleasure," I lied.

"By way of thanks, I'd like to give you one of my pieces." He must have seen my reaction because he said, "Not the paintings in this weekend's exhibition; I know you don't like any of that stuff."

"I wouldn't say—"

"It's okay. They're all rubbish."

"Sorry?"

"It's true. They're awful. I don't know what anyone sees in them." He took out his phone and held it up for me to see. "I'd like you to have one of these."

The images on-screen were all of landscape paintings.

"These are amazing," I said.

"I wish everyone else thought so."

"I don't understand."

"For years, I painted dozens of these landscapes, but I couldn't give them away. That's why, one day, I was so disillusioned that I decided to quit. I took my remaining blank canvasses and basically threw paint at them. I should add that I was very drunk at the time. Anyway, I uploaded images of my new 'creations'—just for a laugh, really. Then, the offers started to come in. People couldn't get enough of them. They put all kinds of interpretations onto them. I couldn't believe it, but then I got a cheque for more money than I'd earned in the previous year."

"That's brilliant." I laughed. "Good for you."

"Will you ever go back to the landscapes?" Jack asked.

"I still do them, but under a pseudonym. I rarely sell one and when I do, it's for a pittance. If you pick one out, I'll have it sent to you."

As we waited for Gregor's taxi to arrive, he said, "I really am sorry about getting so wasted. I've not been that drunk for years."

"It's okay. You weren't all that drunk," I lied.

"I must have been. I was having an in-depth discussion about the art world with that teddy bear of yours." He laughed.

"Really?" Memo to self—kill Humphrey.

"Pretty surreal, eh?"

"That is weird."

After Gregor had left, Jack and I reflected upon his visit.

"He's a funny guy," Jack said. "Nice, though."

"Yeah. He's nothing like his public image, that's for sure."

"I wonder if Kathy knows about his landscapes?"

"I doubt it."

"It was nice of him to give us one."

"I'd rather have had one of his splash paintings." I sighed.

"I thought you didn't like them?"

"I don't. They're complete rubbish, but we could have sold it for a small fortune."

***

After a weird weekend, it was back to work. I'd put the Beasley case to bed, but I still had to find the serial killer responsible for Goldie's murder, and I had to try and get to the bottom of the faulty toy problem that was threatening Joy's Toys' business.

"Good morning, Jules."

"Good morning, Jill. I took the post through to your office earlier, and the Wi-Fi is still flashing. Do you want me to call someone about it?"

"No, it's fine. You could make me a cup of tea, though, please."

"I'm still flashing," Winky said.

"I can see that. I guess those tablets didn't work."

"They would have done if you hadn't shrunk them. I spoke to the pharmacist, and she reckons that by doing that you diluted the effect."

"You were the one who asked me to shrink them."

"It's okay because I managed to persuade her to give me some more."

"But you said you couldn't swallow them before."

"I still can't. I need you to shrink them so I can swallow them, and then turn them back to their full size once I've done that."

"I'm not sure that would work."

"Why not?"

"Because, normally, when I'm casting or reversing the 'shrink' spell, I can see the object in question. That wouldn't be the case once you've swallowed the tablets, so I'll need to check my spell book to see if there's anything different that I need to do."

"Go on, then, what are you waiting for?"

"You really are the most ungrateful—"

"Still waiting."

I took out my phone, brought up the spell book app, and searched on 'shrink' spells. At the top of the list was the spell I'd used thousands of times. Below that were several lesser-known variations on the same spell. One of which had the catchy name: Shrink spell for a concealed object. At first glance, it appeared to fit the bill.

"Well?" said Mr Impatient.

"I think this one might work."

"You aren't exactly filling me with confidence here."

"I need a second opinion."

"How long is that going to take?"

"Not long, hopefully. Wait there."

"Like I'm going anywhere."

I magicked myself over to Grandma's cottage where, once again, I found her seated on the bench in the garden.

"Do you have to pop up out of nowhere like that?" she said. "You made me jump."

"That's rich coming from you."

"What do you want?"

"I need your advice."

"I told you years ago that you should divorce him."

"Not about my marriage! I'm never going to leave Jack. I love him."

"What do you want then?"

"I need some help on a spell."

"Surely, the world's most powerful witch doesn't need my advice."

"Don't start again with that. I've never claimed to know more than you."

"What do you want to know?"

"Can I use the reversal routine for one spell to reverse a different spell?"

"Care to say that again, but in English this time?"

I explained, step-by-step, the situation with regard to the tablets that Winky was trying to take.

"Are you really wasting my time for a dead cat?"

"Winky's a ghost, and the flashing is causing him distress. Please, I need your help."

"Okay, so if I've understood you correctly, you want to shrink the tablets using the standard 'shrink' spell, but then return them to full size, after he's swallowed them, by reversing a totally different spell."

"Correct."

"That definitely *won't* work."

"What can I do then?"

"I would have thought that was obvious, even to you."

"Well, it isn't."

"Give me strength. Before he swallows them, you need to conceal the tablets and cast the concealed object version of the 'shrink' spell on them."

"Conceal them, how?"

"It doesn't matter how provided they're concealed. Just put them underneath something. Anything."

"Okay, I get it. And do you think that will work?"

"It should because you'll be casting and reversing the same spell."

"You're a genius."

"I've been telling you that for years."

"Thanks, Grandma."

"Hang on. Now you're here, you can bring me up to date on Joy's Toys. What's happening?"

"To be honest, I've not made much progress."

"I promised Joy you'd sort this out for her."

"It's not through a lack of trying."

"What have you found out so far?"

"I've looked around the manufacturing unit, and I'm happy that the toys are okay when they leave there."

"The problem must be at the warehouse, then."

"I visited there too, and the toys are fine when they're despatched."

"Have you checked the delivery vans?"

"Of course. All the faulty toys seem to have been delivered by the same driver."

"Then he must be behind it."

"That's what I thought, but having spoken to him, I don't think so."

"Are you sure? It wouldn't be the first time someone has managed to pull the wool over your eyes."

"I'm sure, and besides, the owners of the shops all insist that the toys are fine when they're delivered. It's only later, after they've been purchased, that they develop faults."

"Why didn't you say that at the outset? It's obvious what's happening."

"Not to me it isn't."

"If you're absolutely sure that the toys are okay at the point that they're sold, but then go on to develop faults, there's only one explanation."

"Which is?"

"Someone is casting delayed action spells on them."

"I hadn't thought of that, but I guess it would explain what's happening."

"That type of spell is very difficult to get right, so if I'm correct, this is the work of a master witch or wizard."

"What do you suggest I do?"

"First, you need to confirm that's what's actually happening."

"How am I supposed to do that?"

"You'll need a sniffpecker."

"A what?"

"Don't tell me you haven't heard of sniffpeckers. They're like woodpeckers, but they can sniff out delayed action spells."

"Are you sure you aren't making this up?"

"I have better things to do with my time than to mess with your head. Look them up if you don't believe me."

"Okay, I believe you, but where would I find one?"

"In the local bakery."

"Really?"

"No, not really. They're birds. Where do you think you'll find them?"

"At a pet shop, maybe?"

"Possibly. You should check Candlefield Pages."

"Okay, I'll do that. Thanks, Grandma."

Feeling a little more positive about the Joy's Toys case, I magicked myself back into my office.

"Jill!" Jules dropped the cup of tea she'd been carrying. "Where did you appear from?"

Oh bum! She must have brought the tea through just as I'd magicked myself back to the office. There was no good way of talking my way out of this, so I did the only thing I could: I cast the 'forget' spell.

Still looking a little confused, Jules looked down at the broken cup. "I'm so sorry, Jill, I don't know what happened."

"Don't worry about it."

"I'll go and make you another one and then I'll clear up this mess."

"Okay."

Once she was out of the room, Winky said, "Well?"

"I think I've cracked it. Give me the tablets."

Once he'd handed them to me, I placed them under a folder on my desk.

"Why are you doing that?"

"You'll see." I cast the concealed object version of the 'shrink' spell, removed the folder, and then handed the tiny tablets to him. "Take those and tell me when you've swallowed them."

He took them from me, put them on his tongue, and swallowed. As soon as he gave me the nod, I reversed the spell.

"That should do it."

The words were no sooner out of my mouth than he grabbed his throat.

Oh bum! I must have messed up the reversing of the

spell, and he was choking on the tablets.

"Winky!" I picked him up and tried to figure out how to deliver the Heimlich manoeuvre on a cat. "Don't panic! It's going to be alright."

"You should see your face." He laughed.

"How could you do that?" I dropped him onto the desk. "I thought you were dying."

"I'm already dead, remember?"

***

I magicked myself to Aunt Lucy's house and found her playing in the garden with Barry and Buddy.

"Hey, Jill." Barry came bounding over to greet me.

Buddy managed only a nod of his head.

"Hey, how are you both?"

"I'm great!" Barry said. "Have you come to play?"

"I can't today. I've just come to ask Aunt Lucy a favour. What about you, Buddy? How are you?"

"As well as can be expected under the circumstances."

"What's wrong?"

"Take no notice of him," Aunt Lucy said. "He's just upset because the vet said he needed to lose a little weight."

"That man is an idiot." Buddy sighed.

"What did you want, Jill?" Aunt Lucy asked.

"Just to borrow your Candlefield Pages, please."

"It's inside the house, next to the phone. What are you looking for?"

"Someone who can supply me with a sniffpecker."

"A what?"

"I'm glad that was your reaction. Grandma made me

feel like I was stupid because I'd never heard of them. To hear her talk, she made it sound like I was the only person in Candlefield who didn't know what they are."

"Are you sure she didn't just make it up? You know what she's like."

"She seemed genuine enough, but who knows with her. Let me go and take a look in Candlefield Pages."

"I'll come with you. I'm interested to know now too."

Aunt Lucy picked up the directory. "There are two sections on sniffpeckers: for sale and for hire."

"Let me see." I took the directory from her. "I don't need to buy one. Rental should be fine."

There were two companies listed under sniffpecker rentals: Sniffpeckers R Us and Not To Be Sniffed At. In recognition of the more original name, I decided to give Not To Be Sniffed At a call first.

"N-T-B-S-A. Norman speaking. How can I help you today?"

"Hi, I was hoping to speak to someone about hiring a sniffpecker."

"Then you're through to the right place. How can I help?"

"I've never had occasion to do this before. Might it be better if I pop over there and discuss it with you?"

"Sure. When would you like to come?"

"I can magic myself straight over to you now if that's okay?"

"Absolutely. Do you have our address?"

"I do. I'll be with you in one, two—"

"That was quick," Norman said. "Aren't you Jill Maxwell?"

"I am."

"Just wait until I tell my brother that I've had you in the shop today. He's a massive fan of yours. Mind you, I always thought you were a bit overrated."

"Right, I—"

"I'm just kidding. We both had a poster of you in our bedroom." He blushed. "That sounds a bit bad, doesn't it? It was just one of you fighting a dragon. Nothing, err—you know. Anyway, you said you were interested in hiring a sniffpecker."

"I think so. I've been given to believe that they are capable of sniffing out delayed action spells."

"Then you've been informed correctly. They're the only creature in the sup world capable of such a thing."

"Great. How exactly does it work? How do they do it?"

"It's all very simple. I assume you're familiar with those dogs that are used to sniff out drugs in the human world?"

"Of course."

"It's pretty much the same. You simply allow the sniffpecker to fly free in the area where you suspect a delayed action spell may be present, and if you're right, the bird will soon let you know. Does that sound like the kind of thing you're looking for?"

"It certainly does. What does it cost to hire a sniffpecker?"

"As you might imagine, the sniffpecker's skillset is in great demand, which means their services command a premium price."

I didn't like the sound of that.

"How much?"

"Fifty pounds."

"Per week?"

He grinned.
"Per day?"
"Per hour."
"Fifty pounds per hour? You can't be serious."
"I'm deadly serious, and I should warn you that we're expecting prices to go up within the next month."
"Don't you set the price?"
"No. The sniffpecker's union sets the price. We simply take a small commission for each project we arrange. Are you still interested?"
"I don't really have any choice."
"Excellent. Why don't you come with me, and you can meet the guys, and decide who you'd like to work with."
"Do I get to pick the sniffpecker?"
"Of course. Here at N-T-B-S-A, we believe it's important you find a sniffpecker you're comfortable working with."
"Okay, let's go see them."
Norman led the way across the shop, and through an arch, into a smaller room that was full of cages. I was immediately overwhelmed by the number of tiny eyes staring at me from all sides. Surprisingly, though, the room was quite silent.
"Are these all sniffpeckers?" I whispered.
"They are."
"They're very quiet."
"Sniffpeckers are quiet by nature. Until they get to know you, that is. Then the problem is trying to shut them up."
"I heard that, Norm," said a red and green sniffpecker in the cage closest to us.
"No offence intended, Jimmy." Norman grinned.
"Who's your pretty friend?" Jimmy, the sniffpecker,

enquired.

"This is Jill Maxwell; the most famous witch in all of Candlefield."

"Does that mean you're loaded?" Jimmy said.

"I'm afraid not."

"Pity. I'm thinking of retiring, and I was hoping to find someone who can keep me in the manner I'd like to become accustomed to."

"I'm definitely not who you're looking for, then. I can barely pay the mortgage every month. I am hoping to hire a sniffpecker if you're interested, though."

"Wouldn't you like to check out the others first?" Norman interjected.

"Be quiet, Norman," Jimmy snapped. "The lady wants me." He turned to me. "What's the gig?"

I told him about the issues affecting Joy's Toys, and my suspicions that delayed action spells may be involved.

"What do you think, Jimmy?" I said. "Is that something that would interest you?"

"Definitely. It sounds a lot more interesting than most of the jobs I get these days."

"Great."

Chapter 24

I was becoming increasingly concerned that I'd heard nothing from Edna since I'd hired her to watch Robert Shafto's house. She was supposed to report to me every time he had a visitor, but that was three days ago, and I'd had no communication from her since. I found it hard to believe that no one had visited the house in that time. Edna had always been cranky, but I'd never had reason to question her work ethic. It was always possible that she'd taken ill, so to put my mind at ease, I gave her a call.

"Yes?"

"Edna?"

"Who else would be answering my phone?"

"Right. Sorry. I thought I'd better check in because I haven't heard anything from you."

"That's because there's been nothing to report."

"Hasn't he had a single visitor since last Friday?"

"No. Except for the postman, but I figured you wouldn't be interested in him."

Normally, I would have agreed with her, but based upon my recent experience with Postman Pat, I was no longer so trusting.

"Have you seen Shafto since the postman called?"

"Yeah, he went shopping this morning and came back about ten minutes ago."

"Did you follow him?"

"That wasn't my brief. You told me to report if he had any visitors. Nothing else."

"I'm going to have to change the brief."

"Changes to a brief, once the case is underway, attract an additional charge."

"Course they do," I said under my breath.

"What did you say?"

"Nothing. That's okay, but I want you to follow him if he goes out again. I want to know if he talks to anyone."

"Okay."

"And, Edna, I want you to let me know if anyone comes to the house. Anyone at all."

"Even the postman?"

"Yeah. Anyone and everyone."

"Okay, will do."

I was just about to return to the office when I got a phone call from Jack. He rarely called me during the daytime, so my first thought was that something must be wrong. It turned out that I was right.

"Jill?" He sounded terrible.

"What's wrong?"

"I've had to go home because I'm sick."

"*Throwing up* sick?"

"Yes. Monty and Kiki have come down with whatever this is too."

"Who's manning the store?"

"No one. That's why I'm calling. I wondered if there was any chance you might be able to do it this afternoon. I know it's a longshot, and if you've got stuff you need to do, it's—"

"It's okay. I can do it. I'll get over there as quickly as I can. Do you want me to pick anything up for you on my way back?"

"No, thanks. Gotta go."

Judging by the speed with which he had ended the call, I assumed he was headed back to the bathroom.

After calling Jules to let her know what I was doing, I drove back to Middle Tweaking. Before heading to the store, I parked at the Old Watermill and went inside to check on Jack. I found him lying in bed; he looked even worse than he'd sounded on the phone.

"Don't come too close." He held up his hand. "I don't want you to catch whatever this is."

"Do you need me to get you anything?"

"No, I'm going to try to get some sleep. Sorry about this. I know how busy you are."

"It's okay. Get your head down and I'll see you tonight."

I walked through the village to the store where a certain someone was standing outside the door.

"Why is this place closed?" Grandma demanded.

"Jack is sick. He had to go home."

"Typical human. What about those assistants of his? That Ivers bloke and the pretty young woman."

"They're both sick too. Do you really think Kiki is pretty?"

"Who's going to serve me with my hoops?"

"Hoops?"

"Spaghetti hoops. I thought I had a tin left, but I must have miscalculated."

"I'm here to open up the store."

"You? Do you even know where anything is?"

"Of course I do." Sort of.

I unlocked the door and, as soon as I stepped inside, the alarm began to sound.

"Turn off that awful noise!" Grandma snapped. "It'll damage my eardrums."

"I can't remember the code," I confessed.

"How can you not know?"

"I never open up the store. I'll call Jack."

"What's wrong?" he said.

"I don't know the code for the alarm."

"Three, double one, three."

"Thanks."

I punched in the code, and thankfully, the alarm stopped. I'd expected Grandma to follow me, but she remained outside.

"I thought you wanted some hoops?"

"I do but I'm not going in there. If Jack and the others are all sick, there must be some bug lurking inside."

She was right. Why else would all three of them have gone down with sickness at the same time? Great!

"Hurry up with those hoops, then!" Grandma said.

It took me a couple of minutes, but I managed to locate the spaghetti hoops.

"That'll be one pound twenty-five."

"Put it on my account. I'll pay that human of yours when he's recovered."

I couldn't be bothered to argue, so I handed her the tin and off she went. The last thing I'd expected to be doing that day was running the store, but how hard could it be? Jack would never admit it, but he had the easier end of our partnership. While I was running around the human and sup worlds, trying to solve any number of cases, all he had to do was sit around, waiting for the next customer to appear. Yes, I realise he had to take deliveries and put out stock, but he also had a couple of assistants to help him. The more I thought about it, the more I realised he actually had the life of Riley. The next few hours were going to be a cakewalk for me. I'd just put up my feet and picked up a magazine when the doorbell chimed, and in walked five human-sized penguins.

Was this a dream? No, I hadn't had time to fall asleep.

"Are your cheeses artisan?" asked the lead penguin, who by now I'd figured out was actually a man wearing a costume.

"Sorry?"

"I wondered if your cheeses are artisan."

Artisan was one of those terms which, if I'm being honest, I'd never really understood. Whenever I'd come across shops that included the word artisan in their name, they were always ridiculously expensive. The cheese we sold was quite reasonably priced, so I figured it couldn't be artisan.

"No, it isn't."

"How disappointing." Sighed the lead penguin.

"Are you here for a convention?"

"Indeed. It's Antarctic Con."

"Polar bears and that kind of thing, then?"

"Certainly not," said one of the other penguins. "Polar bears live in the arctic. This con is strictly for Antarctic creatures only."

"My mistake. I guess that's just penguins, then, is it?"

"Absolutely not. There are dolphins, whales, and seals, to mention just a few."

"And many different types of penguins," said the lead penguin. "We're King Penguins."

"I'm honoured to have you in my humble establishment, your highnesses. I'm sorry about the cheese. Is there anything else I can get for you?"

"I have a list." With some difficulty, he managed to produce a list from somewhere inside his costume.

"Normally, we'd help ourselves, but it isn't easy in these costumes, as you can see. Is there any chance you could get this lot together and we'll pop back in an hour to pick it up?"

"I guess so." I took the list from him.

So much for my lazy afternoon. Still, it shouldn't take too long to gather this all together. I'd just made a start on collecting the items on the list when the doorbell chimed again. I returned to the counter to find five penguins standing there.

"I thought we'd agreed an hour," I said.

"Sorry?" said one of the penguins.

"You said you'd come back in an hour to pick up your shopping."

"There seems to be some confusion. We've only just walked into the store."

It was only then that I took a closer look at the penguins.

"You aren't *King* penguins, are you?"

"Certainly not. We're Emperors."

"That explains my confusion. I've just had five King penguins in here."

"That'll be Wayne and his clan. I hope they didn't give you any trouble."

"No, they were fine. They asked me to pick their shopping because their costumes made it difficult for them to do it."

"Because they're lazy asses, more like—pardon my language. They do the same at every con they attend."

"I really don't mind. Would you like me to pick your shopping for you to collect later?"

"We wouldn't hear of it, would we boys?"

The assembled penguins made it clear they wouldn't.

"We'll get our own shopping, but if it's okay with you, we'd like to pay separately."

"That's fine."

In theory, them picking their own shopping should have made my job much easier, but in practice, it didn't quite work out that way. The aisles in the store are wide enough for our regular customers, but it turns out that a man dressed in an Emperor Penguin costume is a totally different proposition. Things became particularly difficult when two penguins tried to squeeze past each other. The result of this congestion was that tins and packets of food were knocked onto the floor, right, left and centre.

"Stop! Stop! You're wrecking the place."

"I'm so sorry," said one of the Emperor penguins. "This store is much smaller than the supermarkets where we usually shop. We'll pick everything up."

"Don't bother. I'll do it, but it might be better if you leave me your lists, and I'll pick your shopping for you."

"Are you sure?"

"Absolutely, but you'd better give me a couple of hours."

"That's very kind. And we're sorry for the disruption."

After they'd handed me their lists, they went on their way.

I'd just finished picking the shopping for the King penguins, and I was about to start on the Emperor penguins' lists when Mrs Johnson came through the door.

"It's happening again, Jill," she said. "But this time it's penguins that I'm seeing. I really do think I should go back to Doctor Fuller and ask him to change my pills."

"There's really no need to do that, Mrs Johnson. Do you remember I told you that it's just people dressed up for a convention?"

"Yes, dear, but that was rabbits and hedgehogs. I've just seen a group of penguins."

"It's still just people wearing costumes. There really is nothing to worry about. I promise."

"If you say so, dear, but it all seems rather peculiar."

I only just managed to put together the orders for the Emperor and King penguins in time. Fortunately, they didn't both return to the store at the same time because I had the distinct impression that they didn't get along too well.

I'd just finished serving a blue whale when a man dressed in a grey uniform came through the door. He had a clipboard in his hand and a puzzled expression on his face.

"What's going on around here?" he said. "There's loads of weirdos walking around dressed like penguins out there."

"They're here for the convention at the hotel."

"Nutters, if you ask me."

"What can I get for you?"

"I have a delivery for you, but I'm new to this route, and I think there might have been a mix-up."

"Oh?"

"Yeah, look." He put the delivery note onto the counter. "See."

"What am I supposed to be looking at, exactly?"

"That item there." He pointed with the tip of his pen. "They obviously got the quantities mixed up."

"The custard creams, you mean?"

"They've got you down for twelve boxes. Even the big supermarkets don't take more than ten. Shall I just leave you the one and take the rest back?"

"No."

"You don't have to take them if you didn't order them. They'll issue you with a credit."

"The quantity is correct."

"Twelve boxes? Really? Are you sure?"

"Positive. The people around here really like custard creams. In fact, there's even a custard cream society in the village."

"Takes all sorts, I suppose. Shall I take everything through to the back?"

"Yes, please, but you can leave one box of custard creams out here because I noticed earlier that we were getting low on stock."

"No problem."

After finally closing the store for the day, I returned to the old watermill where I was surprised to find Jack preparing dinner.

"I thought you'd still be in bed."

"I started to come around a couple of hours ago and I feel fine now."

"Are you sure you're okay to eat? Might you be better waiting until the morning?"

"It'll be fine. I actually feel quite hungry. How did you get on at the store? Any problems?"

"Only the penguins."

"Oh yeah." He grinned. "I should have warned you about Antarctic Con."

"How come they're here already?"

"The convention is being held midweek, apparently."

"Poor old Mrs Johnson was a bit freaked out again." I took four packets of custard creams out of my bag and placed them in the cupboard.

"I hope you paid for those."

"You can take it out of the wages you owe me for this afternoon."

"Hmm."

"Will you need any help in the store tomorrow?"

"No. I'll be firing on all cylinders by then."

"What about Ivers and Lashes?"

"I suspect Monty and *Kiki* will both be okay by the morning."

"You can't know that for sure. People all react differently to viruses."

"It wasn't a virus."

"How do you know?"

"Monty brought in some sausage rolls for us this morning. He'd made them himself."

"He poisoned you all?"

"Not deliberately."

"You didn't mention that when you called me earlier."

"I was too busy throwing up. It wasn't until this afternoon that the penny dropped."

"That's a relief, actually. I was worried I might come down with the virus next. Whatever possessed you to eat something Ivers had made?"

"The sausage rolls looked really nice. I'm sorry I had to drag you away from your cases. Has it caused you any problems?"

"Not really. I've done with the Beasley case."

"What happened in the end?"

"It turned out to be his postman who was trying to blackmail him."

"Has he been arrested?"

"No, Beasley doesn't want the police involved."

"I think you should inform them, anyway."

"That's the policeman in you talking. Have you forgotten you've retired?"

"I'm just saying. What about Goldie's murder? Any progress on that?"

"I'm not sure. I should know more within the next couple of days."

Chapter 25

Jack was eating a bowl of muesli when I came downstairs the next morning.

"If you can eat that mush, you must be feeling okay."

"I feel great, and I've had a text from Monty. He's fine too, and he's already opened the store."

"Have you heard from Lashes?"

"Not yet, but I'm sure Kiki will be okay too."

I'd just poured out a bowlful of my vastly healthier cereal when I received a call from Edna who said, "Milkman."

"Sorry?"

"You told me you wanted to know if anyone went to Shafto's door. The milkman has just been. He left one pint of semi-skimmed if you're interested."

"Did he speak to Shafto?"

"Why would he speak to him? Does your milkman have a chat with you every time he drops off a bottle of milk?"

"I just want to make absolutely sure it was a milkman and not someone pretending to be one."

"It was definitely the milkman. He was driving a milk-float."

"Okay. Keep watching."

"For how much longer? This is really boring."

"For as long as it takes. Let me know if anyone else goes to his door."

"Anything important?" Jack asked.

"I've got someone watching the house of a guy called Robert Shafto."

"As in—"

"Bobby Shafto? Yeah."

"Does this have anything to do with Goldie's murder?"

"We think it might do."

"*We*?"

"Daze and Blaze are working with me."

My phone rang again.

"It's me again," Edna said.

"What's happened now?"

"The postman has just called at the house. And before you ask, I'm sure he was a postman on account of the sack of letters he was carrying."

"Did he speak to Shafto?"

"No, he just put the letters through the letterbox and then left."

"Okay. Keep watching."

"An update?" Jack asked.

"Nothing important."

"Will you be going over there?"

"No, I have an appointment with a sniffpecker this morning."

"A *what*?"

***

The sniffpecker's hourly rate was ridiculously high, but to be fair to Jimmy, he'd been quite flexible in order to keep the number of hours I needed him to a minimum. He'd agreed to meet me outside Joy's Toys warehouse at ten o'clock, which gave me time to pop into the office first.

"Jill, I'm glad I bumped into you," Petty said, as I stepped out of the lift.

That made only one of us.

"Good morning, Mr Petty. I'm really pushed for time

this morning."

I tried to sidestep him, but he was too quick for me, and he managed to block my way.

"This will only take a minute. I wanted to ask for your take on windows."

"I don't much care for it, but then I never was very good with computers."

"No, I mean the windows in the building. You must have some thoughts on them."

My first thought was that I'd like to pitch him headfirst out of one.

"Not really. What do you mean?"

"I mean the standard of cleaning. You must have noticed they're missing the corners."

"I can't say I—"

"You have to wonder what we're paying the management fees for."

"Right, but like I said, I really am pushed—"

"You'll be pleased to know that I've started a petition." He held out said petition and offered me a pen. "I'm sure you'll want to sign it."

A quick glance at it revealed that the only signature so far was Petty's, and although I didn't like the idea of being ripped off by the management company, neither did I want to earn a reputation as a troublemaker because the last thing I needed was to have to relocate offices again.

"I'd rather not." I handed him back the pen.

"But, Jill, what will your clients think when they see the state of your windows?"

"My clients usually have much more important things on their minds than the cleanliness or otherwise of my windows."

"But—"

"Tell you what: If you manage to gather one hundred signatures, come and see me again, and I'll add my name. Now, if you don't mind."

I brushed past him before he had the chance to argue.

"I think they must have fixed the wi-fi, Jill," Jules said. "That awful flashing has stopped."

"That's good. Any messages?"

"Nothing. Tea?"

"No, thanks. I have to go out again in a few minutes."

Winky had stopped flashing.

"I've stopped flashing," he confirmed.

"That's good. The tablets worked, I assume?"

"Like a dream. What did that nutter from next-door want this time?"

"He doesn't think the windows in this building are being cleaned properly."

"To be fair, he has a point." Winky jumped onto the nearest windowsill. "Just take a look in the corners. Very sloppy work."

"I honestly don't care."

"I know some guys who would do a better job for half the price."

"The management company aren't going to employ cats to clean their windows."

"Who said anything about cats? I'm talking about Spick and Span."

"Who's that?"

"A couple of geezers who work out of the arches near the canal."

"And you know them, how?"

"An old buddy of mine, Jonjo, lives with them."

"Is Jonjo a cat?"

"Of course. I could ask him to get them to contact the management company if you like."

"How long is it since you spoke to Jonjo?"

"I'm not sure. Quite a few years ago now."

"Before you died, you mean?"

"Probably. Oh yeah, I'd forgotten I was dead. I guess I won't be able to speak to him, will I?"

"I doubt it."

"It sucks being a ghost."

***

Mickey Michaels had seemed genuinely upset that all the faulty toys had been delivered by his van, and he was adamant that he had no idea how it could have happened. Joy was convinced that Mickey would never do anything to damage the business, and having met him, if only briefly, I tended to agree with her assessment.

Grandma's theory about the delayed action spells made sense, but I needed Jimmy, the sniffpecker, to test out that theory. To that end, I'd arranged to meet him in a bus shelter close to Joy's Toys warehouse. I arrived there a few minutes early, and I was impressed to find Jimmy was already perched on the shelter.

"Hey, Jill."

"Jimmy. All set?"

"Absolutely, what's the plan?"

"The toys are all perfect when they leave this warehouse, but a considerable number develop unexplained faults after they've been delivered to the shops. I suspect someone is casting delayed action spells on some of the toys before they leave the warehouse. I need you to go inside and check out all the toys waiting to be despatched, to see if you can sniff out any delayed action spells."

"I can do that."

"The thing is I don't want the people in the warehouse to know that you're there because you might spook whoever is behind this."

"I'm not sure how we can avoid that. People are bound to see me flying around."

"Not if I make you invisible."

"*Invisible*?" He gulped. "I'm not sure about that. Won't it hurt?"

"No, you won't feel a thing, I promise. Watch." I made myself invisible for just a few seconds. "See. Nothing to it."

"Okay, I guess. What's the plan, then?"

"Do you see that open window up there?"

"Yeah."

"That's in the main despatch department. After I've made you invisible, I want you to fly through it and check out all the packages in there. When you're done, meet me back here and tell me what you've found."

"No problem."

"Any idea how long it will take you?"

"Shouldn't take long. Half-an-hour tops."

"Great. Are you ready?"

"As ready as I'll ever be."

I cast the 'invisible' spell on him.

"There. All done."

"Is that it?"

"Yeah."

"Can't you see me?"

"I can, but no one else can."

"Cool. Just wait until I tell the guys back at the shop about this." He flew up to the open window and disappeared inside.

The wait was excruciating because everything hinged on what Jimmy discovered. If, as I suspected, he found evidence of delayed action spells, I would know someone inside the warehouse was responsible for the sabotage.

After just under twenty minutes, Jimmy reappeared and flew down to join me in the shelter.

"That was amazing," he said. "No one had a clue I was in there even though I flew right by them."

"What did you find?"

"Nothing."

"*Nothing*?"

"Zilch! There are no delayed action spells in there."

"Are you sure?"

"Absolutely. One hundred per cent."

To say I felt deflated would have been an understatement. I'd been sure that he was going to find evidence of delayed action spells in the warehouse. It seemed that Grandma's theory was wrong after all, and I was back at square one.

"Okay. I'd better make you visible again."

"Pity. I was having fun being invisible. I'm really sorry that I didn't find anything helpful."

"That's okay."

***

"Why the long face?" Winky asked.

"I thought I'd cracked the toy case but the sniffpecker drew a blank."

"The *what*?"

"Sniffpecker. It's a bird, a bit like a woodpecker that can sniff out delayed action spells."

"I'll just pretend that sentence made even a lick of sense, shall I?"

"The bottom-line is I'm all out of ideas with that case."

Winky was just about to respond—no doubt with some wisecrack—when his demeanour changed, and he shot under the sofa. That could mean only one thing.

"Grandma, how many times do I have to ask you to come up in the lift like everyone else?"

"I'm not everyone else, and besides, I have exciting news."

"Really."

"Aren't you going to ask me what it is?"

"No."

"My patent application has been approved."

"Whoop de doo."

"You could at least pretend to be pleased for me."

"Why should I care when I don't even know what the patent is for?"

"I can tell you now that it's been approved: It's for a wandroom."

"A what?"

"It's a combination of the words wand and broom: Wandroom."

"And what does it do, exactly?"

"I would have thought that was obvious, even to you. It's a broom that can convert to a wand, and vice versa. Every witch in Candlefield will want one."

"I won't."

"The biggest problem is going to be keeping up with demand."

"If you say so."

"What's wrong with you today? Why are you being so grouchy?"

"I'm still getting nowhere with the Joy's Toys case."

"I told you what was happening there: it's delayed action spells."

"I thought you were right at first, particularly after I took a jigsaw home from Joy's Toys. It was perfect when I got it to the office, but then later that same day, one of the pieces went missing."

"Exactly. A delayed action spell if ever I've seen one."

"Yeah, but I've just had a sniffpecker check the warehouse and he found no evidence of delayed action spells."

"In that case, someone must be casting the delayed action spells while the toys are in transit. Have you had the sniffpecker check the vans?"

"No. It would be a waste of time."

"Why do you say that?"

"Because the jigsaw I took home had never been inside one of the delivery vans. Joy had handed it personally to the toy shop owner, with a batch of others, by way of an apology for all the problems he'd experienced."

"That is weird. I wish I could stay around and help, but I have to find someone who can manufacture the wandrooms in quantity. I know something that will cheer you up, though."

"What's that?"

"When I get the first batch of wandrooms, I'll let you

have—"

"I don't want a free wandroom."

"Who said anything about *free*? I was going to say that I'll let you have one at twenty percent discount."

Chapter 26

"Wandrooms!" I huffed.

"I think your grandmother has finally lost the plot," Winky said. "No one is going to buy her stupid wandrooms."

"If it was anyone else, I'd agree with you, but Grandma has a way of always coming out smelling of roses. Whereas I always end up smelling of—"

I was interrupted by a call from Edna.

"What?" I snapped.

"Who trod on your corns?"

"Sorry. What's happened now?"

"Nothing much, but you said you wanted me to tell you if anyone came to Shafto's door, so that's what I'm doing. The gas man has just arrived. To check the meter reading, I assume."

"Okay, keep watching. Hang on! Did you say *gas* man? Are you sure?"

"That's what it says on his uniform."

"That can't be right."

"Are you doubting my—?"

"I'm coming over there."

After magicking myself to Shafto's house, I looked around, but I couldn't see Edna.

"Up here!" She was perched on a branch of the tree at the end of his driveway.

"Where's the man?"

"He just went inside."

This was terrible; I might already be too late. I didn't waste time trying to explain to Edna what was happening. Instead, I magicked myself inside the house, to find Shafto lying on the floor. Standing over him was a man, dressed in a gas engineer's uniform. The man had a large spanner in his hand, and he was about to strike the prone figure of Shafto.

A lightning bolt to the centre of his back soon put paid to that, as it sent him flying across the room. The impact of his head against the wall was enough to lay him out cold.

"He attacked me," Shafto said.

"You're okay now." I held out my hand and helped him up. He was trembling from head to foot.

"Wasn't it you who came to see me the other day?"

"Yes, and if you recall, I warned you that something like this might happen."

"What did you just do to him?"

"I tasered him. He'll be okay in a few minutes."

"Who is he?"

"I don't know, but I have reason to believe he's already murdered a number of people."

"Was he going to kill me?"

"I believe so. You've had a nasty shock. Why don't you go and make yourself a drink while I secure this gentleman."

"I think I will. Do you want one?"

"No thanks."

While Shafto was in the kitchen, I used magic to tie up the man who had attacked him, then I made a call to Daze.

"Jill? What's happening? Any news from Shafto's?"

"Yeah, the murderer just made his move, but I was able to intervene before he had the chance to hurt Shafto."

"Thank goodness for that. We'll come straight over and drag his sorry backside to Candlefield."

Moments later, Daze and Blaze came to the door. I'd just let them in when Shafto came out of the kitchen.

"Who are these people?"

"It's okay, Mr Shafto, these are my colleagues. It might be best if you stay in the kitchen while we sort this lot out."

"Okay."

"Hey, buddy." Blaze gave the prone man a slight kick. "You're going to spend the rest of your miserable life behind bars."

"Well done, Jill," Daze said. "We'll take this lowlife off your hands now."

"Do you recognise him?"

"I can't say I do, but we should be able to put a name to him once we're back in Candlefield."

"About that."

"Yeah?"

"I don't want you to take him to Candlefield."

"What do you mean?" Blaze said.

"I brought this case to you because my client has been charged with the murder of his ex-wife. He's innocent. It was this lowlife who killed her, but the only way I can clear my client's name is if I can hand over this guy to the police here."

"We really should take him back," Daze said.

"I'm pretty sure he's committed other murders here in the human world. If you take him to Candlefield, those murders will remain unsolved. We owe it to the relatives of the victims to bring this guy to justice. It's the only way they'll get anything resembling closure."

"I hear what you're saying, Jill, but you're forgetting one thing."

"Which is?"

"The man is a wizard, so he'll be able to use magic to escape custody here."

"Not if you apply a magic-blocker."

"That's a drastic step. We'd have to get authorisation from the very top to do it."

"Then try. Please."

"Okay, I'll see what I can do. Let me make a couple of calls, but don't get your hopes up."

Daze stepped outside, leaving Blaze and me alone with the murderer, who was starting to come around.

"What did you do to me?" he said. "I'm in agony. I need a doctor."

"Shut up," Blaze said. "You're lucky Jill didn't finish you off."

"I have rights," he moaned.

Daze returned bearing good news. "They've agreed. We can block his magic and leave him for the authorities here to deal with."

"You can't do that!" the man protested. "I want to go back to Candlefield. I know my rights."

"You relinquished your rights when you decided to murder innocent people here in the human world," Daze said, then she turned to me. "You'd better go and stay with the victim while we sort this guy out."

"Okay. Thanks, Daze."

"What's happening?" Shafto said when I joined him in the kitchen.

"My colleagues are just processing the prisoner."

"What about me?"

"You'll have to make a statement."

"What's going to happen to the guy who attacked me?"

"He'll be charged with murder and attempted murder."

A few minutes later, after Daze had given me the thumbs up to indicate she'd blocked the wizard's magic, I made a call to Washbridge police.

Fifteen minutes later, Big Mac and a number of uniformed officers came to Shafto's door.

"What have you got for me this time, Maxwell?" Big Mac said. "My people said something about murder and attempted murder."

"That's right. The gentleman tied up through there attacked this man." I pointed to Shafto who had come out of the kitchen to find out what was happening.

"And who are you, sir?" Big Mac asked.

"My name is Rob Shafto. She's right. He attacked me. If it hadn't been for her, I'd most likely be dead."

"Okay, sir. This constable will drive you to the station, where the doctor will check you over. If he says you're okay to talk, we'll have a little chat later." Big Mac waited until Shafto was out of the room, and then said, "Care to tell me how you just happened to be here, Maxwell?"

"Because you recently charged my client, Liam Locks, with the murder of his ex-wife, Goldie Barr."

"Oh yes. I remember now. What's that got to do with any of this?"

"The guy in there, dressed as a gas engineer, came here to kill Rob Shafto. He's actually the person who murdered Goldie, and it's quite likely that he's responsible for at least another two murders. If you check his DNA, I'm sure you'll be able to confirm that."

"How come you just happened to be here when he made his move against Shafto?"

"I've been keeping a watch on Shafto's house for some

time, and when I spotted the gas man, I knew it was my man."

"How?"

"Because these houses don't have a gas supply. They're all electric."

"You mentioned a connection between the murders. Care to elaborate?"

"Sure. All of the victims have names connected to nursery rhyme characters: Goldie Locks, Cole King, Beau Peep and now Bobby Shafto."

"*Nursery rhyme characters*? You can't be serious."

"I'm deadly serious, but don't take my word for it. Run a check on the DNA found at all of those murder scenes. My guess is that it will match our friend here."

"We'll see."

As we spoke, two constables brought the attacker out in handcuffs.

"She attacked me with a thunderbolt!" he shouted to Big Mac.

"A *thunderbolt*?" Mac laughed.

"It's true. She's a witch. Ask her."

"I'll be sure to do that, sir. Take him away."

"You can't arrest me. I'm a wizard. I don't live in this world."

Big Mac waited until the man was out of the house, then said, "Something tells me he'll be pleading insanity."

"Looks that way."

"He called you a witch."

"I've been called much worse. Is it okay if I get off?"

"For now, but don't leave the country. I have a feeling I may need to talk to you again."

***

When I walked into the house, I could hear voices coming from the kitchen. I hoped Jack hadn't invited anyone over because I really wasn't in the mood for entertaining guests. Only when I put my ear to the kitchen door did I realise who he was talking to.

"Why are you talking to that teddy bear?" I said.

"Humph and I were just talking about—"

"I don't want to know what you were talking about. He's a teddy bear!"

"Don't mind me," Humphrey said. "Just act like I'm not here."

"Quiet, you!" I snapped. "Well, Jack?"

"Humph just happened to mention ten-pin bowling, so—"

"What does he know about ten-pin bowling?"

"You'd be surprised."

"I'm a big fan of bowling," Humph said. "Jack said he'd take me the next time he has a match."

"You said *what*? Are you insane? What will people think if you turn up with a teddy bear?"

"I'll say he's my lucky mascot. Lots of the guys have them."

"I give up."

By the time we sat down at the kitchen table, I'd managed to persuade Jack to take Humphrey upstairs, so we could eat in peace.

"I don't know why you're being so down on yourself," Jack said as we tucked into the pizza that we'd ordered in. "Two out of three isn't bad."

"I know, but I really wanted to get to the bottom of the toy case. Joy is such a lovely lady, and I hate to see her business being destroyed."

"I thought your grandmother had given you a lead there."

"She did, and I thought she was onto something, but that theory didn't pan out. Talking of Grandma, I discovered that her patent is for a wandroom."

"What's a *wandroom*?"

"You might well ask. It's a hybrid broom and wand."

"Is there a demand for those?"

"Grandma seems to think so, but I'm not convinced."

"Do you think they'll release Liam?"

"They'll have no choice if the DNA proves the guy who tried to kill Rob Shafto committed all of the other murders."

"How was your buddy Big Mac?"

"Not as big a prat as usual, but that isn't saying much. I think he was a bit distracted by the murderer claiming he was a wizard and that I was a witch."

"I wish I could have been there to see that. Won't he just be able to use magic to escape, though?"

"No. Daze got authorisation to put a block on his magic."

"This is really good pizza." Jack took the last slice out of the box.

"Hey, that's my piece," I said.

"No, it isn't. There were six slices, and you've already had three."

"Are you sure? I thought I'd only had two so far."

"I'm positive."

"I think you're wrong. I reckon you've had three

already. How about we split that last piece?"

"Let me think about that." Jack hesitated for a moment. "Nah." Then took a large bite.

"Are you still sulking about the pizza?" he asked ten minutes later when we'd moved through to the lounge.

"I'm not sulking."

"You could have fooled me."

"I never—" I stopped mid-sentence and stared at the completed jigsaw on the coffee table.

"I ought to put that away," Jack said.

"Hold on. It's complete."

"Yeah, I found the missing piece last night."

"Where?"

"It had dropped down behind one of the cushions on the sofa."

"Why didn't you tell me this morning?"

"I didn't think you'd be interested."

"Don't you see what this means?"

"That I was able to finish off the jigsaw?"

"It means that the piece hadn't magically gone missing between the time Winky completed it successfully, and when you and Gregor tried to do it."

"I still can't get over the idea of Winky doing it."

"He's something of a whizz when it comes to jigsaws, but that isn't the point."

"Isn't it? I would have thought a cat doing a jigsaw was a pretty big deal, particularly a dead cat."

"Never mind Winky. This means that Grandma's theory about delayed magic could still hold true."

"Sorry, but you've lost me now."

"It's too complicated to even try to explain. Let's just

say, I'm going to need the services of a sniffpecker again."

"I still have no idea what that is."

Chapter 27

"The name just doesn't make sense," Jack said at breakfast.

"Let it go, Jack. What does it matter?"

"I'm just saying that a woodpecker's name makes sense because the bird pecks at wood, but this bird of yours can't peck at a sniff."

"I've already said I agree with you, so why are you still going on about it? Isn't it time you headed to the store?"

"You're right." He popped one last spoonful of muesli into his mouth, put the bowl in the sink, and then gave me a muesli-flavoured kiss.

"I wish you wouldn't kiss me after you've eaten that muck."

"I'll see you tonight. Good luck with the sniffer bird."

As soon as he was out of the door, I made a call to Not To Be Sniffed At.

"N-T-B-S-A, Norman speaking. How can I help you today?"

"Hi, Norman, it's Jill Maxwell."

"Hey, Jill. I was sorry to learn that Jimmy drew a blank for you."

"It's okay because I've realised I might have been looking in the wrong place."

"Oh?"

"Is Jimmy free today, by any chance?"

"Hold on while I check the diary. He's actually booked up all afternoon."

"Does that mean he's free this morning?"

"Yeah. Until midday."

"Great. Can I book him from nine-thirty?"

"Sure. No problem."

"Would you ask him to meet me at the same place as last time?"

"Will do, and I hope you have more luck this time."

"Me too."

I'd just finished on the call when Daze rang me.

"Are you free, Jill?"

"I have a meeting with a sniffpecker in just over an hour."

"I've heard of those things, but I've never seen one in action. Are they as good as they say?"

"I hope so."

"Are you at home?"

"Yeah."

"By yourself?"

"Yeah, Jack's just gone to the store."

"Could I pop over there now? I'd like to update you on our friend, the nursery rhyme guy."

"Sure. I'll put the kettle on."

I'd no sooner put the water in the kettle than there was a knock at the door.

"You didn't have to knock, Daze. You could have just come straight in."

"I don't like to do that."

"Come in. Tea will be just a minute."

Once we had our drinks, we sat at the kitchen table.

"What did the police say?" Daze asked.

"They were happy to arrest him for the attack on Bobby Shafto, but Big Mac was more sceptical about him being some kind of serial killer."

"*Big Mac*?"

"He's the head honcho. He's a pain in the backside most

of the time, but once he's seen the DNA evidence, I have a feeling he'll come around."

"I have some info on the murderer."

"Have you identified him?"

"Yes. He goes by the name of Horatio Northwind."

"Does he have a criminal record in Candlefield?"

"He does, but not under that name. His real name is Georgie Porgie."

"Seriously?"

"Yeah. By all accounts, he had a miserable childhood. Kids picked on him because of his name. Understandably, he changed it as soon as he was old enough, but the experience had taken a toll."

"So, he decided to murder people who also had nursery rhyme names?"

"Apparently."

"That doesn't make any sense."

"To him it clearly does."

"Why did he attack people in the human world rather than in the sup world?"

"I'm not sure we'll ever know, but I'd speculate he thought there would be less chance of being caught here. Or maybe because the nursery rhymes originated here."

"I can sympathise with what he went through as a child but that doesn't excuse what he did. That was pure evil."

"Agreed." She stood up. "I'd better let you go and meet your sniffpecker."

"Thanks for the update, Daze."

***

Jimmy, the sniffpecker, was waiting for me at the bus

shelter.

"I didn't expect to hear from you again, Jill. I was really surprised when Norman told me you had another job for me."

"It's actually the same job."

"Really? I checked the despatch department thoroughly last time. Do you think someone has cast spells in there since then?"

"No. I now believe that the delayed action spells are being cast while the toys are en route. I want you to check the packages in the van."

"Do you think the delivery driver is doing it?"

"His name is Mickey Michaels, and he's a werewolf, so he can't be the one casting the spells. But someone is doing it and I'm sure it's happening in the van."

"Okay. What do you need me to do?"

"Mickey's van is scheduled to leave in about twenty-minutes."

"How do I get inside?"

"Same as last time. I'll make you invisible and then magic you inside. How long will it take you to check all the packages?"

"Impossible to say without seeing them."

"I've checked Mickey's delivery schedule. His first drop-off is about an hour away at Gregg's Toys and Games. How about I meet you there, and you can tell me what you've found?"

"Sounds like a plan."

Once I'd magicked the invisible Jimmy into Mickey's van, I magicked myself to Gregg's Toys & Games. Two doors down from there was a small coffee shop where I availed myself of coffee and cake, to keep me going while I waited.

What? Okay, it wasn't all that small. Satisfied?

The coffee shop was practically empty, so I was able to sit on a stool by the window, from where I had a great view of the toy shop. After an hour, I began to wonder where Mickey's van was. After ninety minutes, I was beginning to get worried. Had something happened? Had Mickey been involved in a traffic accident? I was on the verge of calling Joy, to see if she'd heard anything when the van came around the corner and parked outside the shop. I watched as Mickey opened the doors and began to unload the packages. As soon as he was inside, I hurried towards the van.

"Jimmy! Where are you?"

"I'm here." The invisible bird suddenly perched on my shoulder.

I quickly reversed the 'invisible' spell on Jimmy and demanded impatiently, "What happened?"

"As soon as we set off from the warehouse, I checked every package in the van."

"And?"

"Nothing."

"Again?" I was devastated. "Oh well, I guess I got—"

"Hold on. I haven't finished yet. The driver stopped for breakfast at a roadside café."

"That explains why it took him longer than I expected to get here. I'd forgotten Mickey called at Kat's for breakfast."

"The bacon smelled amazing. It was torture having to stay in the van while he was enjoying a fry-up."

"That's all very interesting, but it doesn't help my

investigation."

"If you'd just allow me to finish, you might change your tune."

"Sorry. Carry on."

"While I was waiting in the back of the van, wishing I had one of those bacon sandwiches, some geezer wearing a purple suit suddenly appeared. And guess what he did?"

"Cast delayed action spells?"

"Got it in one."

"When you say he *appeared*?"

"That's exactly what happened. He appeared out of thin air. And, after he'd done casting his spells, he disappeared again. Puff! Just like that."

"He was a wizard, then?"

"I would guess so."

"Can you describe him?"

"I can do better than that." He handed me a photograph. "We sniffpecker's always carry an instant camera."

"You're a genius, Jimmy."

"You're only saying that because it's true."

***

When I called Joy to let her know that I'd solved the mystery of the faulty toys, she was delighted, and she asked me to go to the shop. As soon as I arrived there, Leaf ushered me straight through to see Joy.

"Is it true, Jill?" Joy said. "Have you really got to the bottom of it?"

"I have but I'm not sure you'll be too pleased to hear

what I've discovered."

"What do you mean? Why wouldn't I be?"

"I could kill for a cup of tea. I don't suppose—"

"Leaf!" She yelled at the top of her voice.

"Yes, Joy?" A breathless Leaf came rushing through the door.

"Make us some tea, would you? And bring in the custard creams."

Over tea and biscuits, I brought Joy up to date.

"I checked the manufacturing unit and the warehouse, and it was obvious that both were operating to the highest standards. It was only when I talked to the shop owners that a pattern began to emerge. It became clear that toys, which had arrived at the shops in perfect condition, were developing faults later—often after they'd been sold to their customers."

"But how can that be? If a toy is in perfect condition when it arrives at the shop, how can it then develop a fault?"

"That had me stumped too. It was my grandmother who worked out what was happening. She realised that someone must be casting delayed action spells on the toys, causing them to develop faults later."

"I had no idea there were such things as delayed action spells."

"They're very advanced and only a few witches and wizards are capable of casting them."

"Are you telling me that someone in the warehouse is casting these spells before the toys leave the building?"

"I thought that might be the case, but the sniffpecker ruled that out."

"The *what*?"

"Sniffpecker. They're birds who can detect the presence of delayed action spells. I had one check the warehouse and it came back all clear."

"If the spells aren't being cast in the warehouse, that must mean it's happening while the toys are in transit."

"That's correct."

"Are you saying Mickey has something to do with this?"

"No, he has no idea that this is happening."

"I'm confused. Who is doing it?"

"After leaving the warehouse, Mickey calls for breakfast at a roadside café called Kat's. While he's inside the diner, someone magics themself into the van, to cast the delayed action spells."

"Do you know who it is?"

"I do. That brings me to the part that you might not like." I took out the photo, which Jimmy had given me and handed it to her.

"James? Are you sure?"

"Positive. My assistant, the sniffpecker, took this photo while James was in the back of the van, casting the delayed action spells."

Joy looked as though all the wind had been knocked out of her.

"James and I have known each other for more years than I care to remember. I thought we were friends. Why would he do something like this?"

"Only he can answer that. Might it have something to do with his failed bid to buy your company?"

"I don't know. I suppose it could have."

"The question now is what you want me to do. Would you like me to take what I know to the authorities here?

I'm not sure exactly what crime he's committed but he must have committed at least one."

"No, don't do that."

"Why not?"

"The recent batch of faulty toys has already sparked some bad publicity. I don't want any more."

"What do you intend to do, then?"

"I think it's time I spoke to James, don't you?"

"Definitely. Would you like me to be with you when you do?"

"No, thanks. You've done your part, Jill. Now it's up to me to sort this out once and for all."

"Will you let me know how you get on?"

"I will, and you must let me have your invoice."

***

I was a little late getting home for dinner. Jack must have seen me arrive because he met me at the door.

"We have a dinner guest," he said.

"It's not Kathy, is it?"

"No. Come on through."

I followed him into the kitchen where I was delighted to find Florence seated at the table.

"Darling!" I threw my arms around her, but then pulled back. "What's wrong?"

"Nothing is wrong, Mum. Can't I have dinner with my parents once in a while?"

"Of course you can. Are you sure nothing is wrong, though?"

"Positive. Helen Peep told me that they've arrested someone for her father's murder. Apparently, the guy has murdered several other people too. I assume you must have had something to do with it because the police didn't seem to have a clue before."

"Your mother worked out that the killer was targeting people who had names based upon nursery rhyme characters," Jack said.

"He killed them because of their names?" Florence looked understandably horrified.

"It seems that way," I said. "Do you remember Goldie who lived just down the road?"

"Of course. Don't tell me she was one of his victims too?"

"I'm afraid so. Hopefully, this means that her ex-husband, Liam, will be released now. How is Helen?"

"Still not great, but she seemed relieved that they'd caught her father's murderer at least."

"It'll take her some time to recover. You'll need to support her."

"We will. Can we eat now?" Florence turned to Jack. "I really miss your dinners."

"What about mine?" I said.

For some unknown reason, that made them burst out laughing.

Chapter 28

The next morning, Jack was subdued over breakfast, and I thought I knew why.

"Are you wishing Florence was still here?" I said.

"Yeah, I'd forgotten how much I miss her."

"Me too. It was nice to have her with us for dinner last night, wasn't it?"

"Yeah. Do you think we did the right thing letting her go to CASS?"

"For who? Not for you and me, obviously; we'd both rather she lived here full time. But it's what she wants and that's what matters."

"You're right." He picked up the newspaper. I wasn't sure if he actually wanted to read it, or if he'd just done it to hide the tears I could hear in his voice.

We ate in silence for a couple of minutes and then he said, "What's our postman's name?"

"Sorry?"

"Do you know what our postman's name is?"

"Err, no. Why would I? I barely ever see him."

"There's an article here about a poor guy, named Pat, who fell downstairs and died. He's a postman, apparently."

"I don't believe it!"

"It's true. That's his name."

"I'm not talking about his name. Give me that." I snatched the paper from him.

"Hey, I was reading that."

"This is the postman who was blackmailing Beasley."

"The guy whose mother fell down the stairs? Hang on, you don't think—"

"That's precisely what I think." I stood up and started for the door.

***

Perhaps I was wrong. Perhaps it was just a coincidence. Plenty of people fell downstairs to their death. Who was I trying to kid? From the outset, Beasley had insisted he didn't want to go to the police for fear that they might think he'd killed his mother. Even when I'd unmasked his blackmailer, he'd insisted the police should not be involved. I was now convinced that he'd used me to identify his blackmailer, so that he could deal with him in his own way.

It was time to have a serious conversation with Mr Beasley.

When Beasley answered the door, I barely recognised him. He was clean-shaven, smartly dressed, and standing upright. He looked ten years younger than the last time I'd seen him.

"Hello, Jill, I didn't expect to see you again." He grinned. "Are you here to give me your invoice? You could have just posted it."

"That's not why I'm here."

"I'd invite you in for a drink, but I'm off to the gym in a few minutes."

"What about your bad back?"

"It's so much better, but thanks for asking."

"I suppose you heard what happened to your postman."

"Pat? Yes, I read about it. Such a tragedy."

"Do you take me for a fool, Bobby?"

"I don't know what you mean, Jill."

"I don't like being used, and I especially don't like being made an accomplice to a murder."

"I have no idea what you're talking about."

"You know exactly what I'm talking about. You killed Pat after I'd stupidly led you to him."

"What a vivid imagination you have."

"And, unless I'm very much mistaken, you killed your poor mother too."

"What an awful thing to say. I loved my mother."

"Tell that to the police."

He smirked. "I'd rather not."

"You won't get away with this."

"I rather think I might. Now, enjoyable as this has been, I really do have to get to the gym."

He brushed past me and climbed into a brand-new Audi that was parked on the road outside his house.

***

"What time do you call this?" Winky said. "I didn't realise you were working part time now."

"Don't start on me. I'm not in the mood for it."

"What's wrong? Why don't you tell Uncle Winky?"

"That Beasley guy has done me up like a kipper. He killed his mother and now I've helped him to kill another innocent man."

"What did I tell you? I said he had murderer written all over his face the first time he came in here."

"We can't all be as smart as you."

"That's true, so what are you going to do about it?"

"I'm not sure what I can do. I have no proof he killed anyone."

"So, you're just going to sit here feeling sorry for yourself, are you?"

Winky was right. Sulking wasn't going to change anything. I had to come up with a plan, but before I could even make a start on it, my phone rang with a call I'd been dreading from Queen Moonlight.

"Jill, I'm really sorry to bother you but it's Ringabell the day after tomorrow, so I wanted to check if you'd had any luck repairing the mace."

"I'm really sorry, your highness. I've tried everything I can think of, but I've had no success."

"That's disappointing, but not altogether surprising. I'm grateful to you for at least trying."

"What will you do now?"

"We'll have to withdraw from the Ringabell parade."

"That's such a shame. Couldn't you go ahead without the mace?"

"I'm afraid not."

"I really am sorry."

"Don't beat yourself up, Jill. You did your best."

"Another satisfied client?" Winky said.

"Shut it!"

"Would you like me to cheer you up?"

"How? By moving out and going to live in GT fulltime?"

"That's a horrible thing to say." He disappeared under the sofa and began to sulk.

"I'm sorry. I didn't mean it."

"Your words cut deep."

"Would salmon help?"
"Red not pink?"
"Obviously."

Jules came through to my office just after Winky had finished his bowl of salmon. She glanced at the empty bowl and shook her head.

"This really isn't healthy, Jill. You have to put that cat behind you. Why don't you let me throw that old bowl away?"

"Don't you dare!" Winky screamed at me.

"I can't let you do that, Jules. It holds a lot of sentimental value for me."

She shook her head and sighed. "I just came in to tell you that a Mr Makepiece rang while you were on another call. He'd like you to call him back."

"Okay, will do."

"Are you absolutely sure I can't throw that bowl away?"

"I'm positive."

Arnold Makepiece picked up on the first ring.

"Thanks for getting back to me, Jill."

"No problem. Any news?"

"The best. Liam has been released."

"That's amazing. What happened?"

"They've arrested another man. My understanding is that he's going to be charged with a number of murders, including that of Goldie Barr."

"Excellent."

"Liam asked me to call and thank you, even though we didn't need your help in the end."

I didn't see any reason to tell Makepiece about the part

I'd played in the arrest of the murderer because I had no intention of taking money from Liam for the work I'd done.

"No problem. I did it for Goldie."

Once I'd finished on the call to Makepiece, I called Washbridge police station and asked to speak to Big Mac. I didn't really expect him to take my call, but much to my surprise, he came straight on the line.

"What can I do for you, Maxwell?"

"I understand Liam Locks has been released."

"That is correct."

"Does that mean you're going to charge the man I apprehended with Goldie's murder?"

"I'm afraid I'm unable to discuss an ongoing case with you."

"You must think he was responsible for her murder, or you wouldn't have released Liam."

"As I said: I'm unable to comment."

"What about the other murders? Did his DNA match that found at those murder scenes?"

"No comment."

"Okay. Bye."

"Before you go, Maxwell, there is just one thing I wanted to say."

"What's that?"

"Thank you," he said, then ended the call.

It was a good thing I was sitting down otherwise I would probably have collapsed with shock.

***

"I still can't believe that someone would kill people over

something as trivial as their names," Jack said that evening, after we had retired to the lounge.

Before I could agree with him, Humphrey chipped in, "Me neither. There are some weirdos out there."

"There's at least one weirdo right here in this room." I fixed him with my gaze.

"I don't understand why you're so hostile towards me, Jill," said the bear.

"I'm not being hostile. I would just like to be able to have a conversation with my husband, without some stuffed toy chiming in every five minutes."

"That's a bit harsh, Jill," Jack said.

"I might have known that you'd take the bear's side."

"I'm not taking anyone's side, I'm just—"

"Don't bother. I'm going for a walk." I stood up and started for the door.

"Don't be silly, Jill," Jack shouted after me, but I ignored him.

If I'd realised how cold it was, I would have put on a coat, but there was no way I was turning back.

As I did a circuit of the mostly deserted village, the vicar appeared out of the shadows.

"Out for your evening constitutional, Jill?"

"Something like that."

"It's rather chilly out here. Aren't you cold?"

"Nah, I don't feel the cold." I shivered.

"Jack still at the store?"

"No, he's at home, talking to the teddy bear."

"Teddy bear?"

"I'm kidding. He's watching TV."

"I'm glad I bumped into you."

Something told me I wasn't going to be.

"Why's that?"

"It's the church fete in three weeks' time and I was hoping you might agree to lend a hand."

"I suppose I could do the tombola or something like that."

"That's not what I had in mind."

"What then?"

"I thought it would be nice to put on a few local acts to entertain visitors."

"And you'd like me to work backstage? I can do that."

"Actually, I was hoping you'd agree to be one of the acts. Mrs Juicetime has already agreed to sing; that woman has the voice of an angel."

"I can't sing if that's what you're about to suggest."

"It isn't. Your grandmother has kindly volunteered to work on the organising committee, and she told me that you do a magic act."

"*Magic act*? Grandma said that?"

"Yes, she said you could perform some amazing tricks."

"I—err—"

"I'll pencil you in for now, shall I?"

"I—err—"

"Don't stay outside too long or you'll catch your death."

Memo to self: kill Grandma.

"You have goosebumps," Jack said when I walked back into the house.

"Where's the bear?"

"I took him upstairs."

"Good."

"I know you don't like him, but he's quite good company."

"Better company than me?"

"Now you're just being silly. I thought you'd be on top of the world tonight after you caught Goldie's killer."

"I am, but I'm still fuming about the way Beasley used me."

"What are you going to do about it?"

"I'm not sure yet. Something really amazing did happen today, though."

"What's that?"

"Big Mac said thank you to me. *Thank you!* Can you believe it?"

Chapter 29

By the next morning, I was feeling much better, and do you know why? I'll tell you: I had formulated a plan so cunning that it would have won an award if only there were awards for cunning plans.

"You look a lot happier than you did last night," Jack said.

"I've figured out a way to put Beasley behind bars."

"I told you last night that you should go to the police."

"And I told you that I have no proof to show them. The cassette was the only solid evidence and like a fool, I handed that over to Beasley, who will no doubt have destroyed it."

"What are you going to do, then?"

"Resurrect the dead."

"Huh?"

"I'll fill you in tonight."

***

"Have you stopped feeling sorry for yourself?" Winky said.

"I have, and I'm grateful for the pep talk you gave me. It was precisely what I needed."

"Does this mean you've come up with a plan to sort out that Beasley guy?"

"It does."

"And may I ask: Is it by any chance a plan of the cunning variety?"

"It's cunning with a cherry on top."

"That's more like the Jill Maxwell we all know and

love."

"Thanks, Winky."

"Don't mention it. Just break open the salmon."

I'd just finished feeding Winky when my phone rang; it was Joy.

"Have I caught you at a good time, Jill? If not, I can call back."

"Now is fine."

"I had a meeting with James this morning."

"How did that go?"

"Pretty well, all things considered. He had the audacity to try to deny everything at first, but when I showed him the photo that you'd given me, he soon changed his tune and became quite aggressive. Would you believe he had the nerve to blame me?"

"For what?"

"For rejecting his offer to buy our business. He insisted it was the only way to save it."

"I bet that went down well."

"I was livid, and I told him I was going to report him to the police. That got his attention."

"That's exactly what you should do. He deserves everything he has coming to him."

"Actually, I've decided not to go to the police."

"Why not?"

"Because I gave him another option."

"Which was?"

"To sell James' Games to me."

"I didn't see that coming."

"Neither did he. And, if I'm being honest, neither did I, but then it occurred to me that his business would gel nicely with ours."

"What did he say?"

"I wouldn't like to repeat his actual words, but let's say he wasn't very receptive to the idea. But when he realised that I was serious about going to the police, he pretty quickly changed his mind."

"Does this mean that you now own James' Games?"

"Not yet, but I will soon."

"That's amazing, Joy."

"James was right about one thing: I've allowed Joy's Toys to fall behind the times in terms of systems and technology. By acquiring James' Games, we'll be able to utilise theirs across both businesses."

"How do your sons feel about it?"

"They're thrilled."

"Even Roy?"

"Yes. He's been frustrated at our antiquated systems, and he's excited at the prospect of adopting the technology from James' Games."

"That's great. I couldn't be happier for you, Joy."

"It's all thanks to you, Jill. If you hadn't got to the bottom of what was causing the faulty toys, it would only have been a matter of time before Joy's Toys folded. I'm so grateful."

"It was my pleasure."

"I assume you'll send me your bill."

"I will."

"And, Jill, if there's ever anything I can help you with, don't hesitate to give me a shout."

"Thanks, Joy."

***

I magicked myself to Turnip Shed Road and took up a position from where I could see Beasley's house. Only when I was sure he was inside did I make a move. My plan, although cunning, was also fraught with risk, mainly because it relied heavily on my memory.

First, I magicked myself into the basement, which was just as dark and cold as I remembered. After switching on the light, I put the next part of my plan into action. This is where my memory came into play: I had only glanced briefly at the photograph of Beasley's late mother, and so I had to rely on the image I had in my head when I cast the 'doppelganger' spell. I would only know if I'd been successful when I saw how Beasley reacted.

I climbed the steps and, once at the top, I knocked on the door. Judging by his footsteps, Beasley initially assumed that there was someone at the outer door. When he discovered there was no one there, and realised the sound was actually coming from the basement, he shouted, "Who's there?"

Instead of replying, I simply knocked on the door again.

"Who's in there?"

Again, I responded with another knock.

This time, the key turned in the lock.

"I have a hammer," he said.

I remained silent and waited.

Slowly, very slowly, he pulled the door open. When it was open wide enough for him to see me, he took several steps backwards before falling in a heap onto the floor.

"Why did you do it, son?" I said.

Slumped, with his back against the wall, he was shaking, and blubbing like a baby.

"Leave me alone."

"Didn't I always love you, son?"

"You're not real." He closed his eyes tight shut for several seconds, but when he reopened them, I was still there.

"I'm sorry," he pleaded. "It was an accident."

"You pushed me."

"Please go away."

"I can't do that. I'll always be right here for you."

"No! Leave me alone."

"I can only do that after you have done the right thing."

"I'll do anything. Just tell me what I have to do."

"Call the police and tell them what you did to me."

"I can't do that. They'll put me in prison."

"Then I guess I'll just stick around forever. Won't that be nice?"

"No! I'll call the police. I'll do it tomorrow."

"Do it now."

"Okay." He took out his phone.

"And make sure to tell them what you did to Pat too. Such a lovely man."

"How do you know about Pat?"

"Are you going to make that call or not, son?"

"I'm doing it now, Mother. Police, please."

Beasley confessed to both murders over the phone, and when he'd finished on the call, I said, "Good boy. Don't you feel much better now?"

"You promised you'd leave if I called the police."

"And so I will. Just as soon as they arrive."

And, true to my word, as soon as Beasley answered the door to the police, I took my leave.

***

"Do you want me to take Humphrey upstairs?" Jack said after we'd finished dinner and moved through to the lounge.

"No, it's okay. As long as he doesn't try to monopolise the conversation."

"I won't. I promise," Humphrey said from the armchair.

"What happened with Beasley?" Jack asked.

"He's facing two charges of murder."

"Is there enough evidence to convict him?"

"He's already confessed."

"What? Just out of the blue?"

"Yeah. It must have been his guilty conscience."

"What was all that about resurrecting the dead?"

"Nothing. I was just joking."

"A good day, then?"

"Not altogether. I haven't been able to repair the mace for the sunlight fairies, so they're going to have to withdraw their float from Ringabell. Queen Moonlight was very understanding but I could tell she was really disappointed. I can't help but feel I've let them down."

"No, you haven't. No one could have put that mace back together. It was like the world's most difficult jigsaw puzzle."

"What did you just say?"

"I said it's—"

"Never mind. You're a genius." I gave him a kiss and then made a call to Joy at Joy's Toys.

"Jill? I didn't expect to hear from you again quite so soon."

"When you said that if I ever needed anything, I should

give you a call, were you being serious?"

"Absolutely. What can I do for you?"

Chapter 30

It was Saturday morning, and Jack and I were enjoying the same breakfast for once: toast with jam.

"I reckon they've changed this jam," Jack said.

"It tastes the same as usual to me."

"Yes, but then you don't have my discerning palate, do you?"

"Whatever."

"Anyway, I've been thinking," he said.

"Oh dear. Nothing good ever came of you thinking."

"I was thinking that we should get a pet."

"You're joking, I assume?"

"No. Since Florence has been at CASS, this house seems empty."

"I'm not having another dog; I already have two."

"I wasn't thinking of a dog. Anyway, it wouldn't be practical with both of us out of the house most days."

"If you're talking about a cat, you can forget it. One cat is more than enough, even though he is dead."

"I wasn't thinking of a cat either."

"I'm done with goldfish too."

"That's not what I had in mind."

"What then?"

"I was thinking parrot."

"No way."

"Why not?"

"They're too—err—feathery."

"*Feathery*?"

"I don't want feathers all over the lounge. And they probably smell. Why do you want a parrot?"

"You've been able to talk to every pet we've ever had. I

just thought it would be nice if I could talk to our pet too."

"You do understand that parrots can't actually have a conversation with you, don't you? They just repeat what they've heard."

"Even so, I think it would be fun. What do you say?"

"I say no. Definitely not."

"Can't we even talk about it?"

"I thought we just had."

"Can we at least go and look at some? You might change your mind."

"I won't, and anyway, I have to get going. I promised Aunt Lucy I'd go to the Ringabell parade with her."

"What is Ringabell?"

"I have no idea, but from all accounts, it's a really big deal." I gave him a quick kiss. "I'll see you in a few seconds."

I'd arranged to meet Aunt Lucy at Cuppy C, which to my surprise was absolutely packed. Aunt Lucy, who had nabbed a table by the window, waved me over.

"I've never seen it so busy in here," I said. "Where does the parade go?"

"It starts out from Trog Point, which is the most westerly point of Candlefield, through the town centre, and finishes on Sabre Fields."

"That's an awful long way to march."

"Make way for two little ones," Pearl said, as she and Amber joined us at our table.

"Aren't you two supposed to be working?" I said.

"We brought in a couple of extra people, so that we could watch the parade."

"We wouldn't miss this for anything," Amber said.

“What time does it start?” I asked.

“They were due to set off from Trog Point about fifty minutes ago, so the first floats should be coming down the road any time now.”

“It’s a pity Jack couldn’t come with you to watch this,” Aunt Lucy said.

“Yeah, it might have taken his mind off parrots.”

“Huh?”

“He just told me that he thinks we should get a parrot.”

“As a pet?” Pearl said.

“No, for lunch. Yes, as a pet.”

“That sounds like a great idea,” Amber said. “Parrots are amazeballs.”

“I told him no. There’ll be no more pets in the old watermill while I live there. They’re all more trouble than they’re worth.”

“They’re here!” Pearl pointed up the street to where the first float had just come into sight.

I’d been to any number of parades in the human world, but none of them could compare with Ringabell. Because the parade was open to all sups, the size and variety of floats on display was incredible.

“Look at that one.” Aunt Lucy was transfixed by a float in the shape of a castle. Looking through the windows of the castle were vampires with blood (hopefully synthetic) dripping from their mouths.

“Look at the ice nymphs,” Amber shouted.

The ice nymphs’ float was shaped like an iceberg with a slide cut into the side. The nymphs seemed to be having a great time, sliding down the side of the iceberg, then scrambling back up to have another try.

“I don’t believe it.” Aunt Lucy shook her head.

After following her gaze, I could only stare in disbelief.

"How did Grandma get permission to have a float in the parade?" Pearl said. "And what is that she's waving around?"

"If I'm not mistaken, that's a wandroom." I sighed. "It's her new invention: a cross between a wand and a broom."

"She's treating the parade like one big marketing opportunity," Aunt Lucy said. "That goes completely against the spirit of Ringabell."

Grandma had obviously employed a number of sprites who were running alongside the float, handing out what I assumed were flyers for the wandroom.

"As if anyone will want one of her stupid wandrooms, anyway." I scoffed.

"Actually, I wouldn't mind one," Amber said.

"Me too." Pearl nodded.

"Are you both crazy? Aunt Lucy, will you please back me up here? Tell them how stupid an idea it is."

"I quite like the sound of it," Aunt Lucy said. "Obviously it will depend how much they cost."

I couldn't believe my ears.

"Isn't that beautiful?" Pearl pointed to the float directly behind Grandma's.

"It's the sunlight fairies." Aunt Lucy beamed. "It's their first time in the parade and it's all thanks to Jill."

Just then, Queen Moonlight, who was seated on a throne at the front of the float caught sight of me and waved the ceremonial mace, which looked amazeballs.

What? If you can't beat them, join them.

"How was it?" Jack asked when I magicked myself back to the old watermill.

"It was brilliant. I've never seen so many floats in a parade. It took almost three hours from the first one to the last."

"It's so weird when you say stuff like that. You've literally only been gone for a few seconds."

"Grandma did her best to spoil it with her float advertising her wandroom, but apart from that, it was great. In my opinion, the sunlight fairies' float was the best, but then I'm slightly biased."

"I take it the mace was okay?"

"Yes, and that's all thanks to you. If you hadn't said that the jewels were like a giant jigsaw puzzle, I would never have thought of asking Joy for help."

At my request, Joy had allowed me to borrow Nancy who'd been able to assemble the jewels into the correct order. Once she'd done that, it had been a trivial matter for me to use magic to reattach them to the mace. Queen Moonlight had been delighted with the end result, and fortunately she was able to reclaim her place in the Ringabell parade.

"That Nancy woman was amazing," Jack said. "I've never seen anything quite like it."

"And bear in mind that she was actually really nervous because it was her first time here in the human world. She's usually even quicker than that."

"So, my off the cuff remark really helped you, then?" Jack said.

"Yeah, it did."

"Does that mean you owe me?"

"I guess so." I took his hand and started for the stairs.

"Where are we going?"

"I thought you wanted your reward for helping."

"I do. So, about this parrot."

ALSO BY ADELE ABBOTT

The Not-A-Date (a sweet romantic comedy)

I'd just been fired, so the last thing I needed was some guy hitting on me, and I told him so in no uncertain terms. Then he goes and offers me the job of my dreams.

Pushing All My Buttons (a sweet romantic comedy)

I got stuck in a lift with this guy who then tried to hit on me, so I told him he was a jerk. A few days later, I started a new job and discovered he was my boss.

So Not The One (A sweet romantic comedy)

I was devastated when my old boss had to take early retirement. But that was nothing compared to how I felt when I discovered who his replacement was.

The Witch P.I. Mysteries (A Candlefield/Washbridge Series)

Witch Is When... (Season #1)

Witch Is When It All Began
Witch Is When Life Got Complicated
Witch Is When Everything Went Crazy
Witch Is When Things Fell Apart
Witch Is When The Bubble Burst
Witch Is When The Penny Dropped
Witch Is When The Floodgates Opened
Witch Is When The Hammer Fell

Witch Is When My Heart Broke
Witch Is When I Said Goodbye
Witch Is When Stuff Got Serious
Witch Is When All Was Revealed

Witch Is Why... (Season #2)
Witch Is Why Time Stood Still
Witch is Why The Laughter Stopped
Witch is Why Another Door Opened
Witch is Why Two Became One
Witch is Why The Moon Disappeared
Witch is Why The Wolf Howled
Witch is Why The Music Stopped
Witch is Why A Pin Dropped
Witch is Why The Owl Returned
Witch is Why The Search Began
Witch is Why Promises Were Broken
Witch is Why It Was Over

Witch Is How... (Season #3)
Witch is How Things Had Changed
Witch is How Berries Tasted Good
Witch is How The Mirror Lied
Witch is How The Tables Turned
Witch is How The Drought Ended
Witch is How The Dice Fell
Witch is How The Biscuits Disappeared
Witch is How Dreams Became Reality
Witch is How Bells Were Saved
Witch is How To Fool Cats
Witch is How To Lose Big
Witch is How Life Changed Forever

Witch Is Where... (Season #4)

Witch is Where Magic Lives Now
Witch Is Where Clowns Go To Die
Witch Is Where Squirrels Go Nuts
Witch Is Where Rainbows End
Witch Is Where Unicorns Cry
Witch Is Where The Lights Went Out
Witch Is Where Fairies Wing It
Witch Is Where Roses Bloom Early
Witch Is Where Decisions Are Made
Witch Is Where Gnomes Rules
Witch Is Where Cats Always Win
Witch Is Where Chickens Go To Roost

Witch Is The... (Season #5)

Witch is The Nest Now Empty
Witch is The Hardest Pill To Swallow
Witch Is The Joke No One Got

Susan Hall Investigates (A Candlefield/Washbridge Series)

Whoops! Our New Flatmate Is A Human.
Whoops! All The Money Went Missing.
Whoops! Someone Is On Our Case.
Whoops! We're In Big Trouble Now.

Murder On Account (A Kat Royle Novel)

Her boss has been murdered. Now she must find his killer. Smart, sassy and kickass tough, private investigator, Kat Royle, is nobody's fool, but does she have what it takes to keep the agency afloat, and find the murderer?

Web site: AdeleAbbott.com
Facebook: facebook.com/AdeleAbbottAuthor

Printed in Dunstable, United Kingdom

65057451R00184